Death Between The Rivers

DEATH BETWEEN THE RIVERS

EWAN WALLACE

T

The manufacturer's authorised representative in the EU for product safety is Authorised Rep
Compliance Ltd, 71 Lower Baggot Street, Dublin D02 P593 Ireland
(www.arccompliance.com)

Troubador Publishing Ltd
Unit E2 Airfield Business Park,
Harrison Road, Market Harborough,
Leicestershire. LE16 7UL
Tel: 0116 2792299
Email: books@troubador.co.uk
Web: www.troubador.co.uk

ISBN 9781836283645

British Library Cataloguing in Publication Data.
A catalogue record for this book is available from the British Library.

Printed and bound by CPI Group (UK) Ltd, Croydon, CR0 4YY
Typeset in 11pt Minion Pro by Troubador Publishing Ltd, Leicester, UK

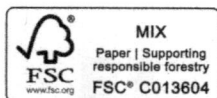

1

7th January

For the third time in an hour, sixty-five-year-old Robert Lennox looked at his bedside alarm. Sighed at the 04:45 displayed. He stared at the flashing colon between the numbers and counted sixty seconds, but realised the vanity of the attempt to regain sleep.

Insomnia had been an early harbinger of his most recent, and worse to date, depressive relapse; it remained stubbornly persistent, despite the modest improvement in many of his other symptoms.

"Moving in the right direction" according to his psychiatrist, Dr Alasdair McLean.

Lennox drew his duvet up and tried to take some comfort from the fact that he was comfortable, warm, well fed and pain-free. He was grateful, too, for the moderation in his clinical condition, though dark thoughts continued to permeate his brain on distressingly frequent occasions.

Self-reproach. Self-contempt. Self-harm.

All perfectly normal symptoms of depression, he had been told, by various members of the mental health team.

But what if they were wrong?

What if at least some of the guilt that weighed him down daily, was as justified as it was inescapable.

He lay motionless in his bed, listening to the all too familiar nocturnal soundtrack of an adult psychiatry ward. He was certainly, by any measure, a different person to when he had been admitted two months previously. So crippling were his anxiety and depressive symptoms, at the time, that he was barely able to move, or communicate. *Catatonic* was the label given by the mental health team; even in their area of expertise a sufficiently rare diagnosis to draw medical students, and psychiatry trainees alike, as if they were viewing a rare animal at a zoo.

His condition had proven resistant to a number of different medical regimens. Now he was two-thirds of the way through a six-treatment course of electroconvulsive therapy (ECT).

He had grown used to the routine on treatment days: a mild sedative in the morning, followed later by the horizontal journey along the corridor on a trolley, only the conveyor belt-like ceiling for distraction. Comforting words, not matched by the serious look in their eyes, from the ECT nurses on arrival at the unit. Electrodes fastened to head and chest. Blood pressure cuffs on one arm and one leg. By now he knew the explanation off by heart; the cuff on the upper arm to monitor his blood pressure, the one on his right lower leg to prevent muscle relaxant travelling past his ankle, allowing his physicians to monitor seizure activity in his foot.

More comforting words from the anaesthetist. A scratch on the back of the hand, followed by total darkness.

Although judged by some as somewhat barbaric, the third- or fourth-line treatment was still seen to have a place in the management of challenging cases. He had started to show a slight improvement after two treatments, and both patient and medical staff alike were relieved to see this maintained over the following two.

The door to his single room afforded some auditory protection, but he could still hear a mixture of coughing, snoring, noise from the devices of other insomniacs and the fire exit door opening and closing at regular intervals; the smokers on the staff taking advantage of the protection offered by a small porch immediately outside. Having satisfied their nicotine demand, they would walk back up the corridor bringing with them a draft of cool January air, carrying, along with it, the faint odour of tobacco. While he appreciated the fresh air, as a former smoker himself, the latter was less welcome. A craving for a cigarette was never far below the surface, and became even more superficial with the right olfactory stimulation.

From time to time, there might also be an acute disturbance from one of his fellow patients. Staff footsteps back and forward. Muffled conversations. The squeaky-wheeled drug trolley being dragged past his room. A gradual return to the background noise as the sedative hit its mark. The rest of the ward breathing a collective sigh of relief. Most would get back to sleep. Lennox would not.

The next hour dragged by, as it did every night. He usually fell asleep between 11pm and midnight, but was reliably awake by 3am. He counted the hours after that, until about 6am; then a new pattern of noise announced the staff preparing their final tea break, before the morning drug round, and handover to the day staff.

He tried to assess his background level of anxiety and low mood, while waiting in anticipation for the sound of clinking crockery from the kitchen. What type of day might he expect? What symptoms would he have to tolerate?

Suddenly, a different, unexpected noise pierced the darkness; the characteristic horn sound he had chosen for incoming SMS messages on his mobile phone. *Who on earth could be messaging at this time of the morning?* Probably the latest offer from Vodafone, or his bank warning him he was about to go overdrawn again.

He ignored the noise until it was repeated after a minute when, as usual, curiosity got the better of him. He turned over, fumbled in the dark, and located his phone on the bedside table. The action of lifting the phone illuminated the screen, but he was unable to read the partial message displayed. Further fumbling. A curse. Finally, his glasses were snared and positioned in place. The blurred message came into focus.

Meet me outside the hospital, in Victoria Park, in 15 minutes. I have something important for you.

Lennox rubbed his eyes and reread the message. Initially he thought it was some kind of joke, or a wrong number, but the accuracy of information it contained made them unlikely. The sender obviously knew where he was. He checked, but their identity was withheld. After a few moments of consideration, he replied.

Who are you?

You don't need to know that. You WILL want to see what I have, however.

It's not even dawn yet. I'm not coming outside, for someone I don't even know.

OK. It's your loss, but this offer will not be repeated. If you are not interested, I'm sure your wife will be keen to hear what I have to say.

What do you mean, my wife? What offer?

I need to show you. Last chance. I'll be gone in 15 minutes.

Lennox hesitated. *Damn this illness.* Always overthinking. Never decisive. He knew he should decline the unsolicited approach, but still…

He couldn't really care, even if there was an element of danger.

OK. Give me ten minutes to throw some clothes on. I'll be over soon.

Fifteen minutes later Lennox, now fully clothed against an Aberdeen winter, did his best to walk noiselessly past the duty room; ongoing muted conversation and a bout of laughter suggested he had done so undetected. Unlike the forensic unit further along the corridor, the doors to the ward were unlocked, and he was soon making sluggish progress along the eerie, night-time corridors of Ashgrove Psychiatric Hospital. Deathly quiet, apart from an occasional muffled sound as he passed the doors to successive wards. Long, bleak walls punctuated irregularly by posters. A faint smell of cigarettes and cleaning agents. He plodded along, like a hooked fish slowly being reeled in by an angler.

Two heavy looking sets of swing doors threatened to block his progress, but were relatively easily negotiated. With a final hiss, they closed slowly behind him as he passed the small shop, and an unmanned reception. Outside, he braced himself against the cold air, his first few breaths condensing into a fine mist in front of his face.

How easy to get out of the hospital.

A short walk took him to one of the exits from the hospital grounds and he looked up and down Westburn Road. There was minimal traffic at that time of day but, habitually, he looked for the traffic lights he knew to be nearby. Light snow had started to fall and a few flakes danced silently around in the halo of light on either side of the crossing. There was virtually no sound apart from the distant rumble of traffic from Anderson Drive, as Aberdeen slowly roused itself for the day.

The illuminated green figure, and auditory signal, invited him to cross the road. Scanning the darkness, he saw no sign of life as he covered the short distance to

Victoria Park, a city centre green space covering several acres, with multiple points of entry and exit. Dawn was still some way off, and large parts of the park were cloaked in a dense blackness, the sporadic lampposts concentrating their efforts on the formal paths.

He was wondering in which direction he should go, when he noticed a torch being flashed on and off, about one hundred yards to his right, in a poorly lit section of the park.

"In for a penny, in for a pound," he muttered slowly to himself, as he set off towards his unknown liaison.

When he was about ten yards away, a masculine voice confirmed the gender, at least, of his mystery texter.

"That's far enough," he instructed.

"What's this all about?" Lennox asked, pillows of his white breath illuminated by the torchlight. He wanted to sound masculine and indignant, but he had not yet recovered the power of his premorbid voice, nor his self-confidence. His ears jarred at the sound of his own feeble voice.

"I have something for you," the torchbearer continued, in a well-spoken, local accent.

Lennox could see just enough of the outline of the man to ascertain he was of average height and build, but his facial features were well hidden behind the torch beam, and what appeared to be a mask.

He wondered if he could detect a hint of something familiar in his voice.

"Do I know you?" he ventured.

"I doubt it. But I know who you are. I know *what* you are."

Lennox felt his mouth go dry, and his pulse quicken.

"I'm not sure I know what you're speaking about… I thought you said you had something important for me."

"I do," he replied, while redirecting the torch beam downwards, to reveal a petrol can and box of matches.

Seconds passed. The wind rustled the nearby trees. A siren sounded in the distance. Lennox nodded slowly as he began to understand what was expected of him. He tried to swallow saliva, but his mouth was too dry. His heart accelerated rapidly and thudded against the inside of his chest wall, his pulse echoing inside his ears. His facial muscles tightened, etching a look of resignation. Despite the cold, small beads of sweat began to form on his forehead and his hands felt clammy.

A tear ran down his face.

He tried to speak, but his voice snagged. He cleared his throat and tried again.

"And if I don't?" he faltered.

"Then I will tell your wife the truth."

"What makes you think she doesn't already know?"

"I will tell her the *whole* truth. Don't forget about your children and the press. I will also tell them. You will be destroyed."

Moments passed with just the whispering noise of the park, and distant city filling the silence. Lennox forced down a feeling of nausea and cleared his throat again.

"Just one thing," he said, in a croaky voice.

"Go on."

"Tell my wife that I'm sorry."

Without saying another word, he picked up the can, poured petrol liberally over himself, and lit a match.

2

9th January

DS Zafar Iqbal had been to the gym, as usual, before breakfast. After an invigorating shower, and choosing his suit for the day, he had a quick breakfast of cereal and coffee, before heading off, on foot, to work. The affable, cricket mad Glaswegian had moved to Aberdeen two years previously to take up his sergeant's post, and an all-rounder position at Aberdeenshire Cricket Club.

Twenty minutes, and half a cricket podcast later, he arrived at the front doors of the main Aberdeen police station. Having made a mental note to tweak his batting grip at his next nets session, he switched the podcast off, removed his earbuds, and waved at reception as he made his way towards the corridor leading to CID.

Although he had a fair idea of his morning workload, he scanned the various whiteboards on the walls to see if anything more interesting had come in during the night. Nothing caught his eye.

Iqbal spotted DC Babinski, engrossed in a PC screen.

"How you doin', Reflex?" he said in his broad Glaswegian brogue.

Babinski, previously named "Reflex" by one of the police surgeons for reasons unbeknown to him, turned to confirm who had spoken, though there was virtually no doubt in his mind. Only one person in the CID had that particular accent.

"Fine, Sarge."

"Anything interesting brewing?"

"Na, not really."

"OK. Fair play. It'll have to be the post-mortem for me, then," he said, with an air of resignation.

Visiting the morgue at the nearby pathology department was not the favourite part of his job. The combination of mouth breathing, and application of menthol cream under the nose, was not always guaranteed to prevent him feeling nauseated when exposed to noxious autopsy smells. It was not unknown for him to have to excuse himself; a subject frequently revisited by his colleagues when they wanted to wind him up.

He used the spare time he had before the post-mortem to grab a coffee and read his emails. When he could leave it no longer – he liked to spend as little time as possible "across the road" – he jogged the short distance to the pathology department, flashed his card at reception, and took his seat in the viewing gallery. Behind him one of the receptionists whispered something in the ear of her colleague, which made her giggle, and then blush.

"So would I," she agreed.

"Ah, cutting it fine as usual, I see, DS Iqbal," commented

Dr Dexter Brewster, one of the local forensic pathologists, as he caught sight of the detective out of the corner of his eye.

Iqbal wondered if Brewster had placed subtle emphasis on the word *cutting* just to wind him up a bit.

"You know me, Doc. Never want to spend too much time here, if I can help it."

Brewster had a mask on, but Iqbal could tell he was smiling by the twinkle in his eyes and the crow's feet spreading out from them. The two men knew each other well, and were comfortable using first or professional names, depending on circumstance. They had first met on a case involving two serial killers from an animal welfare terrorist cell; since then, several other cases had cemented an easy working relationship, which still respected professional boundaries.

The snapping of plastic gloves, stretched over the sleeves of his scrubs, heralded the imminent start of the post-mortem. Brewster, and his anatomical pathology assistant, glanced around in one final check of instruments and scales. A nod to one another confirmed they were satisfied. Without further words, the assistant fitted a PM22B blade to a scalpel handle and passed it to the pathologist.

"The badly burnt body is of a presumed sixty-five-year-old, Caucasian male. ID has still to be confirmed, through dental records and DNA analysis. Found in Victoria Park at 06:20 on the seventh of January. Matches approximate size and description of the patient reported missing from nearby Ashgrove Psychiatric Hospital. There is evidence of extensive thermal damage, especially to the head, arms and upper thorax…"

Iqbal tried not to look directly at the charred corpse, and zoned out from Brewster's ongoing commentary, which was done more for the benefit of his voice recognition software than any police presence. He thought of his cricket podcast and when he might try out the potential gems gleaned. Always trying to improve his averages.

As the procedure drew to a close, he refocussed for what he knew would be the informative part; Brewster's summing up.

"In summary, the corpse is of a badly fire-damaged, middle-aged, Caucasian male. There are clear signs of accelerant use. In addition to soot staining, the upper airways show burns to the tongue, pharynx, larynx and tracheobronchial tree, in keeping with inhalation of hot air."

Brewster looked over the top of his glasses, to check Iqbal had noted the significance of the observation.

"So, he was alive when set alight?" suggested Iqbal.

"Indeed," confirmed Brewster. "In the circumstances, making suicide, by self-incineration, a bit more likely perhaps than homicide, followed by someone burning the body."

"The other thing to note," he continued, "is that I've had a chance to look at his psychiatric records. It's well documented he had suicidal thoughts over the last few months, in particular self-immolation."

Brewster glanced again at Iqbal, but, this time, was met with a puzzled, frowned expression.

"Am I being glaekit, Doc?"

"Not this time," Brewster reassured him, "it's another

term for self-incineration. Not one you're likely to have come across very often."

Iqbal's phone was on silent – he had quickly learnt that lesson at his first post-mortem – but he felt the familiar vibration in his pocket of an incoming message. He quickly scanned the details, before re-engaging with the pathologist.

"Just for your information, Dexter… I mean, Dr Brewster… we now have CCTV footage of a middle-aged man leaving Ashgrove Hospital at 05:02 on the seventh of January. We can also confirm there were only wan set of prints on the petrol can, which are a match to the only two undamaged fingers on the deceased."

"And, was he seen to be carrying anything on CCTV?" enquired Brewster.

"Na, and there's the mystery," agreed Iqbal. "Either he had, somehow, pre-arranged this himself, hiding the petrol can and matches somewhere; or he had outside help. His family are devastated, and we've no' got any indication from CCTV, mobile phone records or car data, that any o' them were anywhere other than at hame at the time in question."

"And, it's hardly likely family would be complicit in such an act, I would have thought," added Brewster.

"That's what we were thinking too, so it is," responded Iqbal. "But why would he do it now when, by all accounts, he was getting a bit better?"

"Ah, well… it might be that it was *because* he was a bit better, he was able to do it," replied Brewster.

"Ach, hawd on there, Doc. You're going to have to explain that wan to me," responded Iqbal.

"Well, sometimes when someone has severe

depression, as I believe the missing patient from Ashgrove had on admission, they are so retarded physically that, even if they are having strong suicidal thoughts, they can't carry out any plan. However, when they are a bit better, and even if thoughts of deliberate self-harm are less intrusive, they are more able to enact a plan. It's a recognised clinical phenomenon."

"You learn something new..." Iqbal whispered to himself, before snapping back his focus, "So, Doc, will you be able to issue a death certificate?"

"Yes," confirmed Brewster, before pausing to gather his thoughts.

"Severe thermal damage. Secondary to self-incineration. Secondary to severe depression."

"Thanks, Doc. That's good for me. No doubt we'll get your full report in due course?" responded Iqbal.

"Of course," replied Brewster, as he tugged sharply down, and then forwards, on his flimsy plastic apron. Two snapping noises confirmed little resistance had been offered. He balled the apron up and threw it in a nearby bin, followed rapidly by the gloves and mask.

Iqbal wasted no time in exiting the pathology department, and getting back to the warmth, and more pleasant atmosphere, of CID. Several years working with Police Scotland had hardened him to all manner of gruesome scenarios, but the sight of the severely burnt body, and the thought of the process that had created it, had still been unsettling. He concentrated on the administration required to move the case on from his in-tray. The familiarity of the routine soon distracted him, and he began to think about his mid-morning cup of coffee.

3

8th February

Kayleigh Peters loved 8 February. It was nineteen years, to the day, since she had entered the world, and it was her favourite day of the year. Not just because of a birthday celebrated, but also because she took great pleasure in taking stock. Assessing the year gone by. Contemplating the year ahead. What plans would she make? How would her exams go? Where would she get a summer job? Who might she date? Who she definitely would *not* date! Was she happy with her pronoun? All matters to daydream about.

Rebellious behaviour had hallmarked her final two years at a private school in North London and, as part of her teenage revolt, she had chosen to go to Aberdeen University to study English Literature, one of the furthest universities away from her home, but still in the UK. In truth, it suited parents and offspring alike as they both, without actually verbalising it, appreciated the distance involved. Trips home were, thankfully, only at the end of term, and the holiday periods were just about tolerable.

Her *look* had evolved during her time at university and her short, dyed blonde hair now also sported a blue fringe. A solitary nose piercing complemented two ear piercings in the right ear, and a further five in the left. Two tattoos stood out on her lean, bordering-on-skinny frame; a teardrop on her left lower forearm, and a butterfly on her right shoulder blade.

She had been on a night out in the city centre with three friends. Angela, who shared a student flat with four others on George Street, had offered it as a venue for pregaming drinks, before heading to Angels Club. Working to a tight budget, Kayleigh normally only drank water after reaching a club, but the passing of midnight heralded her birthday and she needed little encouragement to celebrate. Three rounds of shots, bankrolled by her fellow students, followed in rapid succession.

In good spirits, the four friends left the club in the early hours. All legs and high heels. Unsteady heels. Stumbling and giggling they made their way from the city centre. Angela cleaved off from the group, teetering in the direction of George Street, while the remaining three students decided how they were going to get back to their halls of residence in Old Aberdeen and Balgownie. The last bus had just been missed, and there were no taxis to be seen. Not for the first time Kayleigh bemoaned the lack of an Uber service in Aberdeen. Emboldened by alcohol, they decided to walk the two miles involved. Using each other for mutual support the merry trio negotiated the Kirkgate incline, before turning left towards Mounthooly roundabout, doing a passable impersonation, including out-of-tune singing, of Dorothy, and her ragbag companions, *off to see the wizard.*

Half an hour later, after hugs and resolutions to WhatsApp, Robyn and Jessica disappeared into the darkness of the path leading to Meston Walk halls in Old Aberdeen. Kayleigh stood outside and shivered, suddenly more aware of her solitude. She slipped her hand into her bag. Felt the reassuring presence of pepper spray. Turned it over in her fingers. Emboldened, she set off again towards Balgownie halls, cursing her luck at having drawn a room in the most distant student halls in the annual accommodation lottery. There were now only a handful of people, mostly students returning from their night out, on the cobbled street of Old Aberdeen. The euphoria of the alcohol, and the giddy companionship of her friends, was beginning to wear off, and be replaced by fatigue. Her feet ached. She yearned for her bed. She knew the remaining half mile of her journey could be shortened by taking a shortcut through Seaton Park. She had taken the route many times with friends, but never alone.

What the hell. It's well-lit most of the way, and I've got my pepper spray with me.

With arms folded against the cold, and a tight skirt restricting her step, she click-clacked her way up High Street, the noise of her heels echoing back from the seventeenth century buildings on either side. She passed a bar, the smell of stale alcohol still sweating from the premises after an evening's drinking, before crossing over St Machar Drive into The Chanonry. With thoughts of bed, she kept a reasonable momentum up the picturesque, cobbled road, which ran northwards to St Machar's Cathedral, before descending down the steep hill into Seaton Park. Ear buds were inserted, music chosen and she began to consider if she should get another tattoo this year, or equalise her ear piercings.

It was a direct line towards Balgownie halls and she had soon traversed the park and was ascending the last part, through a wooded area, to get to the exit. The route towards the park gate was darker than the rest, and she quickened her pace as best as her shoes and sore feet allowed. It was with a sense of relief that she saw lights from her halls appear ahead. Taylor Swift was well into her next song, and Kayleigh began to hum the chorus.

She didn't hear the rapidly approaching steps from behind. In a matter of seconds, a ligature had been placed over her head and tightened around her neck. A hand had also been clamped over her mouth to muffle any scream she could muster; in truth the speed of the manoeuvre and the vice-like grip of the ligature prevented any significant vocal effort.

Adrenaline and panic surged through her body. Her eyes reflexly opened as wide as they could; engorged veins popped up on her forehead. She tried to kick and punch, but her assailant was strong, and easily subdued her efforts. She was aware of an intense ring of pain around her neck as she began to see stars in front of her eyes. She thought of her family, as a dark cloud spread across her field of vision. The sound of Taylor Swift in her ears gradually diminished, like someone was turning down the volume. Any residual tone in her muscles melted away. Her limbs fell to dependent, lifeless positions and her unsupported head tipped forwards until her chin rested on her chest. A chest that had ceased moving.

Her small clutch bag dropped to the ground and its contents, including the unused pepper spray, spilled out onto the path.

8 February.

Her first day. Her best day. Her last.

4

10th February

D I Lily Bankhurst cut a lonely figure as she sat on a chair in the corridor of the gynaecology ward at Aberdeen Royal Infirmary. As a busy-looking nurse bustled past, a weak smile whispered across Bankhurst's face, but perished on her lips. In its place, and written large across her features, was the discomfort she was trying to hide. Having been an inpatient for three days, with a significant exacerbation of her long-term endometriosis, she was desperate to get home. She had deliberately underestimated her pain score, when asked, on the morning ward round, and tried not to wince when her abdomen was examined. Her consultant, somewhat reluctantly, agreed with her request to be discharged, and two hours later she was sitting in the monotone, echoey corridor, awaiting her medications from the pharmacy.

"God, I hate hospitals," she muttered.

She pulled out her mobile phone and quickly checked her emails, social media and Tinder. She had updated her Tinder profile just before being admitted and noted, without much interest, that there had been three suggestions for her to consider. Dating, and in particular sex, could not have been further from her mind.

For another day.

Another dreary hour passed in the insipid corridor, interrupted only by the unappealing smell from the food trolley as it went past, before one of the junior nurses arrived, a generous sized paper bag of medications rustling in her hand.

"I hope I haven't cleaned them out," Bankhurst quipped, trying to summon a smile.

"What?" replied the youthful nurse, who looked like she would rather have been anywhere else.

"Never mind."

Bankhurst inspected the bag to make sure all her diabetes and endometriosis medications were correct. A flicker of concern flashed across her eyes before a deeper rummage into the depths of the bag revealed her antidepressants and analgesics. Realising she needed her therapeutic crutches, she was particularly interested to check she had been given a decent supply of dihydrocodeine; a medication she had come to lean on, and not always for its analgesic properties.

Having satisfied herself about the accuracy of her discharge medications, she sent a WhatsApp message to DS Sharon Baxter. A condition of being discharged earlier than planned was that she would be picked up, and her friend had been happy to oblige.

Twenty minutes later, Baxter pulled into the hospital's Rotunda exit. Bankhurst opened the door, and winced slightly as she slumped into the low passenger seat of the ten-year-old Mini.

"God, you look like shit, Lily," declared Baxter.

"Hello to you, too," replied Bankhurst.

"Sorry, but should they be letting you home?"

"I'll be fine in a day or two."

"Let's hope so."

Baxter negotiated a reasonable three-point turn, despite being under the glare of an ambulance driver looking to access an emergency vehicle bay outside the hospital entrance. She acknowledged her transgression with a wave, and hoped a follow-up smile would help, but the unforgiving look on his face suggested it hadn't.

She turned sharply onto the main drag going through the hospital, leaving behind a small trace of tyre rubber on the asphalt in the process. Once she had negotiated the tortuous route, through the hospital grounds and back onto Westburn Road, she leant over and turned the car radio volume down.

"So, how did it go, *really*?" she enquired.

"Much the same as usual. Lots of initial bloods, and a scan, to make sure nothing surgical is required... and then just lying around eating painkillers. Mind you, the IV morphine on the first day was great. Best sleep I've had in ages. Can see why the smackheads like it so much. Morpheus himself would have been impressed."

"Are you still not sleeping well, then?" enquired Baxter.

"Oh, you know, off and on."

"How *off and on*?" pressed Baxter.

"Couple of nights per week… worse if I'm stressed."

"Did you ever finish your counselling following the Zimmerman case?"

"Er…" hesitated Bankhurst.

"That'll be a no then!"

"Well, you know what it's like. Other things get in the way."

Bankhurst was well aware she was hovering on the edge of a PTSD diagnosis following her near-death experience while investigating a previous serial killer, but had ducked out of occupational counselling, and had only given an edited version to her GP. She was determined not to let it govern her life but she wasn't always sure she was winning the struggle. She tried to change the subject.

"What's happening at work?"

"You've heard about the Seaton Park murder?"

"Yes. I saw it on *Aberdeen Live*. Nasty business."

"Yep. It's fairly spooked the uni students."

"Who's the senior investigating officer?"

"Tony Ledingham caught it, but he's actually had a family bereavement since. He's due to go away for a few days later this week. The DCI's not too happy about it."

"I can imagine," replied Bankhurst.

Bankhurst's mentor since she had arrived in Aberdeen, DCI Ken Anderson, had retired a few months previously. Losing his calming, friendly presence was bad enough, but his replacement, DCI Amanda Farrell, being an ambitious sociopath, had only compounded Bankhurst's sense of loss.

Farrell, or DCI Amanda "this wouldn't happen in the Met" Farrell, to give her full Aberdeen Police Station title, had been seconded from the Met for one year. Rumour had it that she had blotted her copybook, and had been farmed out for a year to cool her heels, but no one knew the exact details.

In her relatively short time at the station her unfiltered, sometimes aggressive, approach had alienated most of the staff below her, and even some above, despite her ingratiating behaviour towards the latter. A hint of pleasure spread across Bankhurst's face as she imagined the DCI's squirming response to her SIO going on bereavement leave, thereby placing herself closer to the potentially uncomfortable sharp end of an investigation.

Ten minutes later Baxter pulled into the small lock-block drive outside Bankhurst's Countesswells house, which she shared with her ten-year-old son, Andrew. Baxter collected her colleague's overnight holdall, and the pharmacy bag, before handing them back to her at the front door.

"Jesus, Lily. Have you got enough drugs in there, or what?"

"Aye, it's quite impressive, isn't it? As long as the dihydrocodeine is in there. That's the main thing," she added, with a muted attempt at a laugh.

The clunk of Bankhurst working the key in the door advertised her return home. Her mother, who had travelled from Glasgow to look after Andrew, made her way down the hall. A superficial smile failed to cover her underlying concern. Bankhurst could see Andrew in the background playing on an iPad. His mum's discharge from hospital didn't hold the same interest for him. Familiarity breeding, if not contempt, then certainly a degree of disinterest.

"Hello, love."

"Hi, Mum."

"How are you?"

"Getting there."

Bankhurst detected her mother's subtly raised eyebrow, as if to say, *Really*? She averted her gaze. No need to rise to the bait just yet.

"Well, come on through. You must be needing a cup of tea." Her mother's standard suggestion for any situation.

"Now, Andrew, if you can pull yourself away from Minecraft for a minute, you could give your mum a cuddle."

"Gran! I'm ten years old!"

"Well, OK, a high five, or whatever it is you youngsters do these days, then."

Andrew reluctantly complied, offering his mother a fist pump, which she happily accepted.

"Hi, son. What level are you on now?"

"Four!" he replied, a flush of pride stretching his face.

"Wow. Good for you."

The three-generation family chat continued for another ten minutes; a true hotchpotch of accents. Bankhurst's mother, Gillian, born and bred in Hampshire, had retained her distinctive south coast inflections despite moving to Glasgow with her husband, twenty years previously. Bankhurst, herself, a strange hybrid of Glasgow and Hampshire, and Andrew, born and bred in Scotland, a Scottish brogue, with strong Central Belt influences.

Gradually, Andrew lost interest returning his focus to his iPad. Bankhurst continued chatting with her mother, for as short a time as was politely possible, before excusing herself to take a bath. Wincing in pain as she undressed, she picked up a virginal silver foil of dihydrocodeine. Heard the satisfying pop as she delivered a tablet from its wrapper and dry-swallowed it. With care she slipped carefully into the water and awaited the external and internal warmth.

She retired to bed, earlier than usual, at 9:30pm. Although not in much pain she opted to take another dihydrocodeine to facilitate a good sleep. She quickly checked her social media and Tinder account. Of the three suggestions, two were rapidly swiped left, but one was directed rightwards. Quite a nice looking guy. Right age group. Health professional.

Might be worth another look when I'm more in the mood.

5

12th February

Bankhurst returned to work two days later.

Probably earlier than was wise, but she was keen to get back to some form of normality. Although she had been very grateful for family support at short notice, mother and daughter had reached the limit of a comfortable coexistence under the same roof. Both parties recognised a slight fraying of their relationship edge, and welcomed the development.

Grandma went to Glasgow. Andrew went to school. Bankhurst went to work.

All parties reasonably happy.

At Aberdeen Police Station, Bankhurst dealt with the usual round of polite enquiries about her health. Word had obviously circulated, through the ever-efficient CID grapevine, that she had been in hospital.

So much for confidentiality. Might as well have sent a bloody email!

DS Iqbal beamed his usual, generous smile. The DS and Bankhurst had been through a lot together, and were close. Not as close as she would perhaps have liked, but, for various reasons, not least of which was the fact she was his senior officer, that ship had sailed. Furthermore, it wasn't likely to return to port any time soon.

"How're you doin', Boss?" he said, "Great to see you back, so it is!"

"Fine, thanks," she said, lying. Although she had improved, she was not "fine". Her background struggle with long-term health issues continued.

Don't let the bastards win, her internal voice demanded. Whoever *the bastards* were.

After grabbing a coffee, she sat at her desk. She sighed and rested her chin on steepled fingers as her computer went through the laborious process of logging her in. Finally, she opened HOLMS, the police system used to manage serious crime investigations. She began checking her lengthy list of emails when she noticed a figure entering through the furthest door.

Conversations hushed. Postures straightened. A senior officer was within their midst.

"DI Bankhurst. A word. My office."

A female voice. To the point. No pleasantries. DCI Amanda Farrell had a talent for making even a relatively normal request sound like a rebuke. Today was no exception.

Here we go. What now?

Bankhurst obeyed the instruction, feeling the eyes of many of her colleagues follow her as she crossed the room, before disappearing through the door in the wake of her senior officer. The DI and DCI, an awkward silence hanging between them, went *upstairs*, literally and metaphorically towards Farrell's office. The silence continued as they sat either side of Farrell's desk. She refreshed her computer screen, and typed a few things on her keyboard.

OK, you've made your point.

Finally, Farrell looked up.

"I want you to take over SIO for the Kayleigh Peters murder."

"But I thought Tony Ledingham had that?"

"He did but seems like his bereavement leave is going to last a bit longer than expected."

"OK. No problem. Can I take my own team with me?"

"You can do what you bloody like, as long as you get a result… fast. I'm getting a lot of grief from the Chief Constable over this one. Seems like he's under pressure from the press and the University of Aberdeen. Apparently, there's a lot of unrest amongst the little Generation Z darlings."

"Not without reasonable cause… ma'am."

Farrell glared at her.

"Look, Bankhurst. I just need results on this one. Not backchat. Your reputation counts for nothing with me. Remember that."

"Yes, ma'am."

"I want you to keep me briefed on all developments."

"Yes, ma'am."

"That'll be all."

"Yes, ma'am."

Bankhurst needed no second invitation to leave the room. The door clicked behind her.

"Fucking cow," she whispered.

Two hours later she was looking at her assembled team, a hybrid combination of officers already on the investigation team, and her own chosen few.

DS Zafar Iqbal; her right-hand man. His upbeat Glaswegian personality, allied to his undoubted ability, was a valued combination. Nearest to him, surrounded by his usual cloud of grumpiness, sat DS George Gillespie. A cantankerous, old-school misogynist, but a decent detective; the latter cut him some slack with Bankhurst. In a group, chatting, were up-and-coming DCs Alison Fraser, Hugh MacLennan and Lisa Turnbull. On his own, not unusual for him, sat DC "Reflex" Babinski. Bankhurst had worked with him a couple of times before. Not graced with the best social skills, she assumed he was somewhere "on the spectrum". What he had been blessed with, however, was an ability to see abstracts and patterns which were denied other people. A useful skill set in Bankhurst's mind.

In larger groups, such as an MIT, Bankhurst had become used to knocking her George Ezra mug on her desk to capture attention. This time, George was spared the abuse. Simply by standing up, conversations were hushed and gazes focussed on the SIO. Even George Gillespie shifted his ample frame, accompanied by a creaking complaint from his chair, to pay attention. He was also the only detective in the room old enough to require repositioning his reading glasses towards the end of his nose, looking above them to bring Bankhurst back into focus.

"Thanks, everybody," she started.

"As you all probably know, I've taken over SIO on

this case from Tony Ledingham. Obviously, I've got some catching up to do, as indeed do some of the rest of you."

"Zafar. You're across the case. Can you do the necessary, please?"

"Nae problem, Boss."

Iqbal turned towards the whiteboard, and used its headlines to inform his talk.

Kayleigh Peters
Age: 19
Student at Aberdeen Uni
Family home: London
Found: 07:00 8 February
Seaton Park, Aberdeen
Estimated time of death: 02:30 to 03:30
Cause of death: strangulation by ligature
No sexual assault
No robbery. Phone, bag and purse all found at scene
Last seen alive: approximately 02:20 by two friends
No witnesses
No useful local CCTV
Nothing of interest on local ANPR
Toxicology screen: moderate alcohol. No drugs
Forensics at scene: nothing of note
No weapon found
Digital forensics: nothing so far on phone and laptop, but still being analysed
Timeline created from early evening until 02:20

Bankhurst was struck by the innocent face, adorned

with a cheeky grin, that was looking out at her from the photo attached above Kayleigh Peters' name. A pretty girl, whose life had been cruelly snuffed out before it had a chance to properly flourish.

How can this sort of thing still be happening?

Will it ever end?

She recalled her own carefree student days. Numerous nights out where she had made her way home, worse for wear, late at night. Several times alone.

There but for the grace of God went I.

She was vaguely aware that Iqbal had started his resumé, and forced herself to refocus her attention.

"As you can see from the whiteboard, the victim was a nineteen-year-old student, Kayleigh Peters. Strangled in Seaton Park, in the early hours of the eighth. She had been on, what appears to be, a routine night out with friends. No' much to go on so far. No witnesses, no forensics, no weapon, no motive. We've also drawn a blank with CCTV, ANPR, toxicology and digital forensics."

"And definitely no sign of a sexual assault?" interrupted Bankhurst.

"No, Boss. Dexter Brewster did the PM. No signs at all of sexual interference."

"Doesn't necessarily rule out an attacker with sexual, or robbery, intent… if they were interrupted," she continued.

"Seems a fairly extreme form of attack for robbery, to me," grumbled Gillespie.

"Point taken," agreed Bankhurst.

"What about house-to-house?"

"No' much, so far," replied Iqbal. "Mind you, there's only a smattering of houses along The Chanonry, and none with direct views of the park. On the north side of the park there are just the halls of residence. West is the River Don, and east is Don Street and the A956 northbound carriage. The only thing of note was a brief flash of light, coming from the direction of the park, reported by one of the students in the halls. She didnae think anything of it at the time. Could have been a firework perhaps?"

"Or, someone taking a photo," ventured Bankhurst. "Wouldn't be the first time a murderer has taken a photo of their victim."

"That wouldn't be good," barked Gillespie.

"How so?"

"Well, if you've just throttled someone, you'd have to be pretty cool and collected to take a photo, especially with a flash. Tends to suggest the photo might be very important to the perpetrator, if they were willing to take that risk. Some kind of trophy perhaps."

"Let's hope no," said Iqbal.

"Aye, because a trophy taker might become a trophy collector," suggested Gillespie, with his usual bleak pessimism.

Bankhurst had already, reluctantly, made the deduction herself. Having previously been involved in the last serial murder case in North East Scotland, at significant personal cost, she was in no hurry to repeat the experience. Although she couldn't deny the potential value of any piece of information, no matter how small, at this stage in the investigation, she hoped it was not a bad portent.

"What about family?" she enquired.

"Mum and Dad arrived yesterday, on a red-eye flight

from Heathrow," confirmed Iqbal. "I spoke to them yesterday afternoon. Devastated, as you might expect, so they were. I got a fair bit of background on Kayleigh, but nothing unusual for a teenager. A bit rebellious. Few different boyfriends. Nothing serious."

"And friends?"

"We've interviewed the friends she was out with that night, and also as many of her other friends and classmates, as we've been able to identify. All saying the same thing. Bubbly, likeable, a slight attitude towards authority. No' in a relationship. Drunk alcohol, and occasional recreational drug use. Nothing approaching a motive."

"Just in the wrong place, at the wrong time, perhaps."

Bankhurst's brow furrowed as she took a few seconds to process the information. Her fingers drummed on the desktop as she was caught in a moment of thought.

"OK, let's extend the timeline for a full twenty-four hours before the estimated time of death. I also want to extend the range for the murder weapon search and CCTV footage. Let's try and get everything from the locus right back to, and including, the nightclub. Was anybody acting strangely that night?"

Bankhurst was thinking quickly as threads of the investigation filled her mind.

"Get in touch with Aberdeen uni and request they post safe night-time practices on their social network sites," she continued. "And tell them I want to inspect her room personally."

"Yes, ma'am."

"In the meantime, I'm going to have a chat with my favourite pathologist, to find out what he *didn't* put in the post-mortem report."

In the few years Bankhurst had worked in Aberdeen, she had, by necessity, developed relationships with numerous colleagues. Some could be found in her iPhone contacts list, others most definitely not. Dr Dexter Brewster was the only one on her speed dial list. She had the greatest respect for his professional skills at crime scenes and post-mortems, but also hugely valued his sixth sense. His ability to think outside the box. In a previous case, a Brewster suggestion had led to a major breakthrough in a murder case, and Bankhurst had never forgotten it. He was also, just about, old enough to be her father and, at times, she almost felt his paternal arm around her.

She wanted to know, with Kayleigh Peters, if there was anything to be read between the lines. Something that could not justify on the record comment, but might just have tweaked the Brewster antennae.

Bankhurst was waiting in the coffee room of the pathology department, checking her social media, when a door swung open, and the clip-clop of mortuary room clogs on the parquet floor announced Brewster's arrival.

"Lily. Hello! Our receptionist told me you were waiting in here. Have you tried a cup of the *barely bloody drinkable*?" said Brewster, as he pointed to a jar of cheap instant coffee.

"No, thanks," replied Bankhurst. "Did that the last time. Once bitten…"

"Understood! How can I help you?"

"I was just looking for your thoughts on a post-mortem you did a couple of days ago. Kayleigh Peters."

"Ah. Yes. The student who was strangled. Nasty business."

"I've read your report, obviously. But, you know me, I like to know what you *felt* about it all."

"Well, the main thing about her as I recall is that, apart from her neck, she had barely a scratch on her. We could almost have done without the post-mortem. The post-mortem CT scan had already shown a laryngo-hyoid fracture, and soft tissue haemorrhage, typical of strangulation. The external appearance suggested the use of some form of soft ligature, rather than a manual strangulation. There weren't even any signs of trauma to her fingers, or damage caused by her own nails on her neck. Both, probably, because she was wearing gloves. Of course, we did a full post-mortem anyway, but it didn't turn up anything we didn't already know. All in all, the evidence suggests a sudden attack, where the victim was swiftly overpowered, and succumbed fairly rapidly. Apart from that, I've not much more to add."

Bankhurst pursed her lips in disappointment.

"Sorry," responded Brewster, as he arched his back and stretched his arms.

"I was hoping for a wee Brewster *nugget.*"

"Ha ha. Not this time, I'm afraid."

"Never mind, it was worth a try. Hey, how's Chloe doing, anyway?"

"Good, thanks. Getting really into this yoga malarkey."

"Any chance we'll see you in a leotard sometime soon?"

Brewster didn't reply, but raised an eyebrow, as if to say *What do you think?*

"And, how's my favourite boy, Archie?" continued Bankhurst.

"Oh. You know. Shags everything in sight… if I let him off the lead. That's labradoodles for you. To be fair to him, he's very inclusive. Not just bitches. Dogs too… and even small children of a certain height are fair game!"

"I thought he'd been *done*."

"He has! God knows what he'd be like if he hadn't."

"OK. On that note, I'll take my leave," Bankhurst announced, as she rose from her chair.

Brewster made a show of opening the door for her.

"Any time, madam."

"Why are you so chipper?" she enquired.

"Oh. I don't know. An early finish and a seven pm table for two at Luigi's may have something to do with it!" Brewster responded, with a smile and laughter lines befitting a face in its seventh decade.

As Bankhurst made the short journey back to Aberdeen police station, she hoped, not for the first time, that she would see those wrinkles for a few more years yet.

By mid-afternoon, Bankhurst was running out of steam, her enthusiasm and tolerance reduced in equal measure. She found it difficult to focus on work, and flitted between different social media sites. At 4pm she checked with her team to see if there had been any developments. There were not. Ten minutes later, she was standing at the back door of the station, rubbing her hands together against the cold, scanning the car park for her car. A press on her fob accelerated the process, as an ageing Toyota Yaris obligingly blinked two orange eyes at her. She set off towards Countesswells, but was in no mood for the evening traffic. A taxi, having cut her up, received an angry blast on her horn and a mouthful of abuse.

She wasn't home long before she opened the fridge and retrieved a half-drunk bottle of Sauvignon Blanc. With a generous glass poured she perched on a stool at her breakfast bar, and kicked off her shoes. Absentmindedly she swiped through her phone, but suddenly paused at Tinder. *Nice guy* had also swiped right, and sent a message.

Hi, I'm Tom. Would you like to go for a coffee sometime?

A small smile played across her face.

6

13th February

Unmade bed. Clothes scattered all over the room. A collection of dust motes clinging to the top of the skirting board. A less than fresh smell.

It could easily have been Andrew's bedroom at home. Instead, Bankhurst was standing at the entrance to Kayleigh's room in her hall of residence. Tantalisingly close to the north exit of Seaton Park, and safety.

Her bed had been roughly made, but at least it had been made. Bankhurst recalled her own student days, when domestic tidiness was not a strong suit. Kayleigh's work surfaces were, save for a laptop-shaped space amongst the surface dust, cluttered with typical teenage girl stuff; the portable device having been removed early on for digital forensic examination. Make-up, jewellery, hair bands, perfumes and a picture of, presumably, the family dog, competed for space. A hairbrush, never to be used again, lay on its side with a cocoon of tangled hairs.

For a moment, Bankhurst imagined Kayleigh, with music blaring, singing lustily into the hairbrush, a forever makeshift microphone.

A soft toy had lost out in the crush for space and been pushed onto the floor. By the look of the layer of dust on its surface, it had been there a while.

Bankhurst knew the room had already been assessed by CID colleagues, but she wanted to see for herself. Had they missed anything? Could she get a feel for what type of person Kayleigh was? Would that even help?

She spent half an hour rummaging through the room but, apart from a half smoked spliff at the back of a drawer, found nothing of note. Further thoughts of her own time as a student intruded.

She would never have had a half smoked spliff in her drawer. They were always finished at the first time of asking.

She imagined Kayleigh getting ready for her night out, with the prospect of her birthday after midnight. Anticipation and excitement in the air. She pictured her in front of her mirror applying make-up, adjusting her hair, putting earrings in. Her favourite music in the background. Repeated trips to her wardrobe. Outfit indecision. Finally settling on *the one*. Checking her handbag and phone, picking up her coat, and heading to the door. One final turn and change of blouse. She would likely have left her room in high spirits with not the slightest inkling as to what would befall her.

Unwittingly, she had entered the last act of her life, and was about to be brutally fast-forwarded to the very last scene. At some terrifying point in her ordeal, she would have realised she had no more words to say. And finally, the darkest of all curtains would have come down.

A shiver went down Bankhurst's spine.

"I'm going to get the bastard," she vowed.

They had agreed to meet at Pigments coffee shop, in the West End of Aberdeen. A neutral, public place for a first date. Not too long a commitment. Fast enough for either party to extricate themselves, if necessary.

Lily forced herself, against her natural instinct, to be five minutes late.

Mustn't look too keen.

She parked around the corner and used the rear-view mirror to check her appearance. Last-minute lipstick was applied and, satisfied with her appearance, she set off for her rendezvous. Slight anxiety gnawing at her stomach. It had been a while.

A tall man, about six feet, she estimated, was waiting outside Pigments, his coat drawn up against the cold wind. Fading social distancing pavement marks, a relic of the Covid pandemic, under his feet. Even from across the street, she recognised him from his Tinder picture. The tension in her face and body relaxed slightly. First two hurdles cleared; she hadn't been stood up and his Tinder picture was both current and accurate. Made a change.

"Hi… Lily?" he enquired, with a broad smile flashing handsome teeth.

"Yes. Tom?"

"Yes. Nice to meet you."

"You, too."

He hesitated, searching for a greeting that was neither too formal, nor too familiar. In the end he opted for a one-sided version of a European embrace, keeping a respectable distance between their cheeks.

"Shall we go inside?" he suggested, wafting his hand towards the automatic doors, which swished open obligingly.

The welcoming warm air and smell of on-site, freshly roasted coffee hit them as soon as they entered. The hum of conversation mixed with the noise of the espresso machines. Patrons leant into their discussions, as they luxuriated over morning coffee and pastries. A dog broke with convention and devoured its *pupaccino* in about ten seconds, creating an impressive mess on the floor in the process.

"I'm afraid your usual table won't be free for another five minutes, Tom. There's a couple of others available if you like." The tall, tattooed barista stretched his beard with a generous smile.

"No, you're fine. We can easily wait a couple of minutes."

"On first name terms with the staff," noted Lily.

"Guilty as charged! I'm in here more often than is good for me. I just live a couple of streets away. Usually on my own," he added, with arched eyebrows and cocked head inviting understanding.

Five minutes later, after an elderly couple had left, Tom and Lily squeezed either side of the corner table. With minimal embarrassment, they started the gentle interchange of pleasantries typical of a first date. Information gathering, opinion forming manoeuvres. A keeper... or not? Basically what it boiled down to.

The waiter arrived with their steaming coffee. Lily immediately regretted her choice of pastry. Freshly applied red lipstick and an almond croissant, dusted with icing sugar, were not comfortable bedfellows. A penchant for the French treat, and her craving for the almond paste at its core, had squeezed common sense to the periphery of her decision-making process. Now she had a dilemma. Use a knife to cut it into dainty pieces, like her spinster great aunt… or, just go for it. She had given herself some extra insulin earlier, in anticipation of eating something a little decadent, and could sense her blood sugar dropping slightly. No need to swipe the glucose meter on her upper arm. Not cool on a first date, anyway. She just knew, and she wasn't unhappy that her physiology had effectively taken the decision for her.

"That was impressive," admired Tom, two minutes later, when only a few small flakes of laminated pastry remained on Lily's plate, along with a dusting of icing sugar on her lips. Her natural inclination was to lick her finger and hoover the flakes up too, but she managed to summon a modicum of decorum, and stopped herself in time.

"You might have to get used to that," she said.

Lily realised, in that moment, her throwaway comment carried the subtle implication of future dates. She hadn't meant to make any assumptions, and didn't want to discourage Tom.

Their eyes met.

"Will I, indeed?" he replied, with a grin, exposing a few laughter lines beside his piercing blue eyes.

"So," he continued, "*civil servant* must cover a multitude

of sins," in reference to Lily's vague job description on her Tinder profile.

"The same might be said for *health professional*," she countered. "Could be anything from hospital porter to dean of the medical school. Not that there's anything wrong with being a hospital porter, you understand," she added.

"Busted!" Tom replied.

"So. Which? Or are you pulling my leg?"

"Actually, I'm a doctor. An anaesthetist. Doesn't do to advertise that on Tinder. Tends to attract oddballs like flies to…"

He left the sentence unfinished.

Lily laughed.

"What's so funny?"

"I know where you're coming from."

"Go on," he encouraged.

"I'm police. CID. Tends to put people off, and attract numpties, in equal measure. Especially those who like to fantasise about a woman in uniform."

Tom frowned, and drew his chin back as if to say, *surely not?*

"So, a gasman and plod. What a pair!" he continued.

"Indeed," agreed Lily.

They laughed together.

The tennis ball of safe conversation was struck back and forth for another thirty minutes. Superficial background information was exchanged. Bankhurst, originally from Hampshire, had been schooled in Glasgow, where she also spent her first few years in Police Scotland.

Tom had been born and bred in Huntly, a town thirty-eight miles from Aberdeen and had graduated in medicine from Edinburgh University. After training for several years in England and South Wales, he had returned to his North East Scotland roots to take up a consultant anaesthetist post at Aberdeen Royal Infirmary.

Long finished coffee, and a developing queue, suggested it was time to leave. They stood up and, as a parting gesture, Tom licked his index finger and deftly snagged the remaining crumbs, before placing them in his mouth.

Lily nodded her appreciation of his technique.

Outside, after Tom had repeated his opening greeting, but this time on both sides, they agreed on the possibility of a further date.

"Just one more thing," requested Tom. "I don't suppose there's any chance you could wear your uniform next time?"

Lily's usual response to blokeish humour at work was a raised middle finger. She hesitated for a split second, but was unable to prevent the full vertical salute, in all its unedited glory.

Oh my god, I've blown it.

Tom looked slightly startled for a second, before he tipped his head back and roared with laughter.

"Oh, I *like* you," he declared, as he turned away before announcing, over his shoulder, "I'll be in touch." He walked past the fish shop and Co-op, turning right out of sight.

"I hope so," Lily muttered to herself.

"A doctor!" exclaimed DS Sharon Baxter.

Bankhurst nodded her confirmation.

"A proper, medical one?"

Another nod.

"Bloody hell, Lily. That's got to be a result."

A hint of a blush surfaced on her face.

"What's he like?"

"IC-one. Male. Tall. Brown hair."

"Very funny. What's he actually like?"

"Actually, he's quite cute. And nice with it."

"You're shitting me?"

"No."

"Oh, my god. I've always wanted to date a doctor."

"Why?"

"Well… you know."

"No."

"Their knowledge… of… anatomy." Baxter nodded, and looked down towards Bankhurst's pelvis. Bankhurst knew where the conversation was heading. An opportunity for a bit of sport. She manufactured a confused looking facial expression.

Baxter looked furtively left and right, before leaning forward and whispering, "The G-spot."

"THE G-SPOT," Bankhurst repeated, abandoning any attempt at *sotto voce*.

"Shhh!" implored Baxter. "We're in the bloody canteen!" she hissed.

A pink flush began to bloom on her face.

Bankhurst dissolved into a fit of giggles, so infectious that her friend was compelled to join in.

A few heads turned briefly, but soon returned to concentrate on their food and conversation.

7

15th February

Bankhurst woke up with a start. Her pulse was racing. Pyjamas soaked in sweat. A tingling feeling spread upwards from her body over her head. Her respiratory rate accelerated rapidly. Sharp stabbing pains came and went at various sites in her body. Anxiety gripped her very core.

Something bad was going to happen. She knew it.

Although she had suffered numerous panic attacks since her kidnap, the experience gained never seemed to mollify the next episode. Nocturnal or diurnal, it was always the same. A frightening, all-encompassing, corporal event.

She tried to reason with her adrenalised body, but her physiological responses could not be cowed. Her amygdala, the brain's fear centre, was still in full control.

Be patient, she counselled herself. *Be patient. It will pass.*

And it did. After ten minutes.

Ten very uncomfortable minutes.

And then the insomnia. Cold, clammy pyjamas, and a mind that refused to switch off. Flashbacks. The face of Zimmerman, her captor. His dead face, after she had killed him. The odds heavily stacked against sleep.

All sorts of trivia circuited her brain. Lyrics from a song. Did she need to buy a different brand of toothpaste? Would she be able to cope as SIO in a murder? Had she enough milk in the fridge?

And then the insomnia brought its own pressure.

The *need* to get back to sleep. The *need* to be rested. The *need* to function at work.

Only four hours until the unwelcome melody of her phone alarm would herald the new day.

She turned over and fumbled with a medication foil she had located in her top drawer. *Pop.* A single pill was thrown into her mouth. Three remaining palpable bumps in the foil told of a dwindling supply. She made a mental note to phone her surgery in the morning, to request another prescription.

With the words of her psychologist about stopping her behavioural therapy prematurely, ringing in her ears, she finally drifted off to sleep at 4am.

"OK, where are we at?"

Bankhurst wasted no energy on pleasantries. She wasn't in the mood. Her disturbed night's sleep had not helped her frame of mind.

The room sensed her humour, and were quick to come to attention.

Iqbal cleared his throat and thought, as DS, he should take the lead.

"We've now got a timeline for her last twenty-four hours."

"You mean *Kayleigh's* last twenty-four hours," corrected Bankhurst somewhat sharply, and then immediately regretted it. *Praise in public, criticise in private*, words from her last management seminar sprung immediately to mind. Especially for her trusted first lieutenant, Iqbal.

MacLennan nudged Babinski's leg under the desk, and they exchanged glances, as if to say *Who's rattled her cage?*

"Aye, Boss. Of course. Kayleigh's last twenty-four hours," replied a somewhat chastened Iqbal.

"Nothing particularly unusual," he continued. "The evening before she was at her halls, as witnessed by several students. Her search history indicated she was studying, and dipping in and out of various social media sites. The following morning she was at work at a local bakery. Went to the gym in the afternoon, and then back to her halls, presumably to get ready for her night out."

"OK," acknowledged Bankhurst, while scanning the room for her next source of information.

"Nothing from digital forensics, so far," rasped DS Gillespie.

Bankhurst was relieved to see that the ever grumpy Gillespie seemed to be nursing an even lower mood than herself.

"Usual teenage nonsense," he added, clearly reluctant to use any more words than absolutely necessary.

"What about dating sites?"

"None."

Bankhurst changed tack.

"Any notable miscreants released from jail in the last few months?"

"No, ma'am."

"Debts?"

"Just her student loan. Nothing else significant."

"Any bad habits we should know about?"

"We know she drank and, according to her friends, she was a recreational drug user. Nothing heavy."

"What about CCTV at the club? Anything dodgy?"

"Na, unless you count some of the clothes, and definitely some of the mullets," quipped Iqbal, unable to retard his natural wit.

He escaped with only a *oh, very funny* look from Bankhurst.

"And outside the club?"

"Nothing of note. Just usual weekend madness."

"So, not a lot, then," summarised Bankhurst, with resignation weighing heavily on her words.

"*Not a lot.* More like bloody nothing!"

Iqbal and Bankhurst had gone upstairs to report to DCI Farrell, who wore her unedited dissatisfaction right across her pink face.

"You've been on the case for twenty-four hours, DI Bankhurst, and we're not one bit further on."

"Yes, ma'am. We'll keep at it, and hope to get a break."

"*Hope* shouldn't come into it!" the senior officer retorted. "What am I going to tell the parents... and the dean of the university?"

"Perhaps the comms officer could assist you, ma'am?"

"Don't get clever with me, Bankhurst!"

"Of course not, ma'am."

"Right. You can bugger off now, but I'll be looking to get some concrete developments tomorrow."

A swish of her hand dismissed the two detectives. They wasted no time in taking their leave, but not before hearing, in the wake of the closing door, "this wouldn't happen in the MET".

Iqbal and Bankhurst looked at each other and had to work hard to stifle a giggle.

"Speaking about tomorrow, Zafar. Is there any chance you can give me a lift into work? I'm dropping my car off at the garage tonight for an MOT and service tomorrow. Also, I usually drop Andrew and his friend Gavin off at school on the way, if that would be OK?"

"Nae problem, Boss. What time are we speaking?"

"Eight o'clock?"

"I'll be there."

Bankhurst deposited her car at the garage and caught a bus home. Most passengers had earbuds in or were engrossed in their device screens. Or both. Bankhurst shrugged her shoulders and dug her iPhone out of her bag, tapping the screen and bringing it to life. She started trawling through her emails, and social media, when a ping heralded an incoming WhatsApp message.

Hi Plod,
Really enjoyed yesterday. Fancy hanging out some other time?
I've got some days off next week. Can Police Scotland spare one of its finest for a pie and a pint?
Gasman x

Hey,
You certainly know how to treat a lady!
I might consider it.
Let me check my rota (and babysitter!)
and I'll get back to you.
P x

Great.
G x

True to his word, but not before he had given his car a quick tidy and had unwrapped an air freshener, Iqbal drew into the kerb outside his DI's house at 7:55am.

Bankhurst felt a vibration on her Apple Watch.

"Taxi for Bankhurst!" announced Iqbal's arrival.

Most mornings Andrew needed encouragement, cajoling, and sometimes an overt threat of screen time limitation, to get him out the door. Today was no different, but mother and son finally sunk into the low seats of Iqbal's car at five minutes past the hour.

"Thanks so much for this, Zafar. Really appreciate it."

"Nae problem, Boss."

"A' right, wee man? How're you doin'?"

"Humph," replied Andrew, still in strop mode.

"What about Gavin?" enquired Iqbal.

"I got a text. He's already went to school," grumbled Andrew, proving that he could speak after all.

"He's already *gone* to school," corrected his mother.

"Aw, Boss. The waen's only saying a verb Glaswegian style!"

"Yes. Well. He needn't bother!" affirmed Bankhurst,

before adding, "Do you know the way to the school?"

"Nae problem. I've went there before." He winked at Andrew, who grinned in response. An invitation for Iqbal to turn for a fist pump was accepted.

"You're a bad influence, DS Iqbal!" Bankhurst announced, with a smile stretching her face.

8

5th March

He mopped his brow with a towel, took a swig from his water bottle and adjusted his noise cancelling earphones. He wasn't a fan of gym muzak.

Ten machines done. Two more to go.

He looked at his iPhone. Confirmed his thoughts; only the horizontal leg press and cable biceps bar remained. Twelve reps on each one, the chosen weights calculated to get him to the point of exhaustion.

Having completed his rest period, he started reps on the leg press. Working steadily, he felt his pulse and respiratory rate accelerate. Sweat beads popped on his forehead.

Keep pushing.

He could almost sense his body switching from aerobic to anaerobic respiration, the lactic acid accumulating.

His muscles began to ache.

Feel the burn. Fight the burn, he demanded of himself, as he watched the digital rep counter's ever slower journey to twelve.

Keep going. Keep going.

Finally, gasping for breath, he finished, and started the timer on his app. Two minutes to recover. Allow vital signs to settle. Clean the machine. Hydrate and move on to the last of the twelve exercises.

Exactly five minutes later he had completed the programme, and entered the data in his app. With none of his gym buddies around for a chat, he headed to the changing room and luxuriated in the reward of a long hot shower. Towel dried hair combed neatly into place. Aftershave applied, clothes put on with care and attention. Satisfied with his mirror appearance, he slung his gym bag over a shoulder and exited the gym.

Outside, the lengthening days of March competed against a thick blanket of low cloud for the remaining daylight. A palpable drop in air temperature prompted a shiver and a quick pace as he set off. Four streets later he entered Johnston Gardens, a glance upwards suggesting there was just enough light in the grey sky to traverse the unlit park. Heavily budded azaleas and rhododendrons promised late spring splendour. A mother proudly led a string of four ducklings across the pond, creating a small V-shaped wash in the process. The wind blew a few remaining breadcrumbs from the bridge into the water.

He felt hungry, and grinned as a search of his coat pocket produced an energy bar. Easy access was denied by cold fingers; teeth were enlisted. Against the rustle of the wrapper he thought he heard a noise behind him, but a turn of the head failed to identify any source. There appeared to be only one other person in the park, and they were in front of him heading up towards the monument for the Super Puma helicopter disaster of 2009. He maintained his pace.

After thirty seconds he looked behind again, but all he could see was a myriad of azalea and hydrangea shapes, against the gathering gloom. He felt reassured.

Being aware of the person ahead of him, and not wanting to alarm them, he fell into the rhythm of their stride pattern.

Left. Right. Left. Right.

Keeping a steady distance.

Same stride length. Same footfall noise on the path.

Left. Right. Left. Right.

He finished his energy bar. Carefully scrunched the wrapper and put it inside his pocket. Pulled up the zip.

Left. Right. Left. Right.

Deliberately not closing the gap.

Until he was ready.

He reached into his bag, pulled out a knife and accelerated towards the shape ahead.

The audible change in pace triggered a ripple of fear in Dawn Syme. Before she had time to turn fully, she felt the agony of the first of several deep stabs to the lower back.

She collapsed to the ground, engulfed by crippling pain. A muffled cry barely made it out of her mouth. Her distress was short-lived as massive internal bleeding rapidly emptied her circulatory system of blood. Deprived of vital oxygen, her heart slowed and arrested. She was unaware of the flash of light from a phone camera.

One minute after she died, a vibration, and an auditory alarm, on her Apple Watch went undetected. Her fall to the ground, and lack of recovery after a programmed amount of time, triggered an automatic message to her watch and phone. As there was no response, the system then sent a message to the local emergency services stating the owner, who was over fifty-five years in age, had likely had a fall, and was still lying on the ground.

Greg Smith and Karl Poon had just sat down for a cup of tea and a biscuit in the canteen, at Aberdeen ambulance station. It had been a busy shift, and they were looking forward to a break. Two sips into the tea, the canteen door opened just enough to let one of the traffic controllers stick his head through the gap.

"Ah. Thought you might be here."

The two emergency medical technicians looked at each other, and rolled their eyes. They knew what was coming.

"Look, guys. There's been a pile-up on the Western Peripheral Route. Several units are tied up there. We've been notified of a possible fall in the west side of the city, and I've no one else available at the moment."

"*Possible* fall?" enquired Poon, with slightly raised eyebrows.

"Well, it's one of those bloody automated alerts from a smartphone. Might be something or nothing, but..."

"Most likely nothing," said Smith under his breath.

Both EMTs had been involved with several such "notifications" and had developed a healthy scepticism for their accuracy. More often than not, the phone had simply been dropped, and on one famous occasion, a red-faced, and scantily clad couple were seen getting up from the floor to see what the flashing blue light outside their home was all about.

"Aye. OK, Gus. Give us a couple of minutes to swill the tea down, and we'll be on our way."

"Thanks, guys. The person seems to be in Johnston Gardens. I'll send you the exact coordinates."

The flashing blue light, and piercing howl of the siren, quickly cut a swathe through the last of the rush hour traffic, the cars coming together again behind the ambulance like a giant zip. By the time the crew had arrived at the narrow entrance, the gardens were cloaked in darkness. Unable to take their rig into the garden itself, the EMTs set off on foot, armed with torches and medical kit bag. With accurate GSM coordinates, it only took two minutes to approach the target site. From about twenty yards out both EMTs could see what looked like a casualty lying on the ground. They glanced at one another and quickened their pace. As they approached, they realised their patient was lying face down in a puddle. Only when they knelt down to begin their primary assessment did they realise the puddle was red.

"Fuck's sake!" declared Smith, as he reflexly pulled away, startled.

Poon switched on his portable 800MHz radio and barked into the mouthpiece.

"Unit 32 to control."

"Control. Go ahead."

"Request urgent assistance. Paramedic and police. Severe assault. Possible fatality. Primary assessment ongoing."

"Noted 32. We have the coordinates already. Consider it done."

Robert Syme's annoyance had been displaced by concern. He and his wife went bowling every Wednesday evening. Digestion was not his strong suit, often claiming to be a martyr to his stomach, and he liked to eat early on bowling nights, to "let his tea go down", before playing.

Give or take five minutes, she would normally be home by 6pm. Forty-five minutes later, he had an uneasy feeling in his stomach; his anxiety then reached another level when her co-volunteer at the church office confirmed they left together at 5:45pm. He suddenly remembered that his wife had a find-my-phone app enabled on their Mac. After powering up the machine, and googling how to use the app, he fumbled through the necessary steps.

"That's odd," he said to himself, as the app suggested the phone was in nearby Johnston Gardens. At first, he thought she must have dropped her phone in the park, but then realised, with a growing sense of dread, that she would still have arrived home at her usual time.

He rushed out the door, grabbing a coat as he went, and headed towards Johnston Gardens.

"Please, no. Please, no," he muttered.

A brisk pace took him along several similar granite-house streets. Classic middle-class, semi-detached residences with small, neat front gardens. Blue flashing lights, visible from two emergency vehicles at the entrance to the park, hastened his pace further. Scene of crime tape, and two police officers, restricted admission to all but emergency personnel. Despite his protestations, entry was denied him.

Suddenly, two powerful Dragon searchlights were turned on in the park bathing the ground in bright, silvery light. Even from his peripheral vantage point, he could see a SOC tent being erected.

A tear began to run down his right cheek.

Johnston Gardens, winner of Britain in Bloom Public Park Award 2002, was about to hit the headlines for a much more sinister reason.

The evening traffic had died down and Bankhurst made quick progress across the city to Johnston Gardens. She was due to finish at 8pm and was keen to get the preliminaries, of what sounded very much like a murder investigation, underway. An overt police presence in a quiet Aberdeen suburb, had drawn a crowd. Even this early, Bankhurst noted a reporter from *Aberdeen Live*.

Bloody social media.

The Gardens car park obliged with its last space, next to a recycling point. Bankhurst reversed in, taking extra care, to avoid any embarrassment in front of her watching colleagues. She jogged across Viewfield Road, grateful to recognise one of the policemen on guard duty, sparing her fumbling in pockets with cold hands looking for an ID. He nodded his recognition, and lifted the tape for her to duck under.

A freshening wind was buffeting the higher trees around the periphery of the park, though the more compact members of the rhododendron family below were less disturbed. Like a moth drawn to light, Bankhurst made her way up the tortuous path to the crime scene. The plastic walls of the SOC tent flapped and snapped in the wind, like the sails of a yacht. Bankhurst hoped the anchor points were secure. She started making her way from one plastic SOC stepping stone to another and, even from a few yards out, she recognised the distinctive, rounded silhouette of Dr Dexter Brewster inside the tent.

She took a few deep breaths in. The smell of budding spring growth on the surrounding shrubs filled her nostrils.

Inside was entirely different. A strong coppery smell, from pools of blood, mixed with an even stronger smell of faeces; an opening bowel the last biological act of Dawn Syme's dying body.

Brewster turned, recognised the DI, and shook his head.

"This is grim, Lily. Properly brutal."

"So I see," she replied, suppressing a strong urge to cover her nose.

"Multiple sharp traumas to both sides of the lower back. Massive haemorrhage. Would have bled out in minutes. No obvious trauma elsewhere, but I'll get a better look back in the department."

"Is that where your kidneys are?" she enquired, pointing to the multiple stab wounds.

"Indeed," confirmed Brewster.

"Any defence wounds?"

"No. Looks very much like she was attacked unawares. Nothing obvious under her nails either," he added.

"I know it's early days yet, but do you have any estimate of the time of death?"

"Very likely to be between 5:55pm and 6:10pm," he replied.

"Wow. That's very specific."

"Ah. Well. I've had a bit of help. Her phone records a likely fall to the ground at 5:55pm, triggering the notification to the emergency services. The EMTs were here about fifteen minutes later, and sounds like she was well dead even by then. For what it's worth, her rectal temperature would also fit with that time frame."

"Thanks, Dexter."

"When is the post-mortem likely to be?" she added.

"I'll try and get it done tomorrow morning. Shall we say 10am?"

"Sounds good. Thanks."

Bankhurst forced herself to avert her gaze from the corpse. Although a horrific sight, it was strangely compelling.

Two SOCOs in white uniforms, working diligently in the background, caught her eye.

"Any ID yet?" she enquired.

"Driver's licence for a Dawn Syme in her handbag."

"Any obvious forensics?"

"We've got a good footprint in the blood. Looks about a size nine. Too big for the victim. We've taken photos, and are about to cast."

"Thanks. Sounds promising."

"Soil samples?"

The SOCO looked at his hands, suggesting he only had one pair. Bankhurst held up her own in apology.

"Sorry. Not trying to tell you your job."

"We've another couple of guys coming soon to help out," he said.

"OK. Good," conceded Bankhurst, as she left the tent.

Outside, grateful once again to be in fresh air, Bankhurst fought off a sudden wave of nausea. Her pallid, sweaty face went unnoticed, in the dark, by her colleagues. A nearby wooden bench, dedicated to the memory of Miss Lavina Buchan, offered the chance of a seat and a clear head. Anxiety crawled around her stomach like a sea of weevils. Was she going to have another panic attack?

Surely not here? Surely not now?

She tried to remember what her therapist had said in their sessions, before she had reneged.

Often the fear of the panic attack is worse than the panic attack itself. She concentrated on her breathing. Slow deep breaths. In. Out. In. Out. Slowly the symptoms began to settle, and she abandoned the charade of checking messages on her phone. A cautious rise to her feet passed uneventfully, and she made her way down the path to the park entrance, where the police presence, and with it public interest, had grown significantly. Having confirmed adequate park security, and arranged a dawn fingertip search, she made her way back to her car, through an ever-increasing crowd. Requests for comments from zealous reporters were met with a stony stare.

Having reached the relative sanctity of her car she slumped into her seat, and sighed deeply.

It's a fucked-up world, she said to herself.

She glanced at her watch. Numbers flooded her brain. Thirty minutes to shift end. Fifteen minutes to drive back to the station. Five minutes to drive home. It was a no-brainer. She needed to give Andrew a hug, and see the bottom of a wine glass.

Wouldn't be the first time someone has done a remote handover to the night shift staff, she reassured herself.

She switched on the engine, engaged first gear and

pulled out of the car park. A press photographer risked taking a photo. She glared at him, and made a mental note of his face.

9

6th March

"*Her upstairs* wants to see you."

Iqbal had an apologetic look on his face.

"Thanks, Zafar," replied Bankhurst, before adding, under her breath, "great start to the day!"

She hung her coat up, put her bag in a drawer and switched on her PC. Obligingly it started scrolling through start-up screens, with a familiar soundtrack of computer noises. Having delayed her meeting with Farrell as long as seemed reasonable, she climbed the stairs to the upper floor.

"Come in," shouted Farrell, in response to the knock on her door.

Not for the first time, Bankhurst was hit by the contrast between the diminutive woman sitting opposite her, and the oversized desk.

"Ah. Bankhurst. Sit."

"Ma'am."

No pleasantries. No chit-chat. Straight in.

"I'm going to give you the Syme murder from last night."

"Thanks, ma'am."

"To be honest. You weren't my first choice. The Kayleigh Peters case has gone nowhere fast. I had Tony Ledingham in mind, but he's just gone on bloody holiday apparently! So, as the Peters case is cold, and you've already got a team assembled, we'll see if you can do any better this time!"

Bankhurst gritted her teeth, but managed to squeeze "Thanks, ma'am" through them.

Relieved her encounter with Farrell was over, she descended the stairs two at a time. Despite the DCI's mockery, she was keen to get her teeth into another murder investigation, as she recognised a ring of truth in her assessment of the Peters case. Despite the best efforts of her team, there had been very few substantive leads to follow. At best, the investigation was lukewarm; at worst it was stone cold.

With a slight spring in her step, Bankhurst breezed into the incident room. The overnight team had commenced a whiteboard column for Dawn Syme and she studied the early entries.

Dawn Syme
Age: 62
Married to Robert (64)
Two children (30 and 28) – living in the Central Belt
Retired secretary
Volunteers at local church
Left church at 5:45pm with a co-volunteer. Went separate ways.

Found in Johnston Gardens
Estimated time of death: 5:55pm to 6:10pm
PM awaited but likely cause of death: massive
haemorrhage from multiple stab wounds
No recent arguments/known enemies

<u>Early Forensics</u>
Size 9 footprint near victim
Fits with male (or tall female)
Nike brand. Common variety. Sold in multiple outlets
Dawn fingertip search this morning. Nothing to report

Bankhurst took a few deep breaths in. Ran a hand through her hair.

"OK, here we go," she said, under her breath. "Right. Listen up, everyone."

Heads turned obediently.

"I've been appointed SIO for this murder investigation. My current team for the Kayleigh Peters case will take this on."

Sideways glances and murmurs filled the room.

"I've just had a look at the board. Anybody got anything to add?"

"Yes, ma'am. DC MacLennan. We've just received some early CCTV images showing the victim heading towards the Gardens entrance at 5:52pm. About one minute later, she is followed by another person. Body habitus suggests likely male. Wearing dark clothes. Tall. Carrying a shoulder bag. Face not seen. Unable to determine ethnicity. Not seen on any other cameras in the area."

"Where the hell did he come from?" asked Iqbal.

"Any CCTV in the Gardens?" asked Bankhurst, more in hope than expectation, as she had no recollection of seeing any the previous night.

"No, ma'am." Her fears were confirmed.

"Can you let me have a look at the CCTV footage?"

MacLennan obliged with a soft rat-a-tat of keyboard noises, the final key hit with a slight flourish.

"See what you mean," Bankhurst said softly, "he's made himself difficult to see. Perhaps the gate analysis software might give us something... if he's on the system."

"OK, it's a start," she continued, "obviously, this person on CCTV must be our prime suspect for the moment. We need to extend the CCTV capture area. Perhaps we can find him further away from the scene."

"Let's look at all available CCTV. Aberdeen city street cameras, businesses, residential door cams. Get someone over to the Viewfield area this evening. See if there are any cyclists who use that route regularly on their way home. Some of them might have helmet cameras. We need to look at ANPR. Did the suspect have a car in the vicinity? Are there any plates that ping on the system?"

Bankhurst stared into space as she gathered her thoughts. Tucked hair behind her ears as she concentrated.

"I want that weapon found. Let's extend the search range to a half mile. Every bush, bin, dumpster, burn, and outhouse need to be checked. We'll also need to start house-to-house enquiries. I'll speak to Uniform about that, as we'll need extra bodies on the ground."

"Oh, and let's look into the victim in more detail. I want to know her timeline for the whole of yesterday up to the murder. Where was she? Who did she meet? Who did she speak to? Online or in person. Is she as squeaky clean as she appears to be? The usual stuff-debts, alcohol or drug abuse, online activity, relationships."

Bankhurst delegated the various tasks, and drew the briefing to a close.

"We'll meet again at 4pm."

The low growl that was the voice of DS Gillespie cut across the noise of chairs being swivelled and papers shuffled.

"What about the Seaton murder?"

Bankhurst raised an eyebrow, inviting more detail.

"Could there be a link?" Laconic as ever, Gillespie showed no sign that he was going to expand on his theory.

"You mean, two violent deaths, both in city parks?"

"Aye."

"Well. I suppose 'never say never', but there are very few other similarities. Different part of the city. Different age group. Different time of day. Different MO."

"I'm just saying…"

"Noted, DS Gillespie. Noted."

Bankhurst sought her first coffee of the day. A fortification against her visit to the morgue for the post-mortem. Hot, wet and with a vague taste of coffee, it lived up to its reputation. Only the prospect of a slight caffeine hit persuaded her to drain the last contents from the plastic cup. She quickly checked her social media and messages, in the hope of having received something from Tom, but was left disappointed.

A sudden squall, carrying with it some sleety rain, swept across the courtyard between the police station and the morgue. Unable to afford a delay, for fear of being late for the post-mortem, Bankhurst pulled the collar of her jacket up and jogged across the short distance.

"Hi, Lily."

"Dexter," acknowledged Bankhurst, through the intercom, while taking her seat.

Dr Dexter Brewster was already gloved and aproned, his instruments ready. A red light blinked on his voice recognition system.

Bankhurst looked at her watch. Still only 9:55am.

Brewster noticed the time check.

"Don't worry, Lily. You're not late. I've got a court case later this morning, and I need to get some caffeine before then."

Bankhurst nodded her head.

"Understood." Brewster's partiality to the coffee bean was well known, and might even rival her own.

Never one to cut corners, Brewster went through his normal systematic approach, though Bankhurst noted he was in top gear. Moving efficiently, there was a discernible absence of the usual chit-chat which characterised his post-mortems, especially if Lily Bankhurst was the visiting detective.

Bankhurst listened to the familiar background soundtrack of a post-mortem.

Brewster's commentary, for the clinical record, interrupted by instructions to his anatomical pathology assistant; the clanking of instruments and organ scales; the screwing noise from specimen pot lids.

A long frontal incision allowed recovery, measurement and inspection of the internal organs, before they were placed back within the body. Bankhurst knew the incision was made precisely to allow for organ recovery, but not be visible to relatives when the body was clothed again. A single, transverse incision at the back of the skull would follow, allowing the brain to be harvested, if necessary, again with minimal visible evidence when the body was in a coffin.

To Bankhurst's lay ears, it appeared that most of the findings were in keeping with a sixty-two-year-old, non-smoking lady, who had led a relatively temperate life.

Until Brewster examined the kidneys.

"And now, I'm going to examine the retroperitoneal space," he said, loudly.

This time he did look, over the top of his mask, in Bankhurst's direction, sensing this was likely to be the area of greatest interest.

"You'll probably remember, Lily, that the retroperitoneal space is the area behind the main abdominal cavity, which lies in front, enclosed within the peritoneal sac. The main anatomical features in this compartment are the pancreas, kidneys and the largest arterial and venous blood vessels in the body."

Bankhurst didn't remember, but kept quiet.

Brewster shook his head. "Oh dear. Oh dear," he murmured, more to himself than the wider audience, as he inspected deep inside the body. "This is even worse than I had anticipated."

He tried to remove the kidneys intact, but it proved impossible.

After a few minutes, a stainless steel dish on top of a scale, contained several pieces of amorphous bloody tissue.

"That," announced Brewster, "is the right kidney."

Slop. Slop. Slop. The remains of the left kidney were delivered to a separate dish.

"Not exactly minced, but certainly sliced and diced," he added.

"To be honest, I've never seen such organ destruction, outside of a major accident. For the record, both the abdominal aorta and inferior vena cava have also been breached. Between the blood vessel and organ damage, haemorrhage would have been catastrophic. I estimate she would probably have died within one or two minutes of the assault."

The weight of the information hung in the mortuary air.

Bankhurst let the silence linger for a respectable length of time.

"So, no surprises in the cause of death, and certification?"

"No," agreed Brewster.

"Cardiac arrest. Secondary to hypovolemic shock. Secondary to massive internal haemorrhage. Secondary to trauma to kidneys and major blood vessels. Secondary to multiple sharp traumas in the paralumbar region, bilaterally."

"Thanks, Dexter. Appreciate it."

"No problem. Any time."

4pm

The noisy chatter in the incident room required a double table knock from Bankhurst's ever reliable and uncomplaining George Ezra mug.

"OK. I'll start," she announced.

"Dr Brewster did the post-mortem this morning. No surprises. Massive haemorrhage from multiple wounds to her kidneys and adjacent blood vessels."

Serious faces in the audience reflected the mood in the room.

"Where are we on the weapon hunt, and house-to-house, Zafar?"

"Nothing so far, ma'am, I'm afraid."

"OK. Anything from passive data? Reflex?"

"No pings on ANPR, ma'am."

Bankhurst looked at the wider investigation team.

"Finances?"

"As you might expect for a middle-aged married lady."

"CCTV?"

"Still working through it, ma'am. Largely residential area. Not many businesses. Few domestic cameras and doorbell cams. We also found three cyclists who go through the area daily, one of whom had a helmet cam. So far, we've got the victim on four different cameras, travelling north from the church in the Mannofield area. She's last seen approaching the entrance to Johnston Gardens from Viewfield Avenue. The suspect is only picked up once, heading to the Gardens on Viewfield Road, from the east."

"Significance?" Bankhurst crossed her arms and scanned the room again.

Contributions came in from the floor as invited.

"Suspect was camera aware, while the victim wasn't."

"He parked nearby… or cycled for that matter."

"Some other form of transport took him to the vicinity. A bus, or taxi perhaps?"

"What about the fact that he seems to only start following her from just outside the Gardens?"

"Perhaps he knew her regular time and route, so didn't have to follow her as such?"

"Or maybe," thought Bankhurst out loud, "that he didn't preselect her at all. It was purely opportunistic."

The faces of more senior members of the team lengthened slightly. With experience, came the realisation that spontaneous crimes often remove motive as a potential investigative seam to mine.

"OK," Bankhurst continued, "let's assume he did come from east to west, towards the Gardens. Let's double down on our efforts on that part of the city. There *must* be something we can find."

"Have we missed any CCTV? Recheck ANPR. Get a list of all residential plates, and start looking at any who doesn't belong there; especially if they pinged more than once in the week or two before the murder. He may have reconnoitred the area."

"Check with all the major taxi firms. Did they have any drop-offs or pickups from that area in the hour before, or after, the estimated time of death." Bankhurst glanced at her notes to make sure she hadn't missed anything.

"We need to look at buses as well. Aberdeen city, and any that were passing through the west of the city on their way to Deeside or Donside. On board CCTV, obviously, but worth also enquiring from the bus companies if we can get any data from their payment machines. Nobody pays by cash now, do they?"

The rhetorical question hung unanswered in the air, before Bankhurst broke the silence.

"What about the electric Big Issue bikes? You know the ones scattered all over the pavements."

"Don't even get me fucking started on that!" bellowed Gillespie.

Bankhurst sniggered through her nose. For once she was on the same page as her grumpy DS.

"They surely must have GPS on them. See if any were in the Kepplestone, Seafield or Rubislaw areas on the fifth. If there were, who rented them."

The door at the back of the room opened. Heads turned to see a tall, familiar figure, his pale face framed by thinning, mousy brown hair.

"Ah, Neil. Good timing," announced Bankhurst.

Neil Jardine, head of Digital Forensics, was a regular, and highly valued, contributor to serious crime investigations. His ever-expanding department was often centre stage to an inquiry.

"We've got her iPad, phone and the home PC. Nothing unusual so far. Fairly standard search history. Not on any dating sites. No evidence of any affair. Not very helpful, I'm afraid. We'll have a look at her Alexa and car data in due course."

"OK. Thanks, Neil. Let me know if anything turns up."

Jardine nodded.

Bankhurst clicked her tongue, frustration written across her face.

"Not a lot to show for a day's work," she said, thinking out loud.

She was about to draw the meeting to a close when DC Lisa Turnbull spoke up.

"I think I might have something, ma'am."

10

6th March

"Go on," invited Bankhurst.

"Well. I've been looking at all domestic CCTV from the Viewfield, Seafield and Rubislaw areas. I haven't come across the assumed perpetrator, but I have noticed a peculiarity."

Turnbull turned her PC screen to make it more visible to her colleagues.

"There are three door cams sited on houses on the northside of Rubislaw Park Crescent, which all face Johnston Gardens. I've positioned their data side by side on the screen for you to see."

Glasses were donned by some, and taken off by others, as they worked to get the image in focus.

Iqbal frowned, and looked at Bankhurst, as if to say *What am I missing?*

She shrugged her shoulders.

A pause for dramatic effect over, Turnbull continued.

"All three cameras recorded an event at the same time: 6:01pm. But there are no subsequent recordings of people, or animals for that matter, at the doors of the houses concerned."

"Lorry going past?" suggested Reflex Babinski.

"But, there's nothing recorded," contributed MacLennan.

"Maybe I didn't make myself totally clear," said Turnbull. A trace of annoyance played out on her face, but it wasn't clear if it was directed towards her audience, or herself.

"The cameras were triggered at *exactly* the same time... to the second."

"So, something more generalised must have triggered the cameras simultaneously, rather than something moving along the street?" continued Bankhurst.

"That's what I was wondering," confirmed Turnbull, relieved she had eventually got her message across.

"Like a flash from Johnston Gardens, for instance?" said Gillespie, almost eagerly for him, recognising an opportunity to potentially link the Peters and Syme murders.

"Indeed," confirmed Turnbull.

Bankhurst stuck out her lower lip, and looked pensively at the screen. They had a point.

"OK. Good work, DC Turnbull."

Gillespie rearranged the many lines in his face to convey an *I told you so* message.

Bankhurst made brief eye contact with him to acknowledge his point scored. No words were necessary. The moment passed and she refocussed her thoughts.

"OK. Once gait analysis is finished, recheck the CCTV footage in the Peters case. See if there are any matches, with anyone at the club or, on the streets leading back to Old Aberdeen. And let's look for any other possible links between the murders."

"Seems highly bloody unlikely to me." DCI Amanda Farrell's voice had a slightly high pitch, which made it sound close to a whine most of the time.

"A student, and you know what these potheads are like, *thought* they might have seen a flash, and some random door cams in Rubislaw triggered at the same time."

"Not exactly random, ma'am," countered Bankhurst. "All within one hundred yards of each other, on the side of Rubislaw Park Crescent which faces Johnston Gardens."

Farrell maintained her *not impressed* face. "Could have been anything. A power surge, for instance."

"Yes, ma'am," replied Bankhurst. "I realise it's tenuous, at best, but you wanted to be kept up to date."

"Yes. But this!" Her voice was now in full whine mode, purple neck veins bulging against her collar. "You'll need to do better."

Damned if I do, damned if I don't.

"That'll be all, Detective Inspector."

Bankhurst pulled her seat towards her desk and booted up her computer. With hands in pockets Iqbal sauntered over for an update.

"How'd it go?"

"Oh. You know. The usual."

"So, she was a whining fannybaws then!"

"I couldn't possibly comment, DS Iqbal," replied Bankhurst, although she already had, with the glint in her eyes, and a mischievous look on her face.

11

20th March

They slept together on the third date. Earlier than Lily had intended. She was aware of her chequered history in partner selection, and didn't want to add another entry to the growing ledger of ne'er-do-wells. However, the combination of Andrew being on a sleepover, a modest amount of wine, and the fact that she was between periods, had aligned the stars favourably; the latter not just for practical reasons but, also, because she was much less likely to have endometriosis-related, painful intercourse, mid-cycle. A significant factor in weakening, and then breaking, her resolve. Besides, she was randy.

A dihydrocodeine tablet was surreptitiously taken as insurance against any pain intrusion.

The first time was urgent and relatively brief. Sweaty and breathless. Acceptable, without being memorable. Meeting a need.

The second time, in the morning, was slow and deliberate. Detailed.

And memorable.

Afterwards, Tom got dressed, and bent over to kiss her warmly on the lips, just as his ringtone went off with a vaguely familiar song.

"Who's that?" she enquired.

"Rush. Have you heard of them? Canadian band."

"Can't say as I have. Recognise the tune though, I think."

"Yeh, always been a favourite of mine."

Tom looked at the screen.

"Are you not going to answer it?"

"Na, it's theatre. They'll be wondering where I am for the pre-op assessments. I'm normally very punctual. I'd better get going. You're a bad influence, Lily Bankhurst!"

Grabbing his jacket and car keys, he looked back over his shoulder. "Last night was great. So was this morning! I'll be in touch. Soon."

With a wave, he was gone, leaving behind a fading scent of aftershave and masculinity.

Realising she was a little behind schedule herself, Lily went through to the bathroom, with a lightness of foot unusual for her in the morning. In the shower she washed away the trace of sex, while trying to prolong its pleasant mental embrace. She realised, for the first time in a while, she had slept soundly, free of nightmares and panic attacks.

Not a bad form of treatment.

Having towel dried, she got dressed and finished off her hair with her not-to-be-without hair tongs. Subtle, work appropriate, make-up was applied, before she addressed her diabetic needs. Perhaps because of her unaccustomed nocturnal exercise, her glucose level monitor showed her blood sugar towards the lower end of normal for her fasted state. An extra slice of toast, and a reduced dose of insulin, were allowed. A quick WhatsApp exchange with Andrew confirmed he was *fine!* One word enough to convey his indignation at his mother checking up on him. Lily smiled.

She grabbed her coat, pulled the door behind her, and jumped in the car, reversing out onto the street. Pulling away from the house, exhaust fumes visible in her rear-view mirror, she was surprised to find herself singing along to Radio 2.

Amazing what a good shag will do, she said to herself.

Her good mood didn't last long.

If there was one thing DCI Farrell was good at, it was bursting bubbles.

Three weeks into the investigation, Bankhurst was well used to regular dressing-downs, and less than complimentary comparisons with the capital's finest.

Water off a duck's back, she thought, though the reference to the aquatic bird made for uncomfortable thinking. It brought back images of the pond in Johnston Gardens and, with it, a reminder that the investigation had failed to gain much momentum. Worse, it seemed to be following a similar course to the Peters murder in February. Worse still, DCI Farrell was probably right about the lack of progress.

"So, what's your plan moving forward, DI Bankhurst?"

"Solid police work, ma'am. Crossing the Ts and dotting the Is."

"But that's got you nowhere, so far. With either case!"

"No, ma'am."

"It's not bloody good enough!"

"No, ma'am." Bankhurst internally counted to ten, waiting for the mini tirade to pass.

"Maybe we need to freshen up the team?"

"With respect, ma'am, I'm happy with my team."

"I wasn't speaking about the individual members. Just the SIO…"

Farrell let the words hang and looked over the top of her glasses to watch their impact.

Bankhurst continued to look straight ahead, determined to avoid eye-to-eye contact.

The silence felt awkward. Bankhurst eventually broke it.

"If that is all, ma'am?"

"For now, yes."

Bankhurst nursed her wrath as she descended the stairs from Farrell's office, and decided to seek out Sharon Baxter for an early coffee, and the lowbrow conversation she was in the mood for.

She didn't disappoint.

"So, how was the latest date?"

"Oh. You know. Good," replied Bankhurst, a bloom of pink rising from her neck to her face.

"Is that you blushing, Lily Bankhurst?"

"No!"

"Oh, my god, you are! You slept with him, didn't you?"

"…I might have," she replied, as her face went from pink to almost puce.

"Well. Come on, then. Spill! I want to know everything. Especially… you know… the G-spot expertise."

Bankhurst leant in and whispered, "Never mind the G-spot, Sharon. That man's got a whole alphabet available to him!"

"You're shitting me!"

Bankhurst tipped her head back and roared with laughter, while Baxter gave her a gentle kick under the table.

Later that evening she ceremoniously packed up her Lovehoney 20 and placed it at the back of her bedside drawer.

"Shan't be needing you for a while, hopefully," she said, before laughing at herself for speaking to a vibrator.

12

5th May

Alexandru Balan, a forty-five-year-old Romanian, had moved, with his wife and two children, to Aberdeen five years previously. He had settled into his new home and his English, as well as his ear for the, at times impenetrable, Aberdonian accent, had slowly improved. A variety of part-time and zero-hours contract jobs had helped provide for his family initially, but for the last two years he had a permanent position with a security company, based in the Bridge of Don area of Aberdeen

As part of the redevelopment of Union Terrace Gardens in the city centre, a number of glass-heavy, two-storey pods had been built, to encourage local businesses to move into the regenerated area. The pods, like giant USB-C cable ends, looked down onto the gardens, from their elevated position on The Terrace. One of the units was still to be let, and required a weekly inspection to meet the terms of the developer's insurance policy. Balan was familiar with the routine, and usually allowed himself a ten-minute break before unlocking the pod, and doing his walk-round.

It had been an unusually balmy late spring week in Aberdeen, and the early evening air was still pleasantly warm. He retrieved a packet of L&M cigarettes from his pocket, and tapped the cardboard until an individual cigarette presented itself above the others, inviting retrieval. He lit the cigarette between cupped hands, then took a first greedy drag. The tip glowed brightly, as nicotine-laden smoke was pulled deeply into his lungs. He held it for a few seconds before exhaling, dragon-like, through his nostrils.

After the second draw, he tilted his head up, and propelled the blue-grey smoke skywards, watching it swirl slowly in the gentle, early evening breeze.

He thought of home. Of Romania. Of Bucharest.

He imagined himself sitting in a cafe, by the River Dâmbovița, eating *plăcintă*, *sarmale* or *pârjoale*, although nobody made Romanian meatballs like his grandmother. He could almost taste her juicy pork and potato meatballs, stuffed full of garlic, dill and thyme. His mouth moistened slightly at the memory, and he smiled. He resolved to visit the Romanian store on George Street, after work, to stock up on a few of his favourite foods. It would be a nice surprise for his wife, especially if he could get some of her favourite chocolate.

Satisfied that he could already feel the hit of nicotine in his brain, he deftly moved the cigarette to between his thumb and index finger, and dropped the hand to his side, a trail of smoke drifting upwards. The rest of the cigarette could be taken at a more leisurely pace.

From his vantage point, he looked around the arena of Union Terrace Gardens.

Directly opposite, the Triple Kirks spire, enveloped by a new development, stretched imperiously above its modern neighbours. To his left, three imposing granite buildings watched over the green space. His Majesty's Theatre, the Central Library and St Mark's Church had formed an iconic Aberdeen trio since being built in the nineteenth century and were fondly referred to locally as "Education, Salvation and Damnation".

Just as he looked right, a train, heading westwards to Inverness, threaded itself through the eye of the Union Street bridge, and continued onwards just beyond the Gardens' boundary.

He casually watched as a significant number of Aberdonians, seduced by the unseasonably good weather, continued to enjoy the amenities of the park; those on the grass at the foot of the Gardens appearing like figures in a Lowry painting.

He extinguished the cigarette stub between his fingers and threw it in a nearby bin.

He retrieved the key fob from his inside pocket and pressed it against the external card reader; the sliding door opened with a *swish*. He stepped inside, where he was immediately hit with a blast of heat from the unventilated, greenhouse-like structure. As he let some of the stifling air escape, he thought he could detect an unpleasant odour, a suspicion confirmed when he ventured further into the building.

Could a drain be blocked?

Perhaps a rat, or squirrel had somehow breached the building, and died?

He toured the ground floor, inspecting each space in turn. The taps and toilets seemed to be working well, and there was no smell from any of the sink plug holes.

As he climbed the stairs the smell intensified, to the extent that he had to cover his nose. As he reached the first floor he became aware of a slight buzzing noise, just before a fly hit him on the forehead. Then another on his arm.

He followed the stench, and ever-increasing number of flies, along the upstairs corridor to, what looked like, an office. He began to feel nauseated. Thoughts of his grandmother's *pǎrjoale* seemed a long time ago. The door was slightly ajar. He paused, and swallowed. With growing trepidation, he swung the door open, and tentatively entered the room.

He stopped in his tracks. Despite the oppressive heat in the room, an ice cold shiver ran down his spine.

"La dracu." (Damn)

"La dracu!"

A five o'clock shadow was well established on his face, which was as long as the day had been. DI Tony Ledingham was not in a good mood.

"Cheer up, Sir. It might never happen," commented DS Gary Currie, as he headed to the canteen.

"Humph," was all DI Ledingham could muster.

The forty-seven-year-old had been mulling over his year so far, and it didn't make for happy contemplation. His father had died, in Edinburgh, in February, leaving behind his frail mother, who was known to be in the early stages of dementia. Just how advanced the dementia had been was not obvious until after his death. Kenneth Ledingham had, apparently, been doing a good job in covering for his wife's cognitive impairment. Once exposed to her new, unsupervised life, living on her own, it rapidly became apparent that she would not cope at home without significant assistance. Family support was challenging, with Tony Ledingham living in Aberdeen and his sister, Sandra McBride, a London resident for some fifteen years.

A multitude of tasks kept the siblings busy for three weeks including a social work referral, care assessment, meetings with lawyers, multiple trips to banks and building societies, power of attorney activation, organising delivery of Wiltshire Farm Foods ready meals and selling a car. The list went on and on.

The net effect of his family commitment, apart from leaving him mentally and physically exhausted, was to miss out on being an SIO of a murder case in February. To make matters worse, he missed the SIO boat again in March when he was, paradoxically, away on a week's cruise. Adding fuel to the fire of disappointment was the fact that both cases had ended in the lap of DI Lily Bankhurst. He didn't exactly dislike his colleague, but nor did he like her either.

He couldn't quite put his finger on why.

She was good enough at her job. They hadn't crossed swords in any meaningful way. Was there a, deep down, seam of misogyny that resented a female success story?

Or, was it simply a case of jealousy?

Previously, she had been the successful SIO in the only serial murder case in Aberdeen in a generation. Not only had she cleared the case, but she had killed one of the killers in the process, gaining a degree of cult status in A Division of Police Scotland. An investigation judged her actions to be acceptable within the doctrine of self-defence; indeed, she was awarded the Scottish Police Federation Bravery Award. The fact that she had snared another two murder investigations did not sit well with him. In fact, it was more than that. It distinctly irritated him.

His reflections only darkened his mood.

And, he was hungry.

Low blood sugar did not help his mood.

So lost was he in his brooding thoughts that he hardly noticed the phone ringing on an adjacent desk behind him. Eventually the noise penetrated his thoughts, as did the realisation that there was no one of lesser rank around to answer the phone.

With another "humph" he reluctantly swivelled round in his chair, and reached across to the phone.

"Ledingham," he announced gruffly, before sitting up slightly, when he realised who he was speaking to.

"Evening, ma'am."

The monologue invited no contribution, but as he listened, the expression on his face changed.

13

5th May

Ledingham showed his badge and ducked under the *police line do not cross* tape. Having been in one of the other pods previously, he was broadly familiar with the layout of the building.

"Upstairs, Sir." A uniformed officer gestured with his head.

He took the stairs two at a time, a loose shirt tail flapping behind him. Although the building was now better ventilated and cooler, Ledingham had no difficulty following the smell, and activity of the SOCOs, to draw him to the scene.

"What the actual…?" He left the oath unsaid.

Even though he was expecting a body, the scene took him aback.

A naked, male body was strapped, star-like, across a large table, anchored at each corner by knotted rope. The mouth had been gagged. Lying face up, opaque sunken eyes stared vacantly at the ceiling. His skin was dusky red, liberally studded with an assortment of different sized blisters, some of which were filled with blood. A fly crawled out of his right nostril and flew away.

The tableau reminded him of Da Vinci's *Vitruvian Man*, which he had once seen, as a teenager, in a museum in Venice.

Dr Dexter Brewster noted the new arrival. Pushed his glasses up his nose.

"Evening, Tony. What do you make of this, then?"

"Quite a sight, Doc. I'll give you that."

Ledingham walked slowly around the corpse, ducking at times to see under the table. He noted, what he took to be, reef knots at each corner, tethering the wrists and ankles. He took a look at the face. Even behind the sunken eyes, badly cracked lips and swollen features, he did not think he recognised the man.

He clicked his tongue. "Nasty," he murmured.

Looking up, he scanned the room trying to take in as many first impressions as he could.

"Do we have an ID?" he asked, to no one in particular.

"Not so far."

"Don't suppose there's a phone?"

"No, Sir."

"Any early thoughts, Doc?"

"Difficult one, Tony," replied Brewster.

"The ambient temperature here was very high, and will have significantly speeded up decomposition. At a rough guess, I would say the time of death would be approximately two to three days ago. We'll get more information in due course, and I'll get the entomologists to have a look at the blowfly eggs and larvae. That should help."

"Cause of death?" probed Ledingham, more in hope than expectation.

"Can't say, at the moment. He certainly looks dehydrated, and clearly has heat damage to his skin. There are no obvious signs of trauma. Ligatures, as you can see, have been used, but these have been more for restraint, than lethal effect. There are certainly no obvious bruises around the neck. Only so much I can tell from an in situ examination. Will need a full post-mortem, toxicology, etcetera, before narrowing down cause of death."

"Thanks, Doc."

"Oh, one last thing. Any sign of sexual attack?"

"None so far, but we'll check for rectal semen at the lab."

Brewster stood up and stretched his back.

"That's as much as I can do here," he said. "I'll leave it to the SOCOs. I'm already late for band practice, as it is. I'll give you a call after the post-mortem tomorrow morning."

"Much on just now, Doc?"

"Aye. We've a competition in Glasgow this weekend… and we need all the practice we can get!"

Brewster was a member of the, long established, Grampian Police Pipe Band. Always aspiring to be amongst the best, they were currently settled in Grade 2. It was a long-standing joke, in the band, that he said every year "this will be my last year", but the camaraderie, and powerful music created by the band, had continued to provide the perfect foil for his daytime job. The combination had proven hard to resist.

Within thirty minutes he had taken his place within the ranks of the band, and, with puffed cheeks and deft fingers, was contributing enthusiastically to a stirring Strathspey. The gruesome details of the corpse were soon pushed to the back of his consciousness.

In the Union Terrace Gardens hub, Ledingham wasted no time in getting himself up to speed. Having been appointed SIO by DCI Farrell, he was determined to make the most of his opportunity.

"Who found the corpse?"

"That guy over there," replied ginger-haired DS Hamish MacDonald, in his usual lacklustre manner, as he pointed to Alexandru Balan. The shell-shocked Romanian was sitting on a wall outside, staring into space. His latest L&M cigarette was almost down to the filter. Two crushed stubs lay next to his feet.

"Works for a local security company, Seguridad," he continued. "They inspect the premises once a week."

"When was he last here?"

"The twenty-eighth of April... everything was normal then," continued MacDonald, anticipating the follow-up question.

"Is he clean?"

"No record in this country. We've put out feelers with the Romanian Police."

"Any sign of a break-in?"

"No."

"How the hell did they get in, then? What kind of key system is it?"

"Proximity fob and reader."

"Fairly robust, then?"

"Yes, but with modern scanners, wouldn't be impossible to hack and clone. If you'd been following your target for a while, you could get close enough to him, in a shop or cafe for instance."

"Suppose so," agreed Ledingham.

He sucked the back of his teeth.

"What about CCTV?"

"The cameras inside haven't been activated yet, as the building's never been fully furnished, or occupied. We're rounding up all the CCTV we can get our hands on in the area."

"OK, let's get Uniform going around all the businesses in the area, especially the adjacent hubs. Concentrate on the last two to four days. Somebody must have seen something! I doubt there are any more residents in this area these days, but check that too."

"Will do."

"We need an ID. Anything on the mobile fingerprint analyser?"

"No, Boss."

"OK. Dr Brewster will take samples for DNA tomorrow at the post-mortem. In the meantime, check mispers."

"Sir."

"Oh, and get a sample of the rope over to the forensics lab ASAP."

6th May

"I come bearing gifts." Ledingham held up a slightly grease-stained, paper bag, which produced an immediate smile on Brewster's face. The thought of the likely contents, Aberdeen rowies, was already making him salivate slightly. He had long taken umbrage at the fact that *for health reasons* the rowie had been slightly emasculated over the years, with successive reductions in salt and fat content. *Who the hell eats a rowie to be healthy anyway?*

However, for those in the know, DI Tony Ledingham included, there were still a few city outlets, where full fat rowies could be purchased. Brewster could tell, by the amount of staining on the bag, that these were the genuine article.

"Follow me, young man," he encouraged.

Brewster led the way to the coffee room, where cups were assembled, and the kettle switched on. Dr Roddy Hall, one of Brewster's pathology colleagues, raised an eyebrow. The bakery bag had been clocked, and he was judging whether it might be big enough to offer the possibility of a spare rowie. He kept his counsel, not wishing to alert anyone else to the chance of naughty, but delicious, baked goods.

Brewster knew the drill. One for him, one for Ledingham, toasted. Sacrilege, in his opinion, unless the rowie was two to three days old. Any left over would be cut into halves, and put for general consumption.

Brewster parted the top of the bag, and inspected the contents. *DI Ledingham must be in a good mood.* A small family of four rowies lay nestled together, promising unhealthy tastiness.

He purred at the prospect.

Brewster handed a cup to Ledingham, the coffee still swirling from his circular agitation.

"You know that's disgusting, don't you?" suggested Ledingham.

"It's not that bad. Tesco Finest range," responded Brewster.

"Not the coffee," replied Ledingham. "Stirring it with a scalpel handle!"

"It's sterile, I promise."

"That doesn't matter."

"Needs must, Tony. Needs must. I always carry one in my top pocket. Comes in handy when all the teaspoons are in the sink… and don't get me started on that!"

Coffees and rowies were consumed with appreciative murmurs. Brewster wiped his lips with a paper napkin, brushed flakes of rowie from his scrubs and cleared his throat. He cleaned his glasses on his scrubs and perched them on his nose.

"Thanks, Tony. Now it's my turn."

Brewster knew Ledingham appreciated a summary, rather than exhaustive detail. On many occasions he had distilled two hours work into five minutes for him.

"The corpse was a white male, measuring 177cm and weighing 82kg. Forty to sixty years old. On external examination there were marks from ligatures around the ankles and wrists and from the gag in the mouth. The eyes were very sunken and there was generalised tinting of the skin. In addition to the colour change, there was widespread blistering and haemorrhaging within the skin. The galea, that's the coating on the skull, was noted to be very dry. There was a small mark in the skin over the left forearm consistent with a needle mark."

"Internally, many organs showed significant tissue damage, likely to be due to large volumes of blood being shunted away to the skin, and advanced decomposition due to the hot ambient temperature. The heart and lungs showed surface haemorrhage."

"In addition to the post-mortem findings, we now have some results back from the lab showing elevated levels of sodium, chloride and urea in the vitreous humor sample."

"Eyeball fluid?" enquired Ledingham.

"Correct," confirmed Brewster. "I've also sent samples for toxicology and DNA, including possible semen found in the rectum."

"Bottom line, Doc?"

"Overall, the appearances are highly suggestive that the cause of death was hypertonic dehydration with hyperthermia. Possible rectal semen raises the possibility of anal sex, consensual or otherwise."

Ledingham nodded his head. "Hyperthermia. Is that what it sounds like?"

"Pretty much, yes. If the body's core temperature goes over 40C, its thermoregulatory mechanism is no longer capable of effectively dissipating heat, with consequential organ failure and ultimately, death."

"What about the time of death?"

"Best I can give, I'm afraid, is an estimate of the day… the third of May, I reckon."

"And how long might he have been there before he died?"

Brewster hesitated slightly. "Are you aware of the 'Rule of Three', Tony?"

"Can't say that I am."

"A human can survive without oxygen for three minutes, water for three days, and food for three weeks."

"Go on."

"I estimate it is likely that he was strapped to the table about three days before he died."

"So, basically, he was slow cooked to death."

"Somewhat dramatic… but, yes," agreed Brewster.

14

6th May

DI Tony Ledingham cleared his throat. Ran a hand through his thinning hair.

"OK, everybody. Can I have an update please?"

"Hamish?"

Never in a rush to do anything, DS Hamish MacDonald ambled to his desk and picked up a tablet.

"We're working on a possible ID, Sir. Misper from the twenty-ninth of April. Seems to fit the bill. Oliver Bainton. Known as Ollie. Forty-eight-year-old white male. We've only got an old photograph to work with but, even with the heat-damaged face on the corpse, it looks like a possible match. Lives with his partner in Rosemount. We're getting an up-to-date photograph, and some samples, from his home for DNA. Also, looking into his dental records."

"OK. Sounds promising. If the ID is confirmed, I want to know everything about him. What else have we got?"

"Nothing on ANPR, or business-to-business inquiry. The place has been heaving with the good weather in the last few days, but nobody saw anything unusual, apparently!"

"We've also put out a bulletin on *Northsound* appealing for witnesses."

"What about CCTV?"

"So far, we've been concentrating on the twenty-four-hour period around the estimated time the victim would have been tied to the table," responded DC Alfie Morris.

"And?"

"We've got Bainton on various cameras, from leaving the pub and heading towards the Gardens. While not exactly rushing, he seems to be moving with purpose."

"Like he had a liaison?"

"Yes. We can then see him heading close to the hub, but don't actually see him going in. Unfortunately, the entrance is in a blind spot."

Disappointment etched across Ledingham's face.

"Anything else?"

"Not much, I'm afraid. Usual collection of daytime park users. In the evening, the place is rammed – there are even people drinking *outside*." The intonation in his voice expressed surprise at such behaviour at that time of year in Aberdeen. Not an activity that usually ended well.

"After midnight, there's a smattering of clubbers, drunks and two street pastors. No one is obviously seen to approach or leave the building, though the night-time footage isn't all that clear, to be fair."

"Any word on the rope?"

"Common variety. Synthetic. Combination of polyester, nylon and polypropylene. Widely available, apparently."

"Damn," Ledingham muttered under his breath.

"Any toxicology?"

"Not back yet, Sir."

"OK. Give them a chase."

7th May

Ledingham had slept well and awoke in a good mood. He showered and chose one of his better suits, mindful that he might be required to front a press conference. Passing his teenage children distracted by their devices, he snared a piece of their toast en route to the front door.

"Dad!"

The fine weather was holding, unusual for Aberdeen; it was a pleasant drive into Aberdeen from Westhill, a commuter town seven miles west of the city. Even at 8am the temperature was fifteen degrees centigrade, with the promise to reach twenty-two by early afternoon. The Aberdeen Western Peripheral Route had finally, after years of delay, opened in 2019, and had significantly improved his commute to and from work. As usual he made steady, if unspectacular, progress eastwards towards the city, but at least, nowadays, gone were the previously commonplace long queues of crawling traffic.

The granite houses on the west of the city sparkled in the early morning sun, framed by an azure-blue sky. Pops of late spring colour studded garden after garden; pink-red pieris, deep magenta, early-flowering azaleas and a rainbow of tulip shades. Flowering cherries, laden with blossom, pierced the pavements, the occasional petal fluttering to the ground like pink snow. Small areas of well-tended, verdant, domestic grass provided the perfect foil for the floral displays, with only an occasional artificial lawn, the impossibly correct texture and colour betraying its imposter status. It was hard to imagine these were the same streets that had looked so dank, grey and depressing three months previously.

Winter clothes had ceded to shorter hems and pastel colours, as the population made their way to work. Some of the exposed skin showed clear signs of excess sun in the recent past.

Knowing the fickle Aberdeen weather, Ledingham was aware it would soon change. Images of his favourite grandmother popped into his mind.

"Ne'r cast a clout 'til May is oot" he could see her saying, with a look of wise counsel on her wrinkled face.

He tuned into *Northsound* news to hear what was being reported about the murder, and was pleased to hear only bland, generic information, and an appeal for witnesses. The comms officer had done a good job. The last thing he wanted was for any details of the gory tableau to be leaked to the media, and hence the public.

An interview with a local MP followed. Almost inevitably, it seemed to Ledingham, he tried to make political capital from the string of homicides that had plagued the city since the start of the year.

Ledingham entered the incident room, and nodded his appreciation. Most of the team had arrived promptly, as requested. A previously blank whiteboard had been populated with data from the overnight team.

Oliver (k/a Ollie) Bainton
Age: 48
White
ID confirmed by dental records. DNA awaited
Lives with partner David Glennie (52). Rosemount area
Place of death: Union Terrace Gardens hub
Date of death: 3 May (estimated)
Time of death: not known
Last seen alive: 29 April in The Knockscalbert pub at 11:30pm
Reported missing (by partner): 30 April
Body found: 5 May
Toxicology: alcohol, cannabis, ketamine
No mobile phone located
CCTV/ANPR unhelpful

Ledingham stood in front of the board, with folded arms. He read, and then reread, the information.

He turned to his audience, and spotted Ian Jardine at the back of the room.

"Digital forensics, Ian?"

"We've no phone, but have got the number from his partner. We're waiting to hear back from his provider, but most retain records of phone locations, using mobile-tower triangulation, GPS, Wi-Fi access points, and the like. So, we're hopeful of some useful information. We're also checking the numbers he has been in contact with."

"OK. Let me know ASAP please."

Jardine nodded an acknowledgement.

"What are we thinking about toxicology?"

Hamish MacDonald responded, "Obviously, no great

surprise with the alcohol and cannabis, but the ketamine is a bit unusual. Could fit with the possible needle mark on his left arm though."

"Are we thinking consensual, or not?"

"Who knows?"

"Is it used much in the gay scene?"

"Not widely, but apparently some fisters use it as a muscle relaxant."

Gillespie shifted uncomfortably on his seat.

"I've spoken to Ian Rafferty in the Drug Squad. He says there is some ketamine on the streets currently. Has a variety of names, but tends to be known locally as Special K or K-hole. Most users bump it, but a few inject for a faster high."

"So, a single needle mark wouldn't exclude regular usage, if he was snorting it?"

"Correct."

"Who has legitimate access?" enquired Ledingham, widening the discussion.

"Mostly vets, and a small number of doctors. In the latter, it's mostly used in terminal care and pain clinics, apparently."

"OK. Let's check with all local vets, hospitals and the hospice, to see if there has been any stolen. Also, speak to your snitches. What's the word on the street about ketamine? Who are the main players?"

"And, we'll need to ask his partner if he was known to be a ketamine user."

"Aye, there's a few questions we have to ask him," agreed Ledingham, with the knowing face of someone aware of the statistics on homicides involving close acquaintances.

A voice from the back of the room interrupted his train of thought.

"Sir, you might want to hear this."

15

7th May

DC Alfie Morris, looking a bit like an excited child wanting to tell his teacher something, was holding a phone up in one hand, while the other cupped the mouthpiece.

"I've got the victim's phone provider on the line. The last location for his phone was Union Terrace, at 00:15 on the thirtieth of April."

"OK, no surprise about the location," responded Ledingham, "but narrows down the time frame of interest. Good. Let's have another look at CCTV three hours before and after that time. There must be some footage of him, and hopefully the perpetrator."

"Right, that's it for now. Good work. DS MacDonald and I will head up to Rosemount, to interview Bainton's partner, David Glennie."

As MacDonald and Ledingham walked along the corridor, a serious looking DS Iqbal was heading in the other direction.

"What's up with him?" Ledingham said to his DS, when they were further down the walkway.

"Looks like someone's stolen his cricket bat!"

Iqbal continued along the corridor, before stopping outside DI Bankhurst's door, and listened for a second to see if he could hear any noise within. Silence. Even the echoing steps of his CID colleagues had faded to nothing. He wiped sweaty hands on his trousers, and then went to knock on the door, but stopped himself in the act. He tried to swallow saliva but his mouth was dry.

"Come in if you're coming!" shouted Bankhurst from within her room, making him jump slightly.

He tapped on the door and entered as instructed.

Bankhurst smiled. "Sorry, Zafar. I just can't help myself doing that, if I hear someone coming up the corridor and then standing outside my door."

"Ha ha. Good trick that, Boss. So it is." Iqbal had squeezed out a smile, but didn't look his normal ebullient self.

Bankhurst picked up on his demeanour.

"What's on your mind, Zafar?"

"I just wanted to have a word, Boss."

Bankhurst was about to answer but her phone rang. She picked up the receiver, raising the index finger in her other hand, beckoning her DS to hold on for a minute.

"Ach. Na. You're alright, Boss. It's nothing important. You take the call. I'll see you later."

Before Bankhurst could say otherwise, Iqbal had left her office.

Rosemount was a bustling quarter, north-west of the city centre, embracing several independent shops, cafes and restaurants. The original land was gifted to the burgesses and people of Aberdeen in 1315, by King Robert the Bruce, though the area remained outside the city boundary until Aberdeen extended in 1862. The buildings were largely Victorian granite tenements though at the west end, on the border of Beechgrove, some granite dwelling houses stood.

Bainton and Glennie lived together in Rosemount Square, a newer development dating from just after World War Two. Despite its name, the building was a horseshoe shape, with a central courtyard, the avant-garde European design being somewhat of a departure for the city planners of the era. It was seen as being very modern, and for many of the occupants who moved in, it was their first experience of inside toilets.

The two detectives parked in Rosemount Viaduct and walked the short distance to Rosemount Square, passing under an archway to enter the courtyard. Washing fluttered on criss-cross lines, adults chatted at the entrance to the closes, and a group of young children played tag.

Like a throwback to the seventies, imagined Ledingham.

Under the watchful eyes of the residents, they made their way across to the ground floor, one-bedroom flat that Bainton and Glennie shared. The ringing bell triggered a "Come in" and a dog barking.

MacDonald visibly stiffened, and his face paled.

"I hate dogs," he said, somewhat unnecessarily.

"Ach, you'll be fine," reassured Ledingham. "It's only the small ones you've got to worry about, anyway."

Ledingham led the way into the oppressively hot flat, and was met by a haze of cigarette smoke and air freshener, immediately regretting his choice of suit for the day.

"In here," directed the voice.

Ledingham and MacDonald followed the voice along a short, dingy corridor into the living room. Glennie, looking older than his fifty-two years, sat on a worn, creased, cream leather sofa.

His thinning hair had been coerced into a comb-over, which framed an unshaven, plethoric face. He was wearing a sweatshirt, jeans and trainers. A gold necklace snuggled into the skin creases on the back of his neck, and two chunky rings sparkled on fingers.

On the table in front of him were a *Daily Record*, *TV Times* and an overfull ashtray. On the fireplace sat an empty wine glass, with red dregs staining the bottom, the empty wine bottle standing alongside. Beside his feet was a small, curly-haired dog.

MacDonald looked at the dog suspiciously.

It looked at MacDonald suspiciously.

Sensing the tension, Glennie said, "Dinna worry, she's harmless," but neither human, nor canine looked particularly reassured.

"What's its name?" enquired Ledingham, to defuse the stand-off.

"Gigha."

"After the island?"

"Yes. Ollie has a thing about the islands. *Had* a thing," he corrected himself.

Ledingham and MacDonald used the awkward silence that followed to produce their warrant cards.

"I'm DI Ledingham, and this is DS MacDonald. We're very sorry for your loss."

"Aye. Thanks," replied Glennie, as he nodded to two unoccupied seats. The officers accepted the implied offer.

"I know it's a difficult time for you, but I just need to ask you a few questions," continued Ledingham.

"Aye. OK. I've been expecting yous, ken."

"Tell us about you and Oliver."

Glennie cleared his throat. His eyes moistened.

"Well, I'd kent him for about ten years, and we'd been living together for the last five years. He was a porter at the hospital, and we met after I started working in the laundry there. We've had our ups and downs, ken, like most couples I suppose, but we survived."

"Had he crossed swords, or fallen out with anybody?"

"Na. He was a big saft lump. A'body liked him."

"Any financial worries?"

"Aye, but dinna we all, ken?"

Ledingham and MacDonald nodded their agreement.

"Did he have a drink, or drug, problem?"

"Och, he liked a good dram, now and then... but he wasnae an alcoholic, if that's fit you mean?"

"And drugs?"

"A wee joint, sure, if he could get his hands on one!" A smile stretched his lips, but didn't trouble the rest of his face.

"I need to ask you a specific question," continued Ledingham. "Has he ever used ketamine?"

"No way," replied Glennie.

"Are you sure?"

"Absolutely. No' his scene at all, ken. Why do you ask? Was that in his system?"

"I'm afraid I can't answer that," replied Ledingham, although he knew he already had.

MacDonald changed tack.

"Where were you on the twenty-eighth of April?"

"Here."

"Any witnesses?"

"No. Not unless you count Gigha." He nodded at the cockapoo, who continued to scowl at MacDonald, seeming to sense an unfriendly presence.

"Why didn't you report him missing until the following day?"

"I was in my bed. I didnae ken he hadn't come home until the next morning."

"Was that unusual for him?"

"Aye... and no. Look, I loved Ollie, but at times he could be a fucking raj!"

"Meaning?"

"Well, he was always enough for me, but it wasn't always like that for him. Sometimes he would go with other guys, ken."

"And you didn't mind?"

"Course I fucking minded! But I wanted to stay with him, and, in my mind, that was part o' the deal. He thought I didn't ken, but I'm nae daft, ken."

Glennie's voice snagged slightly and his eyes moistened. A dry cough surfaced, persisted and finally gave way to a wheeze. Spindly nicotine-stained fingers wrapped around a nearby inhaler. SCOOSH. He took as big a breath in as his lungs would allow, and slowly regained his composure.

Ledingham refocussed him.

"How did he pick them up?"

"Mare often than no', through the NEMESIS app."

"NEMESIS?"

"Aye. North East Men Easy Sex in Sixty."

"Sixty?"

"Sixty minutes. Maximum time before you get laid."

Bloody hell, it's a different world. He tried hard not to register any facial reaction.

"Any of these encounters ever turned violent?"

"Nae that I ken o."

"What about Ollie's recent behaviour? Anything unusual?"

Glennie frowned as he concentrated. His eyebrows knitted together, forming a single line of hair.

"No. Nae that I can think of."

"Does he have any family?"

"His parents are long dead. He's a sister who lives in Dundee, but he doesnae really keep in touch with her, ken."

"Just two last things," continued Ledingham. "Do you know if he ever made a will?"

"Na. We always said we would, but never got round to it. And he didnae have any life insurance either, if that's fit you're wondering?"

Ledingham nodded slowly, as he realised his final question had been anticipated.

"Anything you'd like to ask us?"

"Aye. How did he die, exactly?"

"We can't give you exact details I'm afraid, but it was probably severe dehydration."

Glennie looked perplexed.

Ledingham and MacDonald got up, repeated their condolences and made their way out of the flat, glad to get back in fresh air. Still sweating slightly, Ledingham removed his jacket, folded it over his left forearm, and loosened his tie. He dug out his mobile from his trouser pocket, and opened Google Maps. He dropped a pin to his current location and entered an address approximately in the middle of Union Terrace. The app made the instant calculation. He was only four hundred yards from where Bainton lay for three days, slowly being dehydrated to death. Another quick search informed him that The Knockscalbert pub was only six hundred yards from where he was. He sucked the back of his teeth. From what he could remember of Pythagorean theory, the last side of the triangle would be approximately four hundred-and-fifty yards long.

What had happened within this relatively compact city centre triangle?

Somebody must have seen something.

There must be some relevant CCTV.

He punched in the number of the incident room.

"DI Ledingham. Have we got any further result on the possible semen in the rectum?"

"We chased the lab about an hour ago, Sir. Apparently, the sample's very degraded, and difficult to work with. They think it is very likely to be semen, but accurate DNA extraction is proving very challenging."

"Course it is. Bloody hell! OK, keep chasing them."

"Sir."

"And we need to find out all we can about an app called NEMESIS. It's a male sex app used by Bainton. Could possibly have been used to lure him to the hub in Union Terrace Gardens. See if they can give us a list of users."

"Sir."

Ledingham glanced at MacDonald. No words were exchanged but they both knew that false profiles were commonplace in male sex encounter apps. Often names were not even exchanged. A true service industry.

Ledingham looked pensively into the distance. He knew that the team had got off to a sound, if unspectacular start. No breakthrough, but a steady accumulation of hard and soft data. And from the data would come answers. At some point. But he wanted something now.

What were they missing?

Like most detectives Ledingham was aware of Locard's Exchange Principle. Dr Edmond Locard, a pioneer of forensic science in Lyon, formulated the principle that in any contact between two items, there will be an exchange. The physical evidence cannot be wrong. It cannot perjure itself. Only a human failure to find it can render it useless.

"What are you thinking, Boss?"

"I'm thinking we need that bloody DNA!"

DC Alfie Morris's mind was beginning to wander. He'd been reviewing CCTV for several fruitless hours and, with increasing regularity, his mind was wandering to matters involving ballroom dancing. In the previous six months he, and his fiancé, had been attending ballroom dancing lessons; primarily to prepare for their wedding. However, much to his surprise, and somewhat against his better judgement, he had become intrigued by the combination of technique and artistry provided by the discipline. Such that he now not only looked forward to the next session, but had also been seen to practise between lessons, something he would not have anticipated.

He was trying to remember their waltz routine. Did the whisk and chasse follow directly on from the natural spin turn, or was there some kind of connecting step? He ran the routine in his mind's eye, and then reproached himself for not realising, straight away, that there needed to be steps four-to-six of a reverse turn to make the variation work.

Something caught his eye on the screen. He replayed the section several times, both normal size and magnified, noting the time of the recording.

He then opened several more windows and reviewed data from various other cameras, before punching the desk slightly and leaving his chair abruptly.

"What have you got, son?" enquired Ledingham, having been brought to the DC's computer.

Morris took his seat, and opened screens on adjacent PCs. Busy keyboard tapping brought up the relevant files.

Pointing to the left screen, he explained, "This is footage of two street pastors. They are strolling south-eastward towards Union Street. As you can see their high-vis vests are doing their job well, but you can't really make out their faces clearly. They appear to be in conversation. However, at this point," Morris scrolled the footage forwards, "they pass under a streetlight for a few seconds."

"Their faces are much more visible," commented Ledingham, wondering where the presentation was going.

"Correct, Sir. Now, if you watch what happens."

Ledingham, who had now been joined by DS MacDonald, bent towards the screen.

Morris restarted the recording which showed that one of the pastors clearly disengaged from the conversation, and looked across the street for about six seconds.

"Something has caught his attention," commented MacDonald.

"That's what I thought, Sir."

"Now, if we continue watching you'll see that, just as he's leaving the illuminated cone under the streetlamp, he glances back again, in the same direction, for a couple more seconds."

Ledingham nodded his head.

"Indeed he does."

Morris swivelled his chair to position himself in front of the adjacent screen.

"I noted that the time the pastor appeared to be looking across the road in the general direction of the hub was at 02:30, so I reviewed all the footage from other adjacent cameras for that time. Initially I thought I'd drawn a blank, but I think there may be something subtle on this particular camera."

Morris clicked on a button and played footage from a camera looking away from the hub towards the other side of Union Terrace.

"There's nothing, apart from a glimpse of the pastors, captured directly, but if you look at the reflection in the shop window across the street, it seems to show a figure heading north-west along Union Terrace."

He continued, "I think this person is almost certainly what caught the pastor's eye, and could well be someone of interest."

"Play it again," instructed Ledingham, "in slow motion."

Morris obliged, a pink flush of satisfaction creeping up from his neck to his face.

Ledingham looked at MacDonald. They had both seen the reflected image of a quickly moving figure, probably a man. He appeared to be wearing dark clothing and a hoodie.

"Good work, son. Good work," Ledingham said, as he patted him on the back. "Right. Let's get that street pastor in ASAP."

8th May

"Can I ask why you didn't come forward before now?"

Ledingham realised the tone in his voice betrayed a degree of frustration.

The clipped tone did not go unnoticed by Arthur Brown, who looked slightly taken aback. The sixty-one-year-old retired social worker had willingly agreed to attend Nelson Street Police Station to help with enquiries.

He had observed the good and the bad (more of the latter, he usually said) of Aberdeen society during his shifts as a volunteer street pastor, since signing up three years previously. Having witnessed numerous violent incidents, he said he was a little surprised that a seemingly relatively innocuous event had sparked interest from Police Scotland.

"I didn't think it was important," he replied.

"Surely you must have been aware of the murder investigation," continued Ledingham in a direct tone.

"Not really. I don't get a paper these days, and don't dabble in social media either. I'd heard, on the grapevine, that there had been a body discovered in Union Terrace Gardens. I didn't even know it was a murder. In any case," Brown continued, "that was three days later. How was I to know it could possibly link to something I had seen, in passing, seventy-two hours previously? To be honest, after it happened, I didn't give it any more thought, until one of your lot turned up on my doorstep earlier today."

"Fair point," he continued, softening his timbre considerably. With his hackles lowering he took in a slow breath. "OK, let's start again. What do you remember of the events when you walked along Union Terrace at 02:30 on the thirtieth of April?"

"Well. Me and Tommy were just on our final circuit, before packing in for the night. We were making our way back towards Union Street. Just having a chat, as I remember. The streets were quieting down, and there weren't too many folks about. I noticed a movement across the street, and I remember glancing over. I could see it was someone, a man I think, moving fairly quickly in the opposite direction. He was dressed in dark clothes, and had his hoodie up… always a bit suspicious in my view."

"Did you get a look at his face?" interrupted Ledingham.

"Only very briefly. And it was quite dark on the other side of the road. I think he was white; I will say that much."

"OK, that's good," encouraged Ledingham. "Did you notice anything else about him? Build? Height?"

"I would say he was of fairly average build and height. Sorry, I know that's maybe not much help."

Brown looked into the distance, as if he was playing back the images from the night in his head. He raised his right index finger and both eyebrows. A recollection.

"I'm fairly sure he had a small rucksack on his back," he announced, with some gratification.

Ledingham's face registered interest. "Can you describe it all?"

"Not really. Other than that, it was a dark colour, probably black."

"What happened then?" said the Detective Inspector.

"Well, we just carried on walking," said Brown. "I remember glancing back a few seconds later, and he had vanished. I presumed he had crossed the road behind us, and gone up Diamond Place."

"Figures," said Ledingham, clicking his tongue.

He caught Brown's perplexed look. "No CCTV on that street," he explained.

"Ah." Brown nodded his understanding.

"Hope you've no plans for this afternoon," added MacDonald.

Brown quickly re-established the perplexed look which had only just melted from his face.

"We're going to need you to look at mugshots, and have a session with the digital artist."

"But…" Brown truncated his own sentence. The look on the detectives' faces suggested they would brook no dissent.

Brown sighed, and prepared himself for a longer stay at the station.

16

9th May

D I Ledingham had not slept well. Various aspects of the case had ricocheted around his brain like Pong, the original video tennis game. He woke feeling unrefreshed, and was only partially revived by a shower and a cup of strong coffee. He was slightly relieved that the muggy weather had broken, the cool wind and blustery shower that greeted him outside his house being almost invigorating.

More like normal Aberdeen weather, he mused.

He continued to brood over the case on his journey to work from Westhill, aware that the pressure would be building to make a breakthrough soon. When he got to the incident room he wasted no time in calling for updates, hoping for a bit of good news.

"No joy with either the mugshots, or artist's impression, unfortunately," offered DC Alfie Morris.

"Seems like he just couldn't recall enough facial detail to compile anything useful."

"Mm," responded Ledingham, giving nothing away.

"I've been canvassing the gay community," offered DC Andrew Forrest. "There's always a bit of background homophobia, but there doesn't seem to have been any change in the pattern. In particular, no violent episodes have been observed recently, and no specific threats made, as far as anyone is aware. In any case, with the probable semen in the rectum, it seems unlikely there was a homophobic motive. There's been a lot of chat on gay social media sites since the murder, but nothing of obvious use. There's also quite a bit of advice posted about personal security and safe practice."

"Good," responded Ledingham. "What about NEMESIS?"

"Difficult to get any information out of them. Very cagy, as you might expect."

"But this is a bloody murder investigation," snorted Ledingham, visible colour surfacing on his cheeks.

"Doesn't cut any ice I'm afraid. What we have managed to establish is that most users, as we expected, use false usernames and IDs, and even false pictures."

"*Mantelpiece and fire* comes to mind," Morris whispered to Forrest, having leant closer to his colleague to impart the observation.

The naughty schoolboy-type exchange was noted by Ledingham.

"Anything to say, Morris?"

"No, Sir," Morris was quick to reply, before looking at his feet, colour blooming in his face.

"No. I didn't think so," said Ledingham, maintaining a steely stare on his subordinate.

Sensing the admonishment was over, Forrest continued. "The app interacts with the GPS on their phones to pinpoint like-minded patrons in the vicinity. They get told how far away they are, in yards, and coordinates to find them. The rest is up to them."

Neil Jardine, from Digital Forensics, filled the pause that followed.

"If we could find his phone, we could possibly get some more useful data, but without it, there's only a limited amount we can get from the number alone."

MacDonald spoke up.

"I've been looking into ketamine. I've spoken to the guys in the drug squad again. It seems that most of the ketamine comes from Liverpool gangs, who come up and organise local distribution. Anybody who tries to get a piece of the action is viciously dealt with. There's been no obvious change to the supply of, or usage by, the city. They know a few of their regulars who use ketamine, but nobody who would be capable of anything like this."

"How so?"

"Well, they're mostly poor souls, living on the streets. Malnourished. Can barely plan how they're going to feed their dog, never mind something like this."

"What about vets and hospitals?"

"Have sent round emails to all vets, pharmacies, hospitals and the hospice. No reports of any stock missing. Still a few replies to get."

"OK. Chase them up, will you?"

"Sir."

"And, while you're at it, get onto Genetics again. We need that DNA!"

"Sir."

"What about gait analysis?" Ledingham continued.

"The tech guys have had a look. The reflected image isn't great. Certainly not matching anyone on the system."

"Figures," responded Ledingham. "Not a huge database at the moment."

"OK. Well, let's release the video footage to *Aberdeen Live,* and other media, anyway. See if we can't flush out a witness."

Ledingham crossed his arms. Waited. No one spoke.

He changed tack.

"OK, this is clearly a very organised and astute individual. This kind of attack would have taken a lot of planning and preparation. We're assuming he cloned the key to access his building of choice, which in itself had been carefully chosen. It's currently empty and only inspected once a week, which presumably he was aware of."

Ledingham could visualise the scene as he spoke.

"He strapped Bainton to the table of a glass walled room, which is overlooked by the upper floors of the adjacent buildings on Union Terrace. However, these have been vacant for years, so the risk of discovery was minimal. He managed to get in and out of the building almost completely unnoticed. Only a chance recording of a reflected image picked up on CCTV. He's clearly very aware of cameras and has chosen both suitable clothing, and a well-researched route, to avoid leaving any useful footage. It's likely he was carrying equipment and a change of clothing in his bag. Presuming that he accessed the hub during the evening, he was probably wearing summer type clothes to blend in with the crowd who were around at the time, only to change into dark clothes, with a hoodie, for his escape at night."

Ledingham paused and turned to look at the whiteboard.

"The one thing I don't understand is the possible semen in the rectum. He seems to be, forensically, very aware, in that he didn't leave us a single other piece of trace evidence. So, why leave semen as a potential smoking gun?"

"Perhaps he's confident he's not in the system," observed DS MacDonald, "or, had a condom failure."

A few knowing nods in the room suggested it wasn't an unknown experience.

"Maybe so," agreed Ledingham, "but it would still be damning evidence, if he was ever pulled in as a suspect."

Ledingham caught a movement out of the corner of his eye.

DC Elspeth Hamilton had sheepishly raised her arm.

"Go on," encouraged Ledingham.

"DC Hamilton, Sir. May I ask a question about the forensic testing that was done at the scene?"

"Go on."

"Well, it's just that it strikes me the perpetrator must have been there for several hours, between perhaps mid-evening on the twenty-ninth of April and 02:30 on the thirtieth of April, assuming it is him caught on the CCTV at that time."

Ledingham nodded to encourage her to continue.

"So, he must have needed to pass urine in that time frame."

125

"And?"

"Well, I live with two guys, Sir. My husband, and ten-year-old son. Now, I love them both, but let's just say they don't have the most accurate aim when it comes to emptying their bladder. There are *always* drops of urine on the floor in front of the toilet when it comes to cleaning time."

Ledingham looked at the SOC representative, inviting comment.

"We did, actually, check in front of the toilet with UV light, and there was nothing at all picked up," he replied, slightly condescendingly.

"That's kind of my point, Sir. The fact that there was not a hint of urine makes me wonder whether this is another example of the perpetrator's forensic awareness."

"Go on."

"What I mean is, was he sitting down to pass urine?"

Ledingham looked confused.

"To specifically avoid any contamination," she explained.

"How does that help us?"

"Well, when I'm cleaning our toilet at home there's often splashes of urine around the front rim. Talented as I am, they certainly haven't come from me! Any urine in the front of the actual pan would usually be washed away by the flush, but I wondered if there could be any subtle spray around the rim, above the level of the flush."

For the second time in as many minutes Ledingham looked at the SOCO officer, whose confidence, and colour, had suddenly drained from his face.

"I'll get someone on it, Sir."

17

10th May

The Deeside Railway Line was opened in 1853 and closed, as part of the Beeching reforms, in 1966. It originally ran from the Ferryhill Station in Aberdeen westwards to Banchory, but was extended to Ballater in 1866, a total distance of forty-three miles. The line was originally planned to end at Braemar but Queen Victoria, afraid that her privacy at Balmoral would be disrupted by "hordes of tourists", bought land along the route between Balmoral and Braemar to prevent the extension. The Old Deeside Railway was a popular route with Aberdonians for walking, exercising dogs, cycling and horse riding.

Tom Donaldson, with a promise to provide a bike, had persuaded Lily to go cycling along the old railway track. Lily had agreed, but not before asking if Andrew could come along too. A keen cyclist himself, she hoped the shared interest would grease the wheel of their introduction to one another.

It wasn't the best day for cycling. Overnight rain had given way to low clouds scudding across the sky, driven by an easterly wind. The scanty clothing of the recent fine weather had been replaced with sensible layering. Lily pulled the zip of her jacket up to its full extent as she prepared to set off.

Despite her attempt to gain early momentum, her front wheel wobbled worryingly, and she over-adjusted left and right.

"Oh, my god. I've not done this since I was a teenager!"

"Come on," encouraged Tom, "it's like… riding a bike! You never forget."

After another false start, she began to build up a little speed, and with it balance. Some confidence slowly returned, although she still seemed to be drawn towards various obstructions, like a moth to light. Bushes, posts and a small child exerted a magnetic pull, the latter drawing a glare from their mother.

Lily took one hand off the handlebar, holding it up with fingers spread, acknowledging culpability, but only succeeded in destabilising herself on the bike even more. A sharp sideways lurch required her to put a foot on the ground, to prevent a fall. Meanwhile she lost her footing on the pedal on the other side, scraping her shin in the process.

"Shit!"

She narrowly missed a mother walking with her young child

"Do you mind!" objected the mother, as she shepherded her child away, but not before delivering another withering look.

Tom and Andrew shared a glance and a snigger.

After further encouragement, Lily realised that she could, in fact, still ride a bike, and was reminded of why she used to enjoy the experience as a teenager. Smooth, efficient progress with a light, refreshing breeze in the face. A sense of freedom. As confidence built, she began to take in her surroundings more. The banks of the disused railway line were bursting with lush spring growth, with splashes of colour provided by wild garlic, bluebells, buttercups, gorse and hawthorn. A laburnum tree leant casually over the track dripping lanterns of bright yellow flowers, bringing beauty and danger in equal measure. Occasionally, unchecked and unruly *Clemati montana*, tired of the confines of their own garden, spilled over fences like a floral waterfall in search of new adventures. In the background, the horticultural bullies of nettles, sticky willies and ferns were beginning to flex their muscles before dominating summer growth, the latter's coiled leaves ready to unfurl like a party blower in ultra slow motion.

From time to time, the spluttering sound of petrol-driven lawnmowers, from adjacent gardens, drifted onto the line, bringing with it the redolence of newly cut grass, mingling with the aroma of verdant railway bank growth. A variety of fencing, from pristine to the truly higgledy-piggledy, demarcated and defended the gardens.

Birds chirped in the numerous trees which flanked, and occasionally provided a canopy for, the railway line. A woodpecker, often heard but rarely seen, drummed a nearby trunk.

Occasionally, the clouds would relax their stranglehold on the weather, allowing the sun to pierce the tree foliage, producing patterns of dappled light on the fine shale path.

Lily's unsolved murder cases, and PTSD symptoms, began to feel a long way away. For the first time in a while, she was relaxing.

The trio began to make steady progress eastwards though Andrew, frustrated at their slow progress, ventured ahead. He seemed to consider it his duty to swish through every puddle, at as high a speed as he could muster. Without a mudguard on his rear wheel, the inevitable consequence was a spray up the back of his jacket. Lily imagined the size of her washing basket at the end of the day.

Ghosts of old stations appeared regularly, advertised by the sudden suggestion of a geometric platform shape, long overgrown by the chaos of nature. Holburn, Ruthrieston, Cults, Bieldside, Murtle and Milltimber came and went, before increasing saddle soreness made Lily think discretion might trump valour.

She drew to a stop, put both feet on the ground to steady herself, and took a deep breath in.

Tom noticed her flushed cheeks and sweaty hair at the edges of her helmet, which he found curiously attractive.

"Had enough?"

"My bum has!"

"Ah. I forgot. It's been a while."

Lily looked ahead for her son, but despite the arrow-straight line, he was out of sight.

"I'll message Andrew, to say we're turning back."

"OK. Why don't you get him to meet us at the pop-up cafe at Cults station? I noticed they had stovies on the specials board."

"Are you always thinking of your next meal?" teased Lily.

"Well. I'm a man, am I not?"

"I'll give you that," she said, with a twinkle in her eye, memories of their recent energetic sex fresh in her mind.

Having texted Andrew, Lily and Tom set off back towards the city, mindful, as on the way out, of other human, canine and equine users. Tom kept her informed about cycling etiquette: only once did she forget to sound her bell when approaching pedestrians from behind, drawing a rebuke from an elderly couple, fully kitted out in waterproofs, backpacks and ski poles.

Fifteen minutes later, Lily and Tom arrived at the old Cults station, and secured a vacant wooden bench.

"I'll get us a couple of coffees while we're waiting for Andrew," suggested Tom, "Latte, extra hot?"

Lily flashed a smile, and gave a thumbs up. As Tom turned towards the pop-up cafe, she retrieved her phone from her pocket. There was still no reply from Andrew, but she had received one WhatsApp and one SMS. She looked at the senders; Dr Dexter Brewster and the Countesswells Medical Practice, respectively. She knew it was probably unwise to read them, but curiosity trumped common sense, and she opened the message from Brewster.

Hi Lily. Are you at work this afternoon? There's something I need to speak to you about.

Lily was intrigued. It wasn't often her pathology colleague sought her out, the boot normally being firmly on the other foot. She replied:

No. I'm actually off this afternoon. I'm back
tomorrow. L

A swishing noise indicated the reply had been sent, and she moved on to the message from her general practice.

Hello. This is the pharmacist attached to the
Countesswells Practice. Could you please phone
and book a telephone appointment with myself
for a review of your medication use?

That's not going to happen any time soon, thought Lily. The longer the two murders went unsolved the more grief she got from Farrell, the more stressed she felt and the worse were her insomnia and PTSD symptoms. She needed all the support she could currently muster, both physical and pharmacological. She wasn't going to willingly engage in any process that might upset her personal apple cart.

Tom reappeared with two coffees just as Lily slipped her phone back into her pocket. Although the phone had gone, the dying light of concern on her face had not. Tom shot her a glance.

"Are you alright?"

"Yeh. Yeh. Just a couple of messages from work. I should've known better than to look at them."

She tried to recapture her relaxed frame of mind, and smiled at Tom, but it was only a thin veneer. Part of her mind was elsewhere.

"Listen. God knows, I'm no psychiatrist, but if you ever want to speak about it, then I'm your man."

"It's difficult. I can't really speak about my work."

"That's OK. I understand, but I am a good listener. I have to be at work, sometimes. All I can say is, that there would be one or two donkeys without back legs going about if they ever got close to some of the surgeons I work with."

"They'd hardly be 'going about', then," retorted Lily.

"True," Tom agreed, while pointing his index finger towards her in acknowledgement of a point well made.

"Appreciate the offer," replied Lily, as she committed to a fuller smile, a smile that was cut short by Andrew's arrival, with a showy skid-stop, splattering mud onto Lily and Tom's trousers.

"Andrew!"

"Sorreee!"

Tom interjected to defuse the situation.

"About time, wee man, some of us are starving!"

"Do you want some food?"

Andrew, looking sheepishly at his mother, nodded his head, but didn't say anything.

Lily's face changed from anger to *boys will be boys*, and she pretended to clip him around the ear. Andrew relaxed a little knowing if not exactly out of the doghouse, he was at the front door.

Tom returned with three cups of steaming stovies, and a coke. Andrew, looking to identify the source of the steam, peered inside the cups.

"Stovies! Cool! No beetroot?"

"Sadly, no," bemoaned Tom, "though I did get us some brown sauce instead."

Andrew greedily accepted, and immediately scooped up a plastic fork-load of the mixture of lamb, gravy, potato and onion. It was too hot to eat immediately and he impatiently blew on the food trying to get it to an edible temperature.

Eventually the food complied, and was eagerly consumed for its trouble. Nobody spoke, their concentration fully on eating, until a scraping of fork on polystyrene heralded the end of the traditional North East Scotland dish.

Lily glanced at Andrew. She enjoyed watching her son polish off food, and wasn't disappointed when he finished first, and wiped the back of his hand across his mouth.

"That takes me back to my youth," Tom announced. "In fifth and sixth year, we used to get let out of school at lunch, and there was a baker-cum-fast-food shop nearby that cooked up a vat of the stuff every day." He seemed lost in the memory as he began to clear up the debris.

"Right," he said, "anyone for a *fine piece*?"

Andrew looked at Lily, seeking clarification, as if Tom was speaking a foreign language.

Lily caught the enquiring look. "It's the Aberdeen way of saying something sweet and tasty, like a piece of cake, or traybake perhaps."

"Yes, please!" he quickly agreed.

Tom binned the waste and went back to the counter.

Andrew whispered to Lily. "Mum, why does Tom wear a ring?"

"Oh. That's called a signet ring. Some men wear it on their little finger. They've been seen as a bit naff for a while, but are making a comeback, I believe."

"Does it mean anything?"

"No. Not really. Sometimes it's just a fashion statement,

and sometimes they're passed down through generations of the same family. That's why it's uncool to get your own initials engraved, apparently, as you might not be the only owner in its lifetime."

"OK," replied Andrew, whose body language suggested he'd had enough of the subject.

Tom arrived back with three generous slabs of millionaire shortbread. Andrew was admiring Tom's bike.

"Like it?" he enquired.

Andrew nodded enthusiastically.

"It's a Boardman Adventure e-bike. Twelve gears. You can have a shot one day, once your legs have grown a bit."

"Cool!"

Tom held up the millionaire shortbread. Andrew's eyes lit up, and Lily reached for an extra dose of short acting insulin.

They ate the traybake quickly and were getting ready to set off on the last leg homewards, when Lily's phone pinged with an incoming message. It was from Brewster, replying to her earlier message.

OK. That's fine. I'll come over and see you in the morning. D

Lily's emotion changed from her earlier intrigue to worry. She frowned and ran a hand through her hair. What on earth could tempt her friend to leave his natural habitat of the morgue, and come to see her, in what he repeatedly referred to as the "dark side"? She put her helmet on and began cycling, but the question continued to niggle in her mind all the way back to Duthie Park.

18

11ᵗʰ May

Dr Dexter Brewster was due in court in the afternoon. He was smartly dressed in a suit, white shirt and a Royal College of Pathologists tie, the blue colour of which was picked out by the morning sun, as he made his way from the morgue to Aberdeen Police Station.

He identified himself at reception, and said he was there to see DI Bankhurst. The duty officer checked Bankhurst's room extension but, when there was no answer, suggested she would most likely be in the incident room. Brewster intimated that he knew the way, and he was buzzed through the security doors. A long corridor, and two sets of swing doors, took him to the incident room. The door was ajar and he walked in, somewhat sheepishly. He spotted Bankhurst standing in front of, what he assumed, was DS Iqbal's desk. Iqbal saw him, and beckoned him to join them. Bankhurst, watched his progress and he could see she was trying to read his face. Apart from looking like a fish out of water he was giving nothing away.

"Morning Dexter. This surely must be quite important? Coming to our gaff," said Bankhurst.

"Morning, Lily." Brewster nodded at the DS. "Zafar. I'm not sure if I'm second guessing myself or not, but something's been bothering me. I wonder if I may have made a mistake."

"That's certainly not like you, Dexter, but none of us are above errors. Go on," encouraged Bankhurst.

"Well, it's to do with a post-mortem I did in January. You may remember it, Zafar? The patient from Ashgrove Hospital who committed suicide."

"Aye. I do. Horrible death, so it was. Self-incineration."

"That's what I put on his certificate in the end, as the evidence pointed in that direction. But there were one or two loose ends. No suicide note, for a start. I know there doesn't have to be, but it's… em… neater, shall I say, if there is. The second thing was that we don't know where he sourced the accelerant and matches from. He was seen on CCTV leaving the hospital empty handed, but there was a petrol can and a box of matches beside his body. Either he, somehow, sourced them himself previously, and hid them in the hospital grounds somewhere, or he had an accomplice."

"Aye, we looked into that at the time, I remember," said Iqbal, interjecting. "There was no evidence of any outside help."

Brewster carried on. He wanted to get something off his chest.

"Well, I was confident that I made the right decision at the time, but recent events have sown doubt in my mind."

"Recent events?" Bankhurst raised an eyebrow. She wondered where the pathologist was going.

"The spate of murders in Aberdeen. In particular, they seem to have been in very public places. Seaton Park. Johnston Gardens. Union Terrace Gardens."

Bankhurst shifted her weight and continued to eye him closely.

"So, where did this self-incineration take place?" she enquired.

"Victoria Park."

"Fuck's sake!" Bankhurst murmured under her breath.

She shot an accusatory glance at Iqbal, as if to say *Why am I only hearing about this now?*

He put his hands up in a *what can I say?* gesture.

"It was written up, and processed, as a suicide, so I never thought much about it after, except for an occasional image of the post-mortem appearing in my mind's eye from time to time. As you can imagine, it wasn't a very nice spectacle."

"Look, it wasn't Zafar's fault. If anyone's, it was mine," said Brewster. "I don't know for sure whether the suicide verdict was right or wrong, and I haven't come here lightly – I realise the possible implications. But in all conscience, I couldn't keep it to myself any longer."

"Absolutely, Dexter. Thanks for sharing," she said, sporting a weak smile.

A few seconds of silence followed. A giant elephant had just entered, and weighed heavily on, the room.

19

11th May

"Serial killer!"

"You've got to be kidding me." DCI Farrell was already in her high-pitched, stressed-out voice.

After Brewster had excused himself, Bankhurst and Iqbal had shared a coffee, and their thoughts, before deciding the correct course of action. To inform DCI Farrell of their concerns. They went upstairs, to take the bull by the horns.

The omens weren't good. As usual, Farrell looked like she had a bad smell under her nose, an expression that only worsened when Bankhurst laid out her theory.

"Just because you were involved in a serial killer case before, you shouldn't go around wasting time, trying to corral all the Aberdeen shit of the day into another one. You would do better to concentrate on your own two cases. I don't suppose I have to remind you that they are both unsolved!"

"No, ma'am. You don't, but if I could just…"

Farrell cut across her DI. "On what *possible* grounds are you trying to link these cases anyway? As I understand it, the first one was a suicide. The other three were murders, we know that, but they were all completely different. Different parts of the city. Different times of the day. Different MOs. Different victim profiles. Need I go on?"

She did, anyway. "Despite extensive efforts, absolutely no link has been found between any of the victims. In fact, I'd go as far as saying that the only thing that links the cases is the fact that they are unsolved!"

Her face had turned beetroot red, and a small fleck of saliva appeared on her lower lip, as she almost spat out the last word.

"It was Dr Brewster," pointed out Bankhurst, "who came to us today, raising the possibility that the suicide verdict for Robert Lennox may possibly be incorrect."

"So now we're taking suggestions from a pathologist on how to run our department!" It was more an accusation than a question.

"With respect, ma'am, that's hardly what he did."

"Well, as far as I am aware, there was absolutely no evidence of third-party involvement. So, how could it be anything other than suicide? It looks to me that you're scraping the bottom of your investigation barrel, Bankhurst. Smacks of desperation, if you ask me!"

Iqbal shifted his weight from one foot to another, and cleared his throat.

"Something to say, DS Iqbal?" sneered Farrell.

"Well, if, *by any chance*, the Lennox verdict was

incorrect, that means we have a fourth unexplained violent death, to add to the three murders we already know about… and all of them took place in Aberdeen parks or gardens."

"Far too many 'ifs and buts' for my liking!" replied Farrell. "The last thing we want to do is spook the public, by mentioning a possible serial killer… especially based on the flimsiest of evidence."

"The other possible link was a flash of light at two of the murder loci," added Bankhurst, keen to capitalise on any small momentum created by Iqbal.

Farrell's face went to the next shade of red on the colour chart. "What? You mean the testimony of a student, who was more than likely drunk or high at the time, that they *might* have seen a flash, and some grainy footage on a doorbell camera near Johnston Gardens? You'll have to do way better than that, Bankhurst!"

Undeterred by Farrell's intransigence, Bankhurst pressed on.

"We also have CCTV from outside Johnston Gardens and Union Terrace Gardens showing a male of similar build and clothing. At both sites."

"Oh, you mean the average height man, of average build in nondescript clothing," replied Farrell, her tone laced with sarcasm.

Bankhurst realised, herself, that that particular straw had hardly been worth clutching at.

"No. I am not impressed. And I don't want you going around spreading these theories, either! Just get on with your two *unsolved* murders. It's about time you produced some positive lines of inquiry!"

Bankhurst and Iqbal descended the stairs in a subdued mood.

"Well, that went about as well as expected," Bankhurst stated, in a matter-of-fact voice.

"Your naw wrong there, Boss," agreed Iqbal.

Bankhurst took a few paces along the corridor before turning to her DS.

"Are you up for a wee bit of *under the radar* work, Zafar?"

"Nae problem, Boss," he replied, with a slight nod of his head.

"Take a couple of DCs and have another look at the Lennox case."

"Revisit CCTV in and around the park. I know it's a few months ago, but some of the Ring doorbell systems store data for a long time. Also, CCTV from all petrol stations in the city for the few days before his death. See if anyone's filling a jerry can. Wouldn't be too many at that time of year, I wouldn't think. Nobody cuts their grass in January. Check ANPR data. See if there's any commonality with the nights of the other murders. Check to see if his phone ever turned up. If not, see if his wife still has a note of his number. While you're at it see if Mrs Lennox would voluntarily hand over any tablet, PC, etcetera, that he used. We can't get a warrant at the moment, obviously, as we're off record, but I'd love Neil Jardine and his digital forensic guys to have a good look."

"On it, Boss."

A message chimed on Bankhurst's phone.

This is the practice pharmacist...

She ignored the message, and switched the phone into standby mode.

20

12th May

"OK, what've you got?"

Bankhurst was addressing Iqbal, DC Alison Fraser and DC Hugh MacLennan. They had gathered in her office to report back from the surreptitious enquiries into the death of Robert Lennox.

Iqbal cleared his throat.

"Nothing of interest on ANPR, I'm afraid. I was also looking into his mobile phone. Apparently, it was never recovered from the scene, or from his room in the hospital. He was known to have one, so where did it go? Was it taken away by a third party, be they a collaborator or assailant? I phoned his wife. She was able to look up his number. I've passed it on to Neil Jardine, and he's going to take a look. She said his iPad was returned to factory settings, and given to a grandchild, but we're welcome to pick up his PC at any point. She says she hasn't been on it since he died."

"She was a little mystified about the renewed interest in her husband's death. I just spoke in generic terms about 'tying up loose ends', which she seemed happy enough with. She's also consented to being interviewed, if we wish."

"OK, we'll hold off on that meantime, as we're off the record, but we could interview her and pick up the computer at the same time, in due course. Let's see what Digital Forensics can do with the phone number in the meantime."

Bankhurst looked to DC Fraser. "Alison?"

"I've been reviewing all the CCTV from the hospital and surrounding area," said Fraser. "Still quite a lot of footage retained. Good in one way, but time-consuming in another. I haven't found any images of a possible third party, but there is one possible thing of interest."

"Go on," said Bankhurst.

Fraser pointed at Bankhurst's PC. "May I?"

Bankhurst moved her keyboard towards the DC, and rotated the screen slightly so everyone could see. After a few clicks, Fraser brought up doorbell camera footage from a house in Argyll Place, adjacent to Victoria Park.

There was clearly a glow from inside the park with a timestamp to match when the incineration took place. The glow was nebulous and constantly changing, as might be expected from a fireball.

Bankhurst wasn't sure what she was meant to be seeing, her confusion showing on her face.

"I'll run it again in slow motion," Fraser said. "Pay particular attention to the quality and type of light." She restarted the recording, and reduced the speed to fifty percent.

"Now, I think I see what you're getting at," voiced Bankhurst, while nodding her head in appreciation. "There's the background glow from the fire but within that changing light display there's a subtle, transient, but more sheet-like light."

"Like you might get from a flash!" agreed Iqbal. "Somebody taking a photo. A memento, maybe."

"That's what I was wondering," said Fraser.

"There's also similar footage from another doorbell camera on Thomson Street."

A few clicks later the confirmatory recording was displayed.

"Good work, Alison. Keep it to yourself in the meantime. No one out of this quartet."

"Understood, ma'am."

Bankhurst shifted her gaze to DC MacLennan. "What about you, Hugh?"

"I might also have something, ma'am."

Bankhurst felt a slight tingle of excitement going up her spine. "Go on."

"Well, I was looking at CCTV from petrol stations in Aberdeen. Nothing at all, so I decided to broaden the search to include all satellite towns and villages, within ten miles of Aberdeen, who have a petrol station."

"OK. Good idea."

"So, a purchase of petrol, in a jerry can, was made at the petrol station in Portlethen, three evenings before Lennox's death. It's interesting that the purchaser comes into the garage on foot, and uses the furthest away pump which has the poorest illumination. He's dressed in black clothes with a hoodie. He's very careful to keep his face hidden both outside and within the shop, and he appears to pay in cash."

"Interesting," agreed Bankhurst. "Seems very forensically and digitally aware. On foot, so no car registration. Keeps himself well hidden, and leaves no card details. Not unlike the Union Terrace suspect."

"There's actually a bit more," continued MacLennan. "I've got a mate who works in the biometric template department. Owed me a favour. I got him to compare the footage from Portlethen with images captured outside Johnston Gardens and Union Terrace Gardens. Obviously, they had no facial features to compare, but the anatomical and gait analysis were a possible match."

"Right, you bastard," announced Bankhurst looking at the frozen image on the screen, "we're on to you."

She looked at Iqbal. No words were spoken, but they recognised the salient moment. They had been there before; crossed the Rubicon into serial killer territory.

For the second time in twenty-four hours, Bankhurst climbed the stairs to DCI Farrell's office. This time alone. Now she had a confident air about her, quickly making her way to the first floor, two steps at a time. A confidence born from carrying more weighty ammunition to fight the anticipated battle with her DCI.

Outside Farrell's door she knocked with a committed rap.

"Wait a minute!" Farrell ordered in a terse voice.

Bankhurst could hear various noises from within, including what sounded like a filing cabinet opening and closing. *What is she doing in there?*

After about thirty seconds, Farrell spoke again. "Enter!"

Bankhurst did as instructed.

Farrell looked up from her desk looking somewhat flustered.

"Oh, it's you Bankhurst! Wasn't expecting to see you back again so soon. Have you made any progress on your murder investigations?"

"Yes, and no, ma'am."

"What kind of an answer is that!" said Farrell, more as a statement than a question.

Before Bankhurst could answer, she paused slightly. Wafting across from Farrell's side of the desk was the unmistakable smell of alcohol. Bankhurst had smelt enough congeners in her time, particularly when she was married, to instantly recognise the source of the sweet, aldehyde-type smell.

Was that why Farrell had delayed her entry into her office? Was she hiding alcohol in her filing cabinet?

Bankhurst looked more critically at her senior officer. In an instant, she noted slightly bloodshot eyes, a plethoric facial expression and a few red spots on her forehead and nose. Why had she not noticed this before?

Was this the reason she was put out to pasture for a year from the Met? To sort out her problem? Was this also the reason for some of her cantankerous behaviour? Or was it simpler than that? Was she just a class A bitch?

"Well, spit it out, Bankhurst. I'm busy," ordered Farrell. She pointed towards paperwork on her desk, as if to emphasise the point. The only thing it did emphasise, was a fine tremor. Noted by Bankhurst.

Thoughts crowded Bankhurst's mind. She sucked the back of her teeth, and forced herself to focus. She needed to concentrate on her current presentation. Any other potential dilemmas would have to wait.

"I have some more information that suggests there may be a link between the apparent suicide in January, and the three murders since then."

"Not this again!"

Bankhurst ploughed on, afraid that any break might reduce her momentum.

"We now have evidence of possible flash photography being taken at three of the sites, including Robert Lennox in January. In addition, we now have CCTV footage of a person with similar biometrics, with possible links to three of the killings, again including Lennox."

"I thought I told you to concentrate on your own two murders!"

"With respect, ma'am, my team continues to focus on the Peters and Syme murders, but I did delegate a couple of officers to look at the Victoria Park incineration."

"Splitting hairs, Bankhurst. And you know it," she barked.

Bankhurst fleshed out the bare bones of her opening statement, trying to ignore Farrell's darkening features.

"So, with your permission, ma'am, I'd like to formally widen the scope of the investigation, including working with DI Ledingham's team. I believe we should consider setting up a major investigation team."

"Now, hold your horses, Bankhurst. Let's not get carried away with ourselves. I'll give your unit a little leeway in the meantime, but keep DI Ledingham's team out of it. And, no further MIT talk, either! I don't want the press to get wind of any of this, at least not until we have more to go on than your hunches, and a bit of grainy CCTV!"

"Yes, ma'am. Understood. Thank you."

"Don't thank me, Bankhurst. Just bring me some results! Now, if there's nothing else…"

Farrell moved her gaze to the door, apparently anxious to end the meeting. Bankhurst took the hint and left, closing the door behind her.

"Fucking backwater of a place!" she heard Farrell say through the door.

Bankhurst descended the stairs with much on her mind. She had achieved some breathing space for her team, but not the MIT she desired. One step at a time, she told herself.

What to do with her suspicions about Farrell was a different matter altogether.

On the one hand, she had a professional responsibility to take such suspicions to a higher rank, but on the other, for the first time, she viewed Amanda Farrell as an individual, struggling with her own problems. Problems that would always be more challenging in relative isolation. A problem shared is…

She tried to put herself in Farrell's shoes. Isolated by geography, rank and personality. Perhaps life was a struggle for her.

Bankhurst began to check off a mental list of similarities she might share with her DCI:

Failed marriage ✓
Single parent ✓
Police career ✓

Police career as female ✓
Chronic health problems?

She realised that she perhaps had more in common with her senior officer than she would care to admit. No paragon of virtue herself, she felt uncomfortable at being the first to cast a stone. She decided to take no further action. After all, everybody had their secrets. She knew she certainly had.

By the afternoon, Bankhurst had gathered her investigation team in the incident room. By way of preparation for the briefing she had delegated MacLennan to prepare four adjacent whiteboards. One for each of Robert Lennox, Kayleigh Peters, Dawn Syme and Ollie Bainton. Her team were already very familiar with the Peters and Syme cases, had some passing knowledge of the Bainton murder in Union Terrace Gardens, but were completely unfamiliar with the details of Robert Lennox. A buzz of conversation hung in the air, as many pairs of eyes flitted back and forwards between the various boards. Most came to rest on Robert Lennox, in particular his cause of death. Incineration. Bankhurst had specifically instructed MacLennan to remove the prefix self from the mode of death, to encourage open minds.

Robert Lennox
Age: 65
Date of death: 7 January
Time of death: 06:10
Cause of death: incineration

Site of death: Victoria Park, Aberdeen
Married. 2 children. Retired teacher
Inpatient at Ashgrove Psychiatric Hospital (severe depression. Being treated with medication and ECT)
Originally thought to be suicide. No note
Possible camera flash seen on local CCTV
Portlethen Petrol Station CCTV shows man purchasing jerry can of petrol on 4 January
Biometrics suggest possible match with male images captured at Johnston Gardens and Union Terrace Gardens murders

Kayleigh Peters
Age: 19
Student at Aberdeen University
From London
Single
Date of death: 8 February
Found: 7:00am
Time of death: 2:30 to 3:30am
Cause of death: strangulation by ligature
Sight of death: Seaton Park, Aberdeen
No sexual assault
No robbery. Phone, bag and purse all found at scene
Last seen alive: approximately 02:20 by two friends
No witnesses
No useful local CCTV
Nothing of interest on local ANPR
Toxicology screen: moderate alcohol. No drugs
Forensics at scene: nothing of note
No weapon found

Digital forensics: nothing
Eyewitness describes possible flash coming from Seaton Park

Dawn Syme
Age: 62
Date of death: 5 March
Time of death: 5:55pm to 6:10pm
Cause of death exsanguination from multiple stab wounds
Site of death: Johnston Gardens, Aberdeen
Married to Robert (64)
Two children (30 and 28) – living in the Central Belt
Retired secretary
Volunteers at local church
Left church at 5:45pm with a co-volunteer. Went separate ways
CCTV image of possible perpetrator following her into Gardens
Possible flash picked up on nearby doorbell cameras
Size 9 footprint near victim
Fits with male (or tall female)
Nike brand. Common variety. Sold in multiple outlets

Oliver (k/a Ollie) Bainton
Age: 48
White
Date of death: 3 May (estimate)
Time of death: unknown
Cause of death: hyperthermia/dehydration
Place of death: Union Terrace Gardens hub

Lives with partner David Glennie (52). Rosemount area
Last seen alive: 29 April in The Knockscalbert pub at
11:30pm
Reported missing (by partner): 30 April
Body found: 5 May
Toxicology: alcohol, cannabis, ketamine
No mobile phone located
ANPR unhelpful
CCTV shows a reflected image of a likely male, dressed
in black clothes/hoodie. Possible biometric match with
male image on Johnston Gardens and Portlethen CCTV
footage

Bankhurst looked up to see the last of her team enter the incident room.

"Close the door behind you please, DC Fraser," she instructed, thereby raising the level of intrigue in the room.

After giving her a few seconds to get seated, Bankhurst cleared her throat.

"OK, thanks for coming everybody. First of all, I want to make it clear that whatever we discuss here today does not go outside these four walls." She had the full attention of the room. Even DS Gillespie looked moderately interested, no mean feat for him.

"As you can see," she pointed at the whiteboards, " we've added the data of two other violent deaths which have happened in Aberdeen this year. Of course, you know the Peters and Syme case inside out, and most of you will have a passing knowledge of the Bainton case. A couple of days ago, we also became aware of the unnatural death of a Robert

Lennox on the seventh of January. Initially, after the post-mortem, he was certified as suicide by self-incineration, but Dr Brewster recently reviewed his findings, after noting the subsequent pattern of violent deaths across the city."

Bankhurst turned from looking at the white boards to face her colleagues.

"He brought it to my attention this week that there was a possibility his original decision could have been unsound. Incineration, by the use of an accelerant and a match, was, without doubt, the cause of death. But this could either have been suicide, homicide, or coerced death by the hand of Lennox himself, but engineered by a third party. In the latter case, the perpetrator would obviously have to have some form of major hold over the deceased, for him to set alight to himself, against his will." She paused. "Like a threat to his family, for example."

Bankhurst drew in a breath. She could almost hear the air being pulled through her bronchi into her lungs, such was the complete silence in the room. Eager eyes remained locked on the DI.

"Unfortunately, I wasn't able to convince the top floor, initially, that this was worth looking into. Rightly or wrongly, I instructed DS Iqbal and DCs MacLennan and Fraser to have another look at the case over the last couple of days."

Bankhurst thought she detected one or two raised eyebrows at the clear breach of command. Only Gillespie, never one to kowtow to authority, wore a look of grudging respect.

"Their efforts were not in vain. As you can see, although the MOs and causes of death are very different, there are potential links between the cases."

Bankhurst used a laser pointer to highlight her comments.

"The possibility of flashes at three out of the four locations, for a start. Raises the possibility of someone taking photos. Trophies perhaps."

The audience were well aware of the penchant for serial killers to indulge in such behaviour. Two and two were quickly put together. A murmur of conversation started, as it dawned on officers what might be evolving before their eyes. Their DI was building a case for a serial killer.

"The other thing is the CCTV images of probable males at different sites, with biometric measurements suggesting a reasonably high chance they are the same person."

The conversation swelled to a thrum. Bankhurst raised both hands and beckoned silence.

"I went back to DCI Farrell today, and she has now granted us some leeway to extend the investigation. I was keen to combine our team with DI Ledingham's to form an MIT, but she wasn't on board with that idea. Not yet, at any rate. So, for the meantime, it's ours to run with. She wants us to keep a lid on things. Specifically, no leaks to the press. She doesn't want to alarm the public at this stage."

"Perhaps the public should be alarmed," growled DS Gillespie.

Slightly raised eyebrows and a subtle nod towards the DS suggested Bankhurst thought he had made a valid point.

She continued, "The other reason DCI Farrell might want to keep it on a need-to-know basis is what appears to be a high level of forensic awareness displayed by the perpetrator. It wouldn't be the first time that a Police Force had identified one of their own as a seriously bad apple." She paused for a moment to let her comment sink in.

"OK, for the next few days I want us to concentrate on the Lennox case. My gut feeling is it *is* connected to the other murders, but we need more evidence. What are we seeing on these boards? What are we missing?"

No one volunteered an opinion, so she started the ball rolling.

"OK, so we've got four violent deaths spread over five months. All in Aberdeen. All in public spaces, specifically parks or gardens. Three definite murders, and one very unnatural death, that we have a big question mark over. Four very different MOs. Absolutely no connection between the victims… so far. I won't have to remind some of you it took us a while, and a lot of basic police work, before we uncovered the link in the last serial murder case we had. We do, however, have CCTV images of a hooded male, and possible flash photography, linking three of the four loci."

"Do we still have the jerry can and matches from the Lennox case?" enquired DC Alison Murray.

"No," replied Bankhurst, "sadly they weren't retained as the death was ascertained to be suicide."

Iqbal looked at his feet. "Could we ask the digital team to try and enhance the image of the jerry can from the petrol station footage? If we could identify a specific make we could perhaps try and find where he bought it from… if he purchased it for this specific job."

Neil Jardine nodded. "We could give it a go, though when you try to enhance it's often at the cost of clarity."

Bankhurst ran with the idea. "So, where do people buy jerry cans from? Other petrol stations? B and Q? The internet?"

She continued, "I imagine most businesses keep computerised records of their stock, and when individual items are purchased. So they know when to reorder. Obviously, if he ordered one from the internet, we'll have virtually no chance of tracking that, but something tells me he wouldn't have done that."

"Forensic and digital awareness?" suggested Iqbal

"Exactly," agreed Bankhurst. "He wouldn't want to leave any kind of digital trail. Would be much more likely to use cash in some form of shop, than risk an online transaction."

"OK, so we'll look into that."

"I also want to investigate the Portlethen connection more. Does he live there, or did he deliberately travel outside the city to reduce the chance of being discovered on CCTV? If so, how did he get there? Car, bus and train would all be possible. Bike perhaps less likely. We can see from the CCTV that he leaves the petrol station travelling in an easterly direction towards Muirend Road and Mosside Drive, but where did he go next?"

"I live in Portlethen," volunteered DS Sharon Baxter. "That bearing doesn't help much as the bus station and rail station are both in that direction. As could his car, for that matter," she added.

"Fair point," said Bankhurst.

"So," she continued, "we need to look at January timetables for buses and trains, to and from Aberdeen to Portlethen. We'll need CCTV from the bus station, railway station and all the individual buses and trains. I also want ANPR data for every type of vehicle going in and out of Portlethen for six hours either side of the purchase of the petrol. And cross-reference it with data from the other murders. While we're at it, we need to get any CCTV from all the neighbouring streets and those in the direction he was heading."

"What about house-to-house?" suggested Iqbal. "I could speak to Uniform."

"Let's keep it within our team meantime," she responded. "I know it will take longer but I made a commitment to DCI Farrell to keep things low key meantime. Concentrate on the streets adjacent to the petrol station."

"What about releasing the CCTV footage to the media, ma'am, with an appeal for witnesses?" suggested Reflex Babinski, before qualifying his remark with, "under the generic description of investigating an arson, or something like that."

Bankhurst nodded slowly a couple of times, while she weighed up the potential information that might be generated, versus tipping off the perpetrator that they had a lead on him.

"Let's do it," she ordered. "DS Baxter, can you speak to Comms and draft a suitable release to go with the footage?"

"Sure, Boss."

"What about interviewing the petrol station employee who was on that night. Bit of a long shot, but they might have remembered something."

"Sure. Why not?" agreed Bankhurst. "Should be easy enough to check the staff rota to see who was on. Plus, we know what they look like."

"What about you, DS Gillespie? You've not said much so far," said Bankhurst.

Her overweight colleague sat slouched in his chair, the strained buttons of his shirt struggling to contain his belly. His tie, loosened at the top, and stained in the middle, dangled sideways at an angle. His trousers looked like they hadn't seen an iron for a while, and his shoes were in need of a polish. Although the DS had his faults; misogyny, sexism and homophobia amongst them, Bankhurst valued his opinion as a detective.

"Humph," he replied, sending a ripple through his chins.

Bankhurst wasn't sure if he was actually going to volunteer anything else, but she let the silence stretch to see if he would fill it.

"If the first case is related to the others, and I'm not saying it is, then the perpetrator must have had tremendous leverage over Lennox, to get him out of the hospital at that time of night, and do what he did. Some kind of threat to his family has been mentioned. But what if it was something else? What if he had some kind of secret that the perpetrator was aware of? Something that he used to manipulate him."

He paused to take a hacking cough. Bankhurst half expected some sputum to appear, but was grateful to be spared the ordeal.

"I think we need to dig deep into Lennox's past. Interview his wife, colleagues, former pupils. At the moment we don't have any motives for any of the murders. But they possibly started with Lennox. Why? What were his secrets? If we can find out more about that then perhaps we can get a better understanding of how he might link with the other cases."

"Also," – it seemed Gillespie had warmed to the task and had more to say – "if the third party was an enforcer, rather than a collaborator, how did he know to provide the exact equipment that Lennox needed to execute the suicide method he had been ruminating about. I don't believe in coincidence."

Neither do I, thought Bankhurst.

Gillespie continued, "He must have had inside knowledge."

Bankhurst picked up his line of thought. "So, we should be having a look at staff, and fellow patients, in Ashgrove Hospital."

"Aye." Gillespie agreed. "And while you're at it, I would check the hospital firewalls with their IT department. Is there any way that medical records could have been hacked?"

"Thanks, George… eh, DS Gillespie. Very helpful."

DC Babinski raised his arm, looking to make a point.

"Reflex?"

"We know about the violent deaths in January, February, March and May. That's one a month with the exception of April. We've already excluded any murders in the city in April, but is it worth taking another look at all unnatural deaths? Could we have missed something? Just like Robert Lennox. Could another death have gone under the radar? That would then make it one per month."

"Fair point," agreed Bankhurst, while a thin shiver ran down her spine at the prospect of the natural progression of Babinski's theory in June.

He continued. "We've probably got several hundred deaths in the city each month. We could, for the meantime, exclude any thought to be of natural causes. That would take a large chunk out of the equation. All unnatural deaths should have been notified to the Procurator Fiscal in any case, so we could start with them."

"Agreed," stated Bankhurst.

"There's another thing," said Babinski.

"Go on."

"If you look at all the dates of the cases on the boards: the seventh of January, the eighth of February, the fifth of March and the third of May; they're all in the first fortnight of each month."

Bankhurst nodded. Babinski continued.

"So, do we need to look at contract workers? Specifically, those who work two weeks on, two weeks off?"

Everyone in the room was aware of the obvious local connection, but Bankhurst verbally joined the dots.

"The offshore industry."

Babinski nodded. "We could exclude anyone working a shift pattern that puts them offshore for the first fortnight of each month. For those on the opposite shift, of which there must be thousands, we could start by cross-referencing them with a history of any criminal record on the PNC."

"OK, that's good, Reflex. Thanks."

Bankhurst scanned her team for signs of further contributions. Nothing doing. She glanced at Iqbal, often a source of sensible contributions to a brainstorming session, but he looked distracted. She turned and, once more, scanned the boards, a frown forming on her forehead.

"What if" – she started to think out loud, without turning around – "we're looking at the deaths from the wrong perspective? So far, the fact that they are all so different has been an argument against connecting the cases. What if it is precisely because they are so different that actually creates a link?"

A voice from behind her, which she recognised as DS Sharon Baxter, added, "You mean the perpetrator is working through a list of different MOs for every murder."

"It's a chilling thought," agreed Bankhurst, "but, yes."

Bankhurst, who had been jotting down notes during the briefing, delegated tasks and arranged a follow-up briefing for the following day. She dismissed her team, gathered her laptop and paperwork, and walked over to Iqbal's desk. Her DS was gazing out the window.

"Penny for them," she ventured.

"Ach. Sorry, Boss," he replied, and smiled at Bankhurst. But the smile was thinner than usual, and looked a little unnatural.

"Are you OK, Zafar?"

"Aye. I'm fine, Boss. Just some family issues in Glasgow."

"Anything you want to talk about? I've got form when it comes to family issues!"

He grinned, more naturally this time.

"Na. You're alright. Would just bore you to death, so it would."

"Well, you know where I am if you change your mind."

Iqbal gave a thumbs up. "Thanks, Boss."

Bankhurst drove home with thoughts reverberating through her mind. From the mundane to the maleficent. When would she do her weekly shop? Was Andrew up to date with his homework? What motive could connect the murders? Why couldn't the lab isolate DNA from the rectal semen? Who else had to juggle such issues? Why was she still doing this bloody job?

By the time she had stopped at the traffic lights on the junction of Countesswells Road and Springfield Road, nothing had been resolved. The lights seemed to take forever to change and her mind drifted further into her problems. A toot from the car behind, indicating the lights had turned green, snapped her back to attention. She waved an apology before pulling away quickly.

Focus, Lily. Focus.

After a last-minute stop at Aldi, to pick up a bottle of chilled Sauvignon Blanc, she arrived home and parked on her drive. Dark, threatening clouds had gathered over the Countesswells suburb. The first few drops of rain fell, greedily soaked up by the dry ground in her front garden.

With rain splattering on her coat pulled over her head, she scuttled into her semi-detached house. Hung up her coat and kicked off her shoes. A delicious smell, and the sound of joyous laughter, drew her towards the kitchen-diner. Andrew and Olive, his after-school minder, were playing cards on the kitchen table.

"Your son's a shark!" she exclaimed

"Am not," he said, in a fake offended tone.

"Smells good," observed Bankhurst. She put the wine in the fridge, resisting the temptation to open it there and then.

"I noticed you'd defrosted a chilli. Thought I'd put it on a low heat. Hope that's OK."

"Of course. Great. Thanks, Olive."

"I've measured out the rice over there. Good to go, whenever you're ready."

"You're a star!"

"No problem."

Olive rose from the table, and ran an affectionate hand through Andrew's hair.

"Right. I'm off. See you tomorrow… shark!"

At the sound of Olive's throaty car exhaust disappearing down the street, Bankhurst put the rice on, retrieved the bottle of wine from the fridge and poured a generous glass.

She picked up the cards while taking her first sip of the Sauvignon Blanc.

The cool, crisp Marlborough was as fruity and delicious as ever. Well worth, in her opinion, the extra two to three pounds over the price of a mid-range bottle.

"Time for a quick hand before tea," she announced, "and don't forget, I know all of your tricks!"

Bankhurst played cards while enjoying the creeping progression of alcohol through her body. Andrew offloaded about his day. A ping from the microwave advertised the rice was ready.

Andrew, with the typical voracious appetite of a ten-year-old boy, was first to finish, and held his bowl up as if to say *any more?*

"Go on, then!" said his mother.

After tea, having assured her he had finished his homework, Andrew was allowed screen time before being shuffled off to bed at 9pm. Bankhurst changed into her pyjamas and checked her social media, swapping WhatsApp messages with Tom. For the next couple of hours, she flitted between background TV and mindless scrolling, not fully concentrating on either.

Thoughts of her cases intruded regularly. She longed for sleep, and its restorative properties, but dreaded its, now regular, companion. Panic attacks. She decided to postpone her bedtime for another hour.

Perhaps I might take something to help, she considered. *Just for tonight.*

21

13th May

Bankhurst woke up with a start. She felt the first shiver of adrenaline course through her body, and her pulse began to accelerate. A loud noise pierced her brain. *Oh no, not again.* But then she recognised the sound. The familiar, if often unwelcome, noise of her alarm. She had made it through the night without disturbance, giving her a sense of relief. Still somewhat drowsy, and with a low-grade headache, she swallowed two paracetamol and headed for the shower. Half an hour later, and feeling revitalised, she headed to the kitchen for breakfast and her morning diabetic regimen. Andrew was already tucking into breakfast, while scrolling on a phone

"Hoi. That's my phone!" she objected.

"Just having a wee look," he replied, with a cheeky grin.

"Well, you needn't bother. How did you unlock it anyway?"

"Mum, you use the same password and code for everything!"

Busted. She tilted her head slightly in acknowledgement.

"I wouldn't need to do this if I had my own phone," he added.

"Not until you're twelve. We agreed."

"*You* agreed, Mum!" he retorted, adding, "half my class have a phone, by the way."

"And the other half don't!"

"Humph."

"Give it here, please."

Andrew reluctantly ceded the phone to his mother, while putting his lower lip out in an exaggerated fashion.

A pang of guilt nudged at Bankhurst. Caught between sensible parenting and hypocrisy; aware that her own phone addiction gave her, at best, only a flimsy foothold on the mobile phone moral high ground.

She considered checking her search history, to see what sites Andrew had been on, but thought better of it. *Sometimes, ignorance is bliss.*

Mother and son pulled out of the Countesswells estate and joined the morning flow of traffic into Aberdeen. It was a pleasant morning. The car windows were lowered. The groundsman at the nearby school playing fields was already hard at work, and the smell of freshly mown grass wafted into the car. Andrew ignored his sneeze, but Bankhurst made a mental note to order his seasonal hay fever medications from their GP practice. She felt a pang of guilt about not making her review appointment with the practice pharmacist, but dismissed it as she approached the throng of people outside the school.

With Andrew dropped off, Bankhurst crossed the city to Aberdeen Police Station, thoughts of her cases on her mind. A colleague, possibly finishing a night shift, vacated a parking bay, and she gratefully accepted.

With coffee in hand, she made her way to the incident room, where her team was assembled. Neil Jardine, from Digital Forensics, was propped against a wall checking his phone. She hoped his presence might indicate a positive development.

She greeted the room with a customary "Morning".

In reply, she got a few reciprocal "mornings" and a grunt from Gillespie.

"OK," she said, "let's get to it. Where are we now?"

Various detectives looked at each other to see who would speak first.

Hugh MacLennan filled the vacuum.

"I've been looking into the jerry can, ma'am."

"Go on."

"I've looked at similar jerry cans sold within a twenty-mile radius of Aberdeen, the week before the petrol was bought in Portlethen. Of course, he may have bought it well before then, but I thought it was a reasonable place to start. The data is still coming in, but there's already something which has caught my attention. One was paid for with cash."

"Sounds like our man," said Bankhurst.

"That was at a tool outlet on the Westhill industrial estate. They've sent me the CCTV footage, from cameras inside and outside the store."

Bankhurst felt her hopes rising.

"It could be our guy. Once again he was dressed in dark clothes with a hoodie, taking great care to avoid exposing his face to any camera. Also, he didn't appear to have a car with him, and was still on foot when he left the outside camera view."

"I'm even more convinced he's our guy," said Bankhurst. "He's exceptionally careful. Buys a jerry can in Westhill and then, a few days later, buys petrol in Portlethen. Both times dressed to avoid CCTV capture, both times paid with cash and both times either hasn't used a car, or the car has been parked outwith any CCTV coverage."

"Good work, Hugh. Can you look at ANPR data for that day in Westhill, and see if there's any cross-connection with either the Portlethen or murder loci data. One of these days he's going to slip up. Speaking about Portlethen. What about the ANPR data from that night?"

"We've one match between Portlethen and the night of Robert Lennox's death. But the plate belongs to a nurse who lives in Portlethen and works at Aberdeen Royal Infirmary."

"Male or female?" enquired Bankhurst.

"Forty-three-year-old female, ma'am. Mirena Loci. Italian. Scrub nurse in general surgery theatres. Moved to UK ten years ago. Plus, we've confirmed she was on night shift at ARI on the seventh of January, and was picked up on ANPR as she left the hospital complex."

Or her car was, thought Bankhurst.

"OK. I want cyber analytics to have a good look at her. Just in case. Get them to dig deep. Who else could have access to her car? Does she have a partner? Male or female? Any children? Particularly, any adult sons?"

"Who does she associate with? Who are her friends? I want the full monty. Facebook. Instagram. X. Whatever. The lot. We need a decent line of inquiry!"

Bankhurst clicked her tongue in frustration.

"OK. What did we get on the search for people with criminal records living at the Portlethen postcodes?"

DC Lisa Turnbull spoke up. "Quite a hotchpotch as you might imagine, but nothing involving any serious violence. Do you want me to start checking alibis?"

"No, I don't think so. I think the likelihood that he lived in Portlethen was a long shot, at best. Particularly now that we suspect he bought the jerry can in Westhill, it's very likely that he deliberately went outwith the city, to Portlethen, to buy the petrol."

"What about the staff member at the petrol station? Who was looking into that?"

"That's me, ma'am," replied Turnbull. "Twenty-four-year-old male. Showed him the CCTV. Vaguely remembered the sale. Thinks was probably Caucasian, but couldn't be certain. Can't remember if he was local or not. Didn't think he was a regular customer, as he might have remembered him if he was."

"OK." Bankhurst looked around the room. "What else have we got?"

"I checked out the buses and trains for that evening, ma'am," DS Sharon Gillespie said. "There are several he could potentially have caught, but we've no CCTV images of him either at the stations or on the transport. I went down to the stations this morning before I came to work, to have a look at the set-up. If you were wary, you could avoid the cameras on the stations. It would be almost impossible to avoid CCTV on the buses, but you could probably do so on the trains. The one place you couldn't avoid cameras is at Aberdeen train station. Nobody wearing dark clothes and a hoodie that night seen on camera, though he could have changed in the train toilets I suppose. Certainly a few males who could potentially fit the profile."

"OK, let's capture all the images from males of a certain height and build. Run them through facial recognition software. See if there are any hits. If not, then at least we've got some images on file."

"Will do."

Zafar Iqbal took half a step forward to take his opportunity.

"We've had a few people contacting the helpline following the media release – mostly cranks and conspiracy theorists. But there was one guy who sounded quite hopeful. Says he was out walking his dog, and he's fairly convinced he saw our man."

"Good. Let's get someone down there to interview him today."

Iqbal nodded.

Bankhurst looked up. "Neil?"

"We've been able to get some limited information since we got Lennox's mobile number from his wife. We now know he received four texts from an unknown number shortly before he left Ashgrove Hospital in the early hours of the seventh of January."

"Burner phone?"

"Yes," said Jardine.

"Figures," said Bankhurst, thoughtfully.

"Still could be an accomplice, I suppose," remarked Iqbal.

"Could be," said Jardine, "but he'd never had any communication with this number before. You would have thought, if it was an accomplice, they would have some contact before the night in question. Also, why would you go to the extent of getting a burner if you were just an accomplice."

"It's still a horrific thing to be associated with, even if, in some way, they thought they were helping. Might well want to remain anonymous."

"Fair point," agreed Bankhurst.

Gillespie cleared his throat, sounding a bit like a car starting on a cold morning. "I still think we need to know more about Lennox. Looks like, to me, he felt compelled to leave after the exchange of texts. What did they have over him to make him do that? What secrets did he have? Could he have been a closet gay perhaps?" He almost sneered the last question, before adding, "Could he have been a member of NEMESIS?"

"I agree, DS Gillespie. I'm actually going to visit his widow after this meeting," confirmed Bankhurst.

"Humph." Gillespie was less than impressed.

"What about the Ashgrove Hospital interviews? Were you doing them?"

"Aye, I was," Gillespie said.

She waited, trying to resist the urge to fold her arms.

"I've finished the staff. No records. All check out OK. Everybody was very traumatised at the time. Nobody likes a suicide on their watch, particularly that gruesome. They almost seemed relieved that we might be looking at it from a different angle."

"OK, what about his fellow patients?"

"Oh, I have that little delectation to look forward to today," he grunted. Bankhurst smiled internally at the thought.

"Last but not least. Reflex?"

"I've been looking at the offshore workforce whose rotas match the dates in question. Information is very patchy so far. Turns out it's not so easy to get the information we want."

"How so?"

"Well, there are three North Sea drilling sectors – UK, Norwegian and Dutch. In addition to that there are multiple companies, from numerous countries involved in the oil and gas industry, each with different rules and regulations regarding accessing data, etcetera."

"Have you told them it's a murder inquiry?"

"Cuts no ice, ma'am, I'm afraid."

"Bloody hell!"

He paused to refresh his computer screen. "I may have something more interesting on the other thing I was working on."

"Unnatural deaths in April?" said Bankhurst.

"Yes."

"Go on."

"Well, there were nineteen deaths reported to the Crown Office Procurator Fiscal Service in April. Four deaths from RTAs – mostly boy racers by the sound of it. Three suicides. Three accidental overdoses – all known drug abusers. A variety of accidents – electrocution, drowning, a fall offshore and being run over by a tractor. Two deaths after surgical procedures. One death in police custody. One stillborn and one SUDI."

"SUDI?" enquired Bankhurst

"Sudden unexplained death in infancy, ma'am."

"OK. Cot death, as was."

Babinski nodded before continuing. "In view of the Lennox case, I had a good look at the suicides, but they all seemed beyond any reasonable suspicion. It was more the accidental overdoses that caught my attention. One in particular."

"Yes."

"A twenty-four-year-old male, Patrick Heggarty, was found dead on the fifth of April. Known drug abuser. Eight-year habit. Previous convictions for possession. Currently no fixed abode. Was found with a syringe and needle by his side. Needle mark in his arm. Opiates and ketamine on toxicology screen. Dr Roddy Hall did a 'view and grant' external post-mortem. He didn't think, all things considered, there was a need for an invasive assessment."

"I see where you're heading with the ketamine, Reflex, but it's hardly unknown in overdoses."

"It wasn't just the ketamine that caught my eye, ma'am. It was the location."

Bankhurst felt the first prickle of hairs rising on the back of her neck.

"He was found behind an outhouse... in Hazlehead Park."

22

14th May

"That's five deaths, at five different Aberdeen parks, over the last five months. Three definite and two possible murders."

Bankhurst curled her toes as she tried not to raise her voice at her senior colleague. She waited. Her cold blouse stuck to her sweaty back. DCI Farrell sat tight-lipped, saying nothing.

CRACK. Farrell showed no mercy to her knuckles as she interlaced her fingers and hyperextended her joints. Her eyes narrowed.

"OK, let's do it," she announced, a steely look appearing in her previously lacklustre eyes. "I want an MIT set up. We'll combine your team and DI Ledingham's, but I want you to lead, DI Bankhurst."

Bankhurst noted the novelty of her name being prefixed by her rank. "Thank you, ma'am."

"Don't thank me yet. This is going to be tough. You've done it before, so you get the nod over Tony Ledingham… but that also means you carry the can. And I'll be breathing down your bloody neck. Of that you can be sure."

I don't doubt it, thought Bankhurst.

"This needs to be treated with great sensitivity at the moment. Not a word must be leaked. The press are already all over the increase in murder rate in Aberdeen this year, but haven't connected the dots between the killings. And, of course, they are completely unaware about the January and April deaths. We need to keep it that way."

"Ma'am," Bankhurst agreed, but said nothing more. It was refreshing to see Farrell have a positive momentum, and her face and eyes hinted at some relish for the challenge.

"We don't want to spook the public at this stage," said Farrell.

Bankhurst went to say something, but was stopped by Farrell's raised hand.

"I know, I know," Farrell said, "the *public have a right to know* argument."

Bankhurst acknowledged her DCI had guessed correctly with a slight nod of her head.

Farrell lowered her hand, and continued, "We're not actually *sure* we've got a serial killer, and if we broadcast this we'll be tied up with crank calls and press conferences all bloody day, when we could be doing useful police work. Also, our assumed perpetrator is clearly a switched-on individual. We don't want him alerted to the fact that we are on to him. We need him to make a mistake… and that's more likely if he thinks he's still under the radar.

Finally, and importantly, we're now in May. Summer is approaching. The hospitality industry, up and down the country, is only just recovering from Covid. From the little I know about Aberdeen, the parks are an important part of summer life here, for locals and tourists alike. The last thing hospitality, and Aberdeen in general, needs is a scare story at this time of year. It could be an economic disaster for the city."

Bankhurst had some sympathy for the opinion, but couldn't help imagine the bad optics if it ever came out that finance had trumped public safety when moulding a Police Scotland strategy.

Farrell continued. "I'll speak to Tony Ledingham. Explain that you'll be SIO. You know what men are like. I'll need to let him down gently."

Bankhurst nodded, a thin smile creasing her face.

Light of foot and mood, Bankhurst hurried down the stairs from the senior officer's floor and swept into the incident room. Most of her team were engrossed in their mobiles or PCs.

"OK. Listen up boys and girls. If you can pull yourself away from fantasy football for a minute, we've got a green light for an MIT."

A spontaneous din of vocal responses and clapping filled the room. Seats swivelled. Faces locked in on Bankhurst. She let the noise abate slightly. Outstretched arms, palms facing downwards, invited silence.

"Starting tomorrow. The Union Terrace Gardens murder team, under DI Tony Ledingham, will join us to form the MIT."

"Who'll be SIO, ma'am?"

"I will... of course," she replied, summoning her best coy look, and bringing out a further positive response from most of her team.

"Now, I want us to hit the ground running tomorrow. We'll need to brief Tony Ledingham's team where we are to date, and they can do likewise with us as regards their investigation. Reflex, I want as much as you can get on the Patrick Heggarty death in Hazlehead Park, before then. For the rest of you, make sure you've got your data organised and ready to present. And one more thing – absolutely no talking about the investigation outwith the team, especially to anyone even remotely connected with the media. We'll do that through a press conference, as and when it's necessary. That's all for now. We'll meet again tomorrow at 09:00."

Bankhurst left the room, the door swinging behind her, with the sound of excited conversation fading into the background.

23

15th May

Another bad night. It was well after midnight before Bankhurst's mind, racing with thoughts of the impending MIT, relaxed enough to allow sleep. A short, vivid dream about turning up two hours late for the morning briefing, played out on an endless loop inside her head. Eventually, with dawn already broken, she woke with a panic attack. Twenty minutes later, having weathered the anxiety storm, changed from soaking wet to dry pyjamas, and visiting her bedside drawer for a pill, she crawled back into bed, hoping to get another couple of hours sleep.

What seemed like ten minutes later, her alarm went off. While grateful for having had some sleep, the trade-off of lethargy and drowsiness, likely companions for another three to four hours, cloaked her being. As usual, on such mornings, she reduced the heat in her shower and increased the coffee in her cup, but hadn't shaken the effect of the "chemical cosh" as she drove to work. As she neared the police station, a knot developed in her stomach, and she could feel the effects of increased adrenalin circulating around her system. Not the overwhelming and debilitating anxiety of a panic attack, but situational anxiety. She reassured herself it was to be expected. Welcomed even. To be harnessed to her advantage. Slowly, she began to feel more alert, and by the time she was walking down the corridor to the MIT room, another strong coffee in her hand, she felt as ready as she was likely to be to face the day.

"Good morning, everyone."

The room quietened with respectful attention. She scanned her audience. Most were known. Some were not. Her eyes met with those of DI Tony Ledingham. Did they show resentment? She wasn't sure.

An immediate olive branch was warranted.

"Tony, would you like to join me, please?"

He nodded, went to the front of the room, and turned to face in the same direction as Bankhurst, the whiteboards behind them broadcasting information to an eager audience. Earlier, with tired eyes looking back at her, she had rehearsed her speech in front of the bathroom mirror. She hoped her preparation was not wasted.

"As you will be aware, this MIT has been set up to investigate a series of murders, and other unnatural deaths, in Aberdeen, since the turn of the year. Are they all connected? Are we dealing with a serial killer? It's our job to find out. We need to be rational, detached and thorough. No stone unturned. Above all else, I want good communication. Let DI Ledingham, or myself, know if you find anything. No matter how trivial you think it might be. Speak to each other. Share stuff."

A murmur of assent simmered from the room.

"Now, you'll have seen from the whiteboards that these are the five deaths we are interested in. One a month since January. All unnatural. All in Aberdeen parks and gardens. All within the first half of each month. Some you may be familiar with but, particularly for those joining us today with DI Ledingham, some you may not. My team has been looking at the death of Robert Lennox in January. Initially it was thought to have been suicide, but we now believe he may have been forced to kill himself. Yesterday, we also became aware of the death of Patrick Heggarty, from a drug overdose, in Hazlehead Park in April, which prompted this MIT."

Bankhurst looked over her shoulder at the last of the five whiteboards, inviting attention to the latest addition. She noted that some extra information had been added overnight.

Patrick Heggarty
Age: 24
Date of death: 5 April
Time of death: 7–9pm (estimated)
Cause of death: overdose opiate and ketamine (IV). View and grant PM done by Dr R Hall
Death reported to COPFS (Fiscal happy no further action required)
Site of death: Hazlehead Park (behind a group of sheds. Known hang-out site for IVDUs)
Single
No children
Unemployed

NFA
Known IVDU. 8-year habit
No witnesses
No CCTV/ANPR data
Forensics not done (murder not suspected)
No possibility of PM now (cremated)

"Thanks, Reflex."

Babinski nodded.

"I suppose we should send an SOC team to the scene now, but it seems unlikely they'll find anything useful at this time."

"Ma'am."

"What about the needle and syringe?"

"Disposed of at the time."

"And absolutely no witnesses?"

"Not so far, ma'am, though the drugs unit are giving their tree a shake to see what falls out. Not the most reliable group, though," he added.

DS Hamish MacDonald raised his arm. "Any link found between any of the victims, so far?"

"No, nothing," Bankhurst confirmed, "not as individuals, but they were all found in parks or gardens."

"And all entirely different MOs?"

She knew where he was going from his tone of scepticism. "We've actually started to think that it is the uniqueness of each MO that could be a connection."

MacDonald looked puzzled.

"As in, the perpetrator is deliberately choosing a different mode of death each time."

Bankhurst let it sink in.

"The more obvious commonalities seem to be the locations, and the timings of the murders… as in the first half of each month. There's also the possibility that he's taking trophy photos at the scene."

MacDonald retired his confused face, looking like a schoolboy who had been put in his place by his teacher.

Bankhurst continued. "We are looking for anyone with a criminal record in the oil and gas sector, whose rotas would correspond with the killings. We have about twenty so far, but data gathering is quite challenging, and it's early days yet."

Bankhurst looked at her DI colleague. "Tony, what's the latest from your team about the Union Terrace Gardens murder?"

"Still no DNA result from the presumed semen, I'm afraid. Proving very challenging. We might never get it. We did have a SOC team have another look at the site. They found traces of urine under the rim of the disabled toilet, and a partial footprint in the same disabled toilet. Special mention, by the way here, for DC Hamilton, who displayed excellent knowledge of male urination, and pointed us in the right direction on this!"

Bankhurst's team looked confused, but there were a few sniggers from within Ledingham's ranks.

Hamilton tipped her head in acknowledgement.

"The urine's been sent to the forensics lab, but the early word back is that the concentration of DNA in urine isn't great at the best of times, and the sample has apparently degraded quite a bit since the day it was deposited. If indeed it was the perpetrator at all," said Ledingham.

He looked at the SOCO in the room, who managed to avoid his gaze.

"Unfortunately, the partial footprint isn't of sufficient quality to process through the national footprint database."

"Have you been able to approximate size?"

"Yes. Likely to be size nine."

"Same as our print at Johnston Gardens."

Ledingham continued, "We'll maybe get the fingerprint experts to have a look. They can sometimes do naked eye coincident sequencing of prints that aren't of sufficient quality to be analysed by a computer. Perhaps they can do something similar with footprints?"

"OK. Good."

Bankhurst paused, lost in thought for a moment. Her eyes glazed slightly, before she snapped back to attention.

"The print from Johnston Gardens was from a common Nike trainer brand. Yes?"

"Yes, ma'am."

"And, we haven't thrown much resource at that, so far, as they're sold in so many places, and we had other fish to fry."

"Ma'am."

"OK. Maybe we can use the perpetrator's digital awareness against him. He wouldn't have used a card in a shop or bought online, both of which would leave a digital trail. Let's look at cash purchases. I imagine that would be a very small list. I realise there are a lot of outlets out there to check, but we have a bigger team now. Remember, it will be a mistake, or a small detail, that catches this guy out. We cannot afford to miss it."

"What about motive, ma'am? Any thoughts on that?"

"No. Nothing obvious at the moment. Open mind. Happy to consider suggestions."

Bankhurst's eyes swept over her audience. "Any other thoughts?"

"How would he have known about Robert Lennox's self-incineration rumination?"

"Yes. We wondered about that ourselves. Obviously, some of the staff, and perhaps his fellow patients, may have known. We've interviewed all of them, and nothing turned up. Hospital IT assures us it would be very difficult to hack the medical records system, though Neil Jardine says it certainly would not be impossible, with the right skillset and equipment."

"What are our thoughts about his transport?"

"More and more, we're thinking he's either on foot or some form of transport without plates, such as a bike, or scooter. Just to be clear, though, we've no CCTV evidence of the latter, and any footage we think might be him, he is on foot. Also, we haven't had a single number plate duplication on ANPR from the various sites on the nights in question."

Bankhurst turned towards a wall map of Aberdeen studded with coloured pins to show the murder sites.

"As you can see, all the murders to date have been well within the city boundaries. All between The Dee and The Don, in fact… and, therefore, all reachable on foot. Perhaps the safest way to do it, if you think about it. Especially if you have done a reconnoitre beforehand, looking for routes with minimal CCTV coverage."

She turned back.

"OK, there's a lot of interviews to get through today."

"DS Iqbal and myself will go to Broughty Ferry, in Dundee, to interview Jean Lennox, Robert Lennox's wife.

She moved there last month to be closer to family. DS Baxter is going to see Lennox's ex-head teacher in Aboyne, and DS Gillespie will be interviewing patients at Ashgrove Hospital."

"Oh, joy of fucking joy," he muttered under his breath.

"Oh, and we'll need someone to go down to Portlethen," Bankhurst continued, "and have a chat with our dog walker. DC MacLennan?"

"Yes, ma'am. On it."

"For the rest of you, I want you to focus on offshore workers with criminal records. You know the drill. Locate, interview and eliminate. Also, can we recheck the CCTV around Union Terrace Gardens, looking specifically for anything that might indicate a flash photo being taken? Somebody needs to work on the Nike trainers angle, and I also want cyber to create more detailed association charts for all the victims. I want every last friend, associate and colleague detailed, and their social media and phones monitored. If there is any connection between them at all, that will be our best bet of finding it. And remember," she said, knowing, especially for her more senior officers, she was in danger of advising granny how to suck an egg, "assume nothing, believe nobody, challenge everything." She could almost feel the eyeballs rolling.

"One last thing. We need a name for the investigation."

She turned to look at the map of Aberdeen, the arterial trees of the Don and Dee stretching westwards from the North Sea, with the cluster of murders sites lying between them.

"Operation Between the Rivers," she announced, with a certainty which didn't brook any quarrel.

24

15th May

As agreed, Iqbal drove to Dundee, to give Bankhurst time to think. A relative luxury. Freed from the constant interruptions at the station, she had only the pleasant Mearns and Angus countryside to distract her. A patchwork of green and yellow fields, the rape crops in full bloom. Iqbal was in a less chatty mood than normal, which suited her fine. Had she made the right deductions? The right decisions? Was she missing anything? She rechecked her notes on her iPhone, but they offered no fresh inspiration.

Iqbal kept on the right side of the average speed cameras which stud the A90 at regular intervals, between Scotland's third and fourth largest cities, and it took an hour to reach the Dundee city limit. Consecutive left turns took them down to the River Tay, gleaming majestically before them, and then back along the coastline to the residential suburb of Broughty Ferry. Before the construction of the

Tay Railway Bridge in 1878, a ferry ran regularly from Broughty Ferry to Tayport, on the southern side of the river, linking Edinburgh and Aberdeen by rail.

The satnav announced "your destination is on the left". Iqbal drew up outside a semi-detached house, which faced the Tay estuary. Aptly, if unimaginatively, named Tayview, it was a more modest building than its neighbouring mansions, many of whom were built by the Dundee gentry made wealthy by *jute, jam and journalism.*

A WhatsApp chime announced a new message. A glint of excitement appeared in Bankhurst's eyes as she read it.

"It's from DC MacLennan. He's just finished with the dog-walking witness in Portlethen. Apparently, he was suspicious as hell of the guy wearing a baseball cap *and* a hoodie, not to mention the fact he was carrying a jerry can. Turns out he took a photo!"

"What!"

"Yes!"

Bankhurst typed a reply as fast as her thumbs would allow.

Send photo!

Ping.

An image appeared of a hooded man carrying a jerry can, who appeared to be at a distance of approximately one hundred yards from the witness. Bankhurst spread two fingers on the screen to magnify the image, but at the cost of clarity.

"Useful?" enquired Iqbal

"Well. Looks like it could be our guy, but doesn't tell us much more than the CCTV images."

"IC group?"

"Tricky, as it was a dark winter's night. Best I could say is that he's probably not IC3, but all other categories possible."

"Mm."

Bankhurst typed another message.

> *Thanks. Send image to Digital to see if they can clean it up. Find out exactly where photo was taken. Might help us with tracing his route.*

Will do came the immediate reply.

As they exited their car, a twitched curtain suggested they had been spotted. The front door opened as they walked up the garden path confirming the suspicion. A lady, likely to be in her late sixties, smiled and beckoned them forward.

"Come away in," she invited, with a sweep of her hand.

As she turned, and led the way, Bankhurst noted her to be smartly dressed in checked trousers, a cream blouse and, what could only be described as, sensible shoes. Gold was her favoured precious metal, and was generously represented in a bracelet, matching necklace and stud earrings. She wore a little too much make-up for Bankhurst's liking, which seemed to highlight rather than disguise the age changes on her face.

"You must be DI Bankhurst?" she said, more as a statement than a question.

"I am indeed, Mrs Lennox, and this—" Bankhurst turned to look at her colleague "—is DS Iqbal. Thanks for agreeing to see us today."

"You're welcome. I must say I was surprised, and a little intrigued, by your call. Please, have a seat. I'll put the kettle on."

"Oh. You don't need to bother, Mrs Lennox," replied Bankhurst.

"Nonsense! You've come all the way from Aberdeen. Besides, I've made pancakes!"

After Mrs Lennox disappeared into the kitchen, Bankhurst and Iqbal took in their surroundings. She imagined Mrs Lennox had downsized when she moved from Aberdeen and the furniture reflected some difficult choices she would have to have made. Some had perhaps been chosen for sentimental value, without necessarily complimenting neighbouring pieces. In some ways, it resembled a small antique shop, with various period items of furniture bedecked in all manner of antiques. Numerous family photos, including one of Robert Lennox, and spanning three generations, decorated the walls.

Five minutes later, Mrs Lennox returned with a tray carrying a teapot, cups, milk jug, side plates, cutlery and a plate of pancakes, already spread with generous amounts of butter and jam. *How genteel*, thought Bankhurst, before realising it wasn't perhaps too out of place, even now, in the posh end of Dundee. *Not what you might expect elsewhere in the city*, she mused, where a pie and a pint were more likely to be the order of the day.

Bankhurst's eyes and stomach yearned to help herself to a drop scone, but her diabetic head ruled the moment, and she demurred. Iqbal helped himself to two, to the obvious joy of Mrs Lennox.

With all three suitably seated and served, Bankhurst got down to business.

"As you know, Mrs Lennox, we wanted to have another chat about Mr Lennox."

"And, may I ask, why?"

"Of course. As you know it was thought initially to be, and may still be, a suicide. But we have some other cases running in parallel at the moment which share one or two similarities, and we just wanted to make sure we weren't missing anything."

"What kind of other cases?" she enquired.

Bankhurst paused. "Murders."

Mrs Lennox put her lipstick-stained cup down carefully, and sat back in her chair, looking at both detectives in turn with piercing blue eyes. Her make-up could not conceal her concern.

"So, are you suggesting that Robert could have been murdered?"

"Well, at the moment, we're keeping an open mind, but I have to tell you we are considering all possibilities."

Mrs Lennox's eyes visibly moistened, and her chin began to tremble.

"We don't mean to upset you, Mrs Lennox," assured Bankhurst.

"No. No. It's OK," she said, as she pulled a tissue from under her sleeve, and dabbed her eyes. "It's all still very raw, and I hadn't ever considered murder as a possibility... until now. How could he possibly be connected to other murders?"

"We're not at liberty to discuss that, I'm afraid, Mrs Lennox. What we would like to do is get more background information on Mr Lennox to see if there is any possible connection to the other victims."

"Of course. Of course. Anything I can do to help."

Bankhurst gave Mrs Lennox a few seconds to collect herself.

"I'll start with perhaps the most obvious question. Do you know anybody who would want to harm your husband?"

"No. Absolutely not," she answered without hesitation.

"Had he been threatened in any way? Recently, or in the past."

"No."

"Had he fallen out with anybody?"

"Again. No."

"Tell us about him. We want to understand as much as we can about him."

"Well, you know he was a teacher. Thirty-eight years in the profession. We met in Glasgow, when he had not long done his teacher training, and were married two years later."

"What did he teach?"

"Mathematics."

Bankhurst pointed at the photos on the wall.

"Are these your children?"

"Yes, Alan and Barbara. They're both married now. Alan's in England, but Barbara and her family are here in Dundee. That's why I moved here."

"What about your husband's career? Any controversies there?"

"No," she responded, with what appeared to be a hint of defiance.

"We spent ten years in Glasgow, before we moved to Paisley. After another few years we went to Edinburgh, and finally Aberdeen."

"Is that unusual? Moving around the country so much."

"Er. No. Not really. I don't see what you're getting at."

Mrs Lennox's Adam's apple, quite well defined for a female, moved slowly up and down, like a biological dumbwaiter.

"Nothing, Mrs Lennox, I assure you. Just trying to build a picture of your husband, to see if there are any connections with our other cases."

"Perhaps if you told me more about them, I could help."

"I'm afraid we can't do that, Mrs Lennox."

"OK. Sorry. I understand."

Bankhurst changed tack.

"What were your husband's interests?"

"Well, you know. Just the usual stuff. Reading. Fishing. Walking. He liked to do the crossword and sudoku in the paper every day."

"Nothing else you can think of?"

"No." Again, slightly sharp.

"Did he use social media?"

"Robert? No way. Wasn't his cup of tea at all."

"What about a computer? Did he have one?"

"No. He had a laptop which he dabbled with, but I wouldn't call him an enthusiast."

"Do you still have that?"

"No. My daughter, who knows about these things, returned it to its factory settings, I believe. My granddaughter is now using it. I think I already told this to your colleagues recently."

Bankhurst knew she had, but just wanted to check her account was consistent. Her natural scepticism had kicked in when she had heard Lennox's only computer had been wiped clean. Was it just a normal family thing to do, or convenient to erase any possible digital trail?

"Thanks, Mrs Lennox. We're almost finished. Just one or two more routine questions. Please don't be offended but we have to ask them anyway."

She took a breath in as if to fortify herself. "Go on."

"Did your husband have any problem with alcohol or drug abuse?"

"No. He liked a drink socially, but never overdid it... and never took any drugs. Certainly not that I was aware of."

"Was he in any significant debt?"

"Again. Not that I was aware of."

"This last question is somewhat delicate. Mrs Lennox. Is there any way your husband could have been bisexual?"

"Good god, no. What on earth makes you ask that?"

"I'm afraid I can't answer that."

"Did he have any other unusual sexual appetites?"

"Absolutely not!" she replied, her words laced with offence.

"Sorry, Mrs Lennox. These are just routine questions we have to ask."

"None taken, I'm sure," she replied, though by the look on her face the message hadn't been received there.

Iqbal, who had been taking notes, closed his notebook. Bankhurst returned her cup to the tray. The interview was over. Both detectives stood and gave their thanks, before making their way back along the garden path to their car. As on arrival, Jean Lennox's gaze followed the detectives, and she didn't close her door until they had driven off.

"So, what did you make of that?" Bankhurst asked Iqbal.

"The lady doth protesteth too much, methinks," he replied.

She glanced at her colleague, and raised an eyebrow. "I didn't know you were into Shakespeare, Zafar?"

"Is that Shakespeare?" he said, with the voice of an innocent.

"You know damn well it is." She grinned. "I was thinking more of liar, liar, pants on fire, myself. Probably tells you all you need to know about my literary pretensions!"

She continued, "What is she hiding? Did you notice the family photos? Only one of him, the recently deceased husband, but multiple shots of other family members. They were all at least twelve by eighteen, but he only merited what looked like an eight by ten. Also, why did they move around so much? Was he running from something? Or someone?"

"No," she continued, "I suspect 'all is not well, I doubt some foul play'."

"Ha ha. Gaun yersel', Boss. That's a jazzer, so it is. Thought you were strictly lowbrow."

"Oh, I can have the occasional *moment*," she replied, trying not to show her inner delight at dredging up, from the darkest recesses of her brain, not only a Shakespearean quote, but possibly one from Hamlet too.

She remained slightly pleased with herself as they left Dundee and headed northwards towards Aberdeen, but her thoughts soon returned to what Jean Lennox could be hiding. One way or another, she intended to find out.

DS George Gillespie was walking along one of the long corridors at Ashgrove Psychiatric Hospital. Not renowned for a sunny countenance at the best of times, he had a face like a skelped arse. He hated psychiatric hospitals. He hated the sounds, the smells and the feeling that he was always being watched. He hated not being able to tell the patients from the staff.

He walked smartly, avoiding eye contact as best he could, while trying to navigate the bewildering signage back to Kilbrannan Ward. By the end of the morning, he had interviewed most of the patients who were inpatients at the time of Lennox's death, a singularly unhelpful experience. Much to his annoyance, one patient had been away for a chest X-ray, necessitating a return trip in the afternoon.

John Strachan, a sixty-two-year-old Peterhead man, was waiting in the interview room. He was accompanied by a member of staff; at least Gillespie assumed he was a member of staff. Gillespie sat down and put his glasses on, bringing a name badge into focus. Some reassurance, he supposed.

Interviewer and interviewee briefly looked each other up and down, before Strachan's gaze alighted on the table between them. It wasn't often Gillespie saw a man, roughly his own age, who looked more unfit than he did. Almost as wide as he was tall, he didn't appear to have any neck, just a straight line from either side of his head down to his body. Fat arms tapered, only slightly, to fat hands and podgy, heavily nicotine-stained, fingers, splayed out like a fan. He was slightly breathless, even at rest. His lips, a dusky purple colour, and pursing slightly with each expiration, were set against a face that constantly twitched with subtle movements. Gillespie had interviewed a few patients in the morning with similar facial tics, and he assumed they were side effects of some fairly heavy-duty medications.

A wheeze and a deep, prolonged, rattling hawk which promised, but failed to deliver, sputum, was unpleasant for all, even for Gillespie, who was well used to his own musical instrument of a chest.

Christ, no wonder he was away for a chest X-ray.

A nod from the nurse suggested the respiratory embarrassment had passed, and it was appropriate to start.

"Hello, I'm Detective Sergeant Gillespie," he stated, "from the police."

"I know where a DS works," said Strachan in a slow, monotonal voice.

"OK. Good. Sorry. I believe you were an inpatient on the ward back in January?"

"I was." He didn't look up from the table.

"I'm particularly interested in the night that Robert Lennox died."

"Bob?"

Gillespie looked at the nurse, who nodded.

"Yes, Bob."

"I'm not sure I know anything about that."

Undeterred, Gillespie continued, "Do you remember anything at all about that night?"

"I was looking at my plans."

"Your plans?"

"Yes. Have you seen my plans?"

"No," Gillespie replied.

"Of the matrix," Strachan said, this time raising his head to re-establish eye contact. His head and chins oscillated subtly.

"What matrix?"

"The one that will give control."

Oh, here we fucking go. Gillespie tried to resist the temptation to roll his eyes.

"Control of what?"

"You."

"Me?"

"Yes. And him." Strachan pointed a tremulous finger at the nurse.

"Do you want to see them?" he continued.

"Er, OK… I suppose," replied Gillespie, wondering what can of worms he may have just opened.

Strachan reached behind him. Gillespie stiffened slightly, the product of a long-standing distrust of people producing hidden objects from behind their back. He relaxed at the sight of a well-thumbed, stained jotter. Strachan handed it over, enthusiasm showing on his twitching face.

Gillespie made a show of looking through the contents. Page after page of impenetrable equations and diagrams, connected by various lines and arrows, and further decorated by various smudges and coffee cup stains.

"Impressive," was all he could manage, before handing the jotter back.

"Yes, it is," agreed Strachan, as if Gillespie was only stating the obvious.

Convinced that he had wasted enough time, Gillespie began to manoeuvre himself from his chair, and put his hands on the desk to enlist assistance in getting his own generous corporation back over his feet. He was almost upright, his belly spilling over the edge of the table, when Strachan spoke again.

"I did see him that night, you know."

Gillespie stifled a sigh, and sat down again, his belly following just after, with a flop.

"Who?"

"Bob. Bob Lennox."

"What do you mean, you saw him?"

"I was outside, having a cigarette."

"At that time of the morning?" Gillespie asked, incredulously.

"Yes. I have to go outside if I want a cigarette."

The nurse nodded in agreement.

"Go on." Gillespie's attention was captured.

"I was in the gardens. I remember it was cold. I had my hat and coat on. I didn't want the plan to get wet. It was snowing off and on, I think."

The weather description was accurate, at least. Gillespie waited.

"I saw Bob come out of the hospital and walk towards the hospital gate... before he disappeared out of sight."

"Was he with anyone?"

"No."

"Was he carrying anything?"

"No."

"Are you sure?"

"Yes."

"OK. That's good Mr Strachan… er, John. Can you remember anything else? Anything at all?"

"I remember the glow from over in the park a few minutes later."

"And you never saw anyone else? Any car? Anything unusual? Any unusual sounds, or smells?"

"Just the burning smell."

"OK. Thanks, John. That's helpful."

Strachan leant forward. He stared into Gillespie's eyes, unnerving the DS in the process. More involuntary facial movements. A fetid smell from his breath.

"There is one more thing I know which might help you."

"Go on."

"It could be important for your investigation."

"Yes."

"I have the plan… the plan of the matrix."

25

15th May

As DS Gillespie toiled through his afternoon interview, DS Sharon Baxter had been enjoying her trip out the North Deeside Road, towards Aboyne. A typical Deeside town, its three thousand inhabitants lived on the edge of the Highlands, some thirty miles west of Aberdeen. The sun had stood up to, and eventually overcome, the bullying clouds, bathing the last few miles of the A93 route in bright sunshine. The Deeside countryside, already beguiling, was elevated to a higher level. Baxter felt she had definitely drawn the long straw. Transfixed at times, she had to remind herself to concentrate on the road.

Her satnav directed her to a charming cottage on the eastern edge of the town, near to the golf course. A standard Deeside porch, supported by gnarly tree trunk pillars, jutted out like a nose from the front of the granite house. A budded, climbing rose spiralled around the left trunk towards the gutter, promising imminent colour, to add to the pastel shades already supplied by azaleas on either side of the porch. On the roof, a few feet above the gutters, transverse snow guards basked in the sun, their winter duties over for another year.

Baxter rang the bell. A few seconds later the door was opened by a friendly looking, bespectacled man, who looked like he might be in his seventies.

Hector McNeil wore a crisp white shirt, a paisley cravat, corduroy trousers and, despite the warm day, a soft ribbed, cream, sweater-as-scarf around his neck and shoulders. The old-school, gentleman's image was completed by mustard socks and brogues.

"Good afternoon," he announced with the clarity and diction you might expect of someone who had taken many assemblies in his day. "DS Baxter?"

"Yes. Mr McNeil?"

"Hector, please. At your service. Come in, come in."

He guided Baxter through a narrow hall to a small sitting room at the back of the cottage, overlooking the back garden, with Morven hill in the distance.

"Please, have a seat."

"Thank you," said Baxter.

Not yet a total convert to modern ways, Baxter took out her notepad and pen.

"Mr McNeil, er, Hector, I've come to ask you a few questions about one of your former colleagues."

"Go on. I've been dying to know who it is since you phoned. You were a bit cagy, you know," he said with a smile, and a twinkle in his eye.

"Yes, sorry about that. It's actually Robert Lennox, a mathematics teacher we believe you may have worked with at the Edinburgh Institute, when you were the head teacher."

Behind half-moon glasses, a flicker danced across McNeil's eyes. A glint of sunlight from the stream of rays coming through the window? Trying to put a face to a name? Or, could it have been anxiety?

"Bob Lennox. Of course. I remember him well. Excellent teacher. Popular with the kids and colleagues. I did read about his death in the *P and J* a few months back. Terrible business. Such a shame. Could only have been in his sixties."

"Sixty-five, in fact," Baxter confirmed.

"Such a shame," repeated McNeil. "Yes, I worked with him at the institute. For several years, in fact. We were sorry when he left… Aberdeen, I think it was, where he went to."

He paused, moved slightly forward in his seat, and fixed a steely gaze on Baxter, causing the DS to feel she was back in her own school facing the music, after one of her not infrequent indiscretions.

"But, why the interest, now, if I may ask?"

"Information has come to light," she replied, "and we're now treating his death as potentially suspicious."

"Are you, indeed? Suspicious, as in murder?"

"Potentially, yes."

"Oh dear, oh dear. Who on earth would want to murder Bob Lennox?" A look of mild incredulity rippling over his face.

"That's what we're trying to find out. We're trying to build a picture of Mr Lennox."

"Obviously we've interviewed his family, but we're keen to speak to as many people as possible who knew him, socially or professionally."

"Well, I never really knew him socially... the odd school cheese and wine perhaps, but nothing more than that. Professionally? Well... as I said... he was well thought of by myself, and his other colleagues."

"No significant disagreements with anyone?"

"No. Not at all."

"What about the children themselves? Or the parents? Any issues there?"

"No. Again, nothing that I can recall."

"Any disciplinary hearings?"

McNeil shook his head.

Baxter paused, contemplating her next line of inquiry. She had made a few bullet points, as an aide-mémoire, in her notebook, but resisted looking at them. Not the most professional look and one that would, she felt, be immediately noticed by the ex-head teacher, who looked as though he was still sharp as a tack.

"Did he seem to be happy at the institute?"

"As far as I know, yes."

"Why did he leave, then?"

"I've really no idea. People leave for all sorts of reasons. Promotion. Change of scene. Family reasons. Spousal preferences. We didn't interrogate people who moved on. There was always, and will always be, staff turnover. Part of school life."

"So, there was no pressure on him to leave?"

"I don't really know what you're getting at, but his leaving was entirely cordial... on all sides. I do remember, in fact, that we had a nice leaving dinner for him at a restaurant in Bruntsfield." He paused. "Fishing rod, I believe."

"The restaurant?"

"No no, my dear. His leaving gift." A thin smile formed on his wrinkled face, as he looked over the top of his glasses.

Baxter stiffened at the condescending remark, but tried not to show it.

"And did you have any contact with him after he left Edinburgh?"

"No. Not that I can remember."

"None at all."

"As I said."

"OK. Mr McNeil," Baxter returned to his surname, feeling her interviewee had lost the right to informality. "Thank you for your help. We may be in touch again. Here's my card if you remember anything else."

"Of course," he replied, as he accepted the card.

Back in her beloved, if somewhat battered, VW Polo, Baxter spoke to her Apple watch.

"Hey, Siri. Call Lily the Pink."

"Calling Lily the Pink," the device confirmed.

Baxter used the dialling time to check her hair and pout her lips at the windscreen mirror.

Satisfactory.

"Hey, Sharon."

"Hi, Lily. Just checking in. That's me finished in Aboyne."

"How did it go?"

"OK, I guess, though it did feel a bit like being back at school."

"Teacher-pupil type dynamic?"

"Exactly. Took me right back to Torry Academy."

"Anything useful?"

"Can't say that there was. Lennox seems to have been well thought of by staff and pupils. I probed a bit to see if there were any darker edges to him, but didn't really get anywhere."

"OK. Thanks Sharon."

"How are you getting on?"

"Oh, DS Iqbal and I were just having a discussion about Shakespeare."

"Piss off!"

"No, seriously. We were."

"Well, I hope you'll have that out of your system before you get back to Aberdeen. There'll be none of that nonsense at the afternoon cuppa."

"Ha ha. Will do."

McNeil watched Baxter's car disappear over the brow of the hill, heading down towards the main road. When she was out of sight, he walked through to his kitchen and poured himself a measure of Springbank malt whisky. He swirled the amber liquid around the glass and downed it in one go, drawing a grimace from his face as his gullet burnt. He put the glass on the work surface and unlocked a small wooden door towards the rear of the kitchen. Rickety wooden steps took him down to a dark basement. Cold cobwebs cloaked his face and jumper. He brushed away the fine lacework of the web and fumbled for the light switch. A 30W filament bulb cast a pale light on the small, musty room. He took a different key from his pocket and opened a metal strong box, nestled on a shelf, between old, rusting paint cans. Long since dried up drips of paint, on the outside of the cans, advertised the colour inside, but were difficult to make out in the dim light.

The only thing in the box was an analogue phone. He picked it up and was pleasantly surprised when he pushed a button and the screen flickered into life. Two further clicks produced a very small contacts list, he selected a name and dialled a number he hadn't called in years.

The phone rang multiple times, and he was just about to hang up when a hesitant voice answered.

"Eh. Hello."

"It's me."

"Uh-huh."

"Hector."

"Uh-huh."

"The police have been here."

"Uh-huh."

"Asking about Robert."

"Uh-huh."

"Is that all you're going to say, uh-huh?"

"No."

"Well, go on then."

"Destroy this phone, and don't ever call me again."

Click.

The line went dead.

26

15th May

"OK. Can we focus please? Let's see where we're at?"

The MIT lent their attention.

"We'll start with the interviews. I'll kick off. Myself, and DS Iqbal, went to Broughty Ferry to interview Jean Lennox, widow of our first victim, Robert Lennox."

Most of the room noted that Lennox had gone, in the mind of the SIO at least, from *possible* victim to victim.

"To be honest, we didn't really get anything concrete, but we both came away with the impression that she may have known more than she was saying. So, we'll keep an open mind on her."

Bankhurst turned to Gillespie. "What about you, DS Gillespie?"

Gillespie shifted his weight, to the audible distress of his chair.

"I thought it was going to be a royal waste of time..."

"I sense there's a but," said Bankhurst.

"Well, the last patient reckoned he saw Lennox in the gardens, heading out of the hospital grounds."

"Reliable witness?"

"As much as any of the bask… eh, patients in that ward were."

"Any details?"

"He was fairly sure, and for what it's worth I believed him, that Lennox wasn't carrying anything. He didn't recollect anything else useful, but did confirm the light and burning smell from Victoria Park a few minutes later."

"OK, thanks, DS Gillespie. Now that you're known at Ashgrove Hospital, if there are any further interviews, it will be good to send someone they recognise." She broke into a grin.

"Ha fucking ha," he said, and got away with it.

"Sharon?"

"I interviewed Lennox's former head teacher out in Aboyne. Bit like yourself, ma'am. Couldn't really put my finger on it, but did wonder if he was holding something back perhaps."

Bankhurst nodded, and took up the reins again.

"Our eyewitness in Portlethen had the sense to take a photo of the guy he was suspicious of. I've had a look at it. Fairly sure he's our man. We've sent it to Digital for enhancement, but it may turn out to be no advance on the CCTV images from the garage."

"Where are we on the other leads we were chasing down?"

"DC Currie, ma'am. We've had word back from the fingerprint experts. They've had a look at the partial footprint from Union Terrace Gardens and feel it's ninety percent likely to be the same type of Nike trainer."

"OK. Good. And what about similar Nike trainers bought for cash?"

"Still working on it, ma'am. A lot of retailers to get around."

"OK. Keep on it."

"Reflex. What about offshore workforce?"

"Again, working on it, ma'am. We've managed to eliminate eight from our original list. Working on the others, but the list is getting bigger all the time, as more data comes in."

Bankhurst scanned the room, but the flow of information seemed to have dried up.

Then Gillespie growled, "We need to look at profiling."

"Agreed," replied Bankhurst, "and I know just the person to help us with that."

Dr Louise McEwan, criminologist to A division of Police Scotland, was on a shopping trip to Edinburgh. For some years she had treated herself to a six-monthly day trip to the capital, though in recent times, due to the demise of shopping in Aberdeen, she saw it more of a necessity than a luxury. She liked the quality things in life. Boutique hotels, decent restaurants, fine wines and clothes. Especially clothes. As usual, her husband had been left behind, which suited both parties. His shopping tolerance, on a good day, was about two hours, before a weary gait and tired eyes told of a man at the end of his forbearance.

She had caught an early train from Aberdeen, and arrived mid-morning into Edinburgh Waverley. Pushing through the tourist throngs on Princess Street she had headed straight towards Stockbridge, attracted by its independent shops and cafe culture. A loyalty card and "to die for" almond croissants ensured her return trade to a particular cafe, where she was warmly welcomed by the owner.

Feeling the benefit of her latte and croissant, she made a few small gift purchases as she meandered through Stockbridge and up towards the New Town.

As she crossed over Queen Street the skirl of pipes advertised a wedding party going into the Royal College of Physicians. She stopped to observe proceedings from a distance, a smile forming on her face as she recalled her own wedding reception in the same venue.

By the time she had navigated George Street, bulging bags from Jigsaw, Lulu Lemon and Me + Em hinted at expensive tastes and the means to satisfy them. In need of further refreshment, she had taken a light lunch and a large glass of wine at Harvey Nichols, the latter as she was no longer allowed to have a drink on the train back home.

Mindful of the fact that she still had a few of her favourite brands to seek out, she headed along Multrees Walk towards St James Quarter. Just before entering the shopping centre, a ping on her phone announced the arrival of a WhatsApp message.

She glanced at the name of the sender.

Lily Bankhurst.

Interested, she opened the full message.

Hi Louise, I was hoping to enlist your expertise again!
We've set up an MIT to look at a string of murders which have happened in Aberdeen this year. You may have heard about some of them.

We're now beginning to think they are connected.
Possibly five in total. Of course, that means
serial killer territory. Not sure how you are
fixed just now, but would love your input ASAP.
Please keep this strictly to yourself meantime.
Regards, Lily

Already a good day, it had just got even better for McEwan.

She had worked with DI Lily Bankhurst a few times before, but notably on the last serial killer case in Aberdeen, her involvement in which spawned a clinical paper and invites to speak at several criminology conferences.

Without hesitation she replied.

> *Hi, Lily. Just getting some much-needed retail*
> *therapy in Edinburgh. Home tonight. Would*
> *tomorrow morning 9am be OK?*

Bankhurst replied.

Jealous! Tomorrow am would be great. See you
at MIT room. Do you remember where it is?

> *How could I forget?*

"So, there I was in the virtual waiting room, counting my last few tablets, without realising the pharmacist had started the online consultation... and was watching me!"

Bankhurst paused for a sip of canteen tea.

"No way! Sneaky so-and-so," replied Baxter.

"Yes, caught in the act. At least, that's what it felt like."

"Ha ha."

"So, how did it go after that?"

"Oh, she gave me a hard time about still being on dihydrocodeine, and ignoring previous communications."

"Both true!"

"Well, yes, but that's beside the point! I said the endometriosis was still giving me jip."

Baxter looked dubiously at her friend.

"Of course, she then said, if that was the case, I needed to make a review appointment with my GP."

"And?"

"Oh, I played the murder investigation card. You know. Serious crime. Senior investigative officer. Too busy. Blah, blah, blah."

"Course you did."

"Bought me another month, but only if I book a review appointment."

"And have you?"

"Don't be daft."

"Lily!"

"I know. I know."

Realising she was hitting a dead end, Baxter changed tack.

"So, how's it going with Dr Dreamy?"

Bankhurst started to blush. "Very good, actually."

"Are you speaking about the sex, or the relationship?" probed Baxter.

"Wouldn't you like to know?" Bankhurst tried to muster a coy expression. She drained the last tea from her cup, rose from her chair and headed back to the MIT room, leaving her friend lost in imagination.

27

16th May

The MIT door opened and an elegant lady, perhaps in her early forties, entered the room. Heads, especially male ones, turned as she walked gracefully towards Bankhurst, her Jo Malone perfume arriving just before she did, at the DI's desk. Dr Louise McEwan was on time, to the minute.

Bankhurst, having been through a lot with her criminologist, felt a hug would not have been inappropriate, but settled for a more professional handshake. Up close she noticed a few facial wrinkles and grey hairs had developed since they had last met, which gave her a sense, not exactly of schadenfreude, but of relief. Even the most attractive people were not spared the consequences of time, it seemed.

"Hi, Louise. Thanks for coming."

"You're welcome, Lily. Your WhatsApp was certainly intriguing! Can't wait to hear the details."

"OK, let's do it."

Bankhurst turned to address the MIT.

"For those of you who don't know her, this—" she indicated with her hand "—is Dr Louise McEwan. An eminent criminologist we have consulted from time to time."

Dr McEwan smiled, and nodded her head in acknowledgement.

Bankhurst turned to the whiteboards and, with the help of a laser pointer, flitted between the various data sets as she brought McEwan up to date.

"So, that's where we are to this point, Dr McEwan. We'd be delighted for your overall assessment, and particularly any help you can give with profiling."

"Thanks, DI Bankhurst, and thanks again for inviting me."

She looked at the boards for some time in silence, occasionally clicking her tongue or replacing a stray strand of hair behind her right ear. Finally, she turned to the MIT, who had been waiting in respectful silence.

"OK. This is very interesting. Horrific, but interesting. It certainly looks like, with the evidence gathered thus far, this is a serial killer."

She paused. A murmur went round the room.

"Of the four recognised types of serial killer, I think we can probably rule out the visionary and mission-oriented varieties. The former because they are likely to be psychiatrically very unwell and incapable of the precision planning and execution that this killer exhibits. The mission-oriented killer is also unlikely, I feel, as they target specific types of people who they deem as unworthy of living. The victims here are so diverse and without any connection, that this seems unlikely, though there is a slight caveat here. At times, and some of you have experience of this, the link between victims can elude detection for some time."

A few officers nodded acknowledgement, all thinking of the case she was referring to.

"No, I think they are likely to be either a hedonistic or power-oriented killer. The hedonist kills for pleasure, including possible sexual arousal. Power-oriented killers, however, are motivated by exerting ultimate control over another person. And, what greater control than deciding if someone lives or dies."

Spooling through her past experiences, she walked slowly back and forward creating a profile in her head.

"I think our man, and it will be a man, may well be a narcissist or have narcissistic tendencies. He is likely to feel entitled. Used to getting what he wants, manipulating anybody he sees fit in the process. He will be intelligent and likely be in employment. He will not feel guilty about what he is doing and will stop at nothing to achieve his desire, be that the act of killing itself, or the pursuit of total power. He will be persuasive, and charismatic when he needs to be."

A pause.

"He is likely to be between twenty and fifty and could be in a relationship, which could be with a man or woman. The rectal semen is interesting. Does that mean our killer is homosexual, or could that be a form of ultimate domination of an individual, prior to taking their life? There could have been a condom failure, or it may be that his grandiose self-opinion is so high, and he feels beyond capture, that he was willing to take that risk. He is obviously forensically aware, so if he chose to take that risk, he must have been confident he was not in the PNC system."

"In summary, this is an extremely dangerous individual who is very likely to kill again. He is obviously intelligent, organised and methodical. However, that doesn't mean he can't be caught. He will have a weakness. He will make a mistake, if he hasn't already done so. Look for patterns of behaviour. It is human instinct to follow routines. You've already identified the pattern of monthly deaths, specifically at parks and gardens in Aberdeen. What else are we missing?"

She continued, "Put yourself in his shoes. What will be his next move? Will he be planning a June strike already?"

"The other thing you could consider is phishing his unregistered phone. Obviously, most of the time it is switched off, but if he hasn't already got rid of it, and it was switched on again in the future, he would get a message popping up from you. You could appeal to his high self-belief, and feelings of invincibility, into perhaps opening a link with a hidden programme that would give full access to his device. If you taunt him or challenge him, he may be unable to resist responding, and any response at all would trigger the cyber invasion of his phone."

Bankhurst looked at Ian Jardine to see if this was possible.

He noted the unsaid question. "Possible, in theory," he replied, "but he's likely to have a few different cheap Nokias that he will use as burners. If he's any sense, he'll change them every month. Worth a try, though."

"Any questions for Dr McEwan?" asked Bankhurst.

"What do you make of the possibility of a photograph being taken of the victims?"

"Ah, yes. A souvenir," said McEwan. "Something to enable him to relive the scenario multiple times for further gratification. Not a good sign I'm afraid."

No further questions were asked

"OK, Dr McEwan. As always, that's been very helpful. We'll keep you up to date about any developments, and hopefully can invite you back for further analysis in due course."

"Any time," she replied. "I'll leave you to it, then." With her usual effortless poise she left the room, leaving behind the Jo Malone scent to slowly dissipate.

That night Bankhurst tossed and turned in bed, revisiting McEwan's comments. What had she said? What were they missing? What patterns of behaviour should they be looking for?

She finally slept at 1am but awoke, almost predictably, two hours later with a panic attack. The usual flight and flight combination. Blood coursing through her system, driven by raised blood pressure and a fast pulse. Profuse sweating. A feeling of dread. She rode out the storm, and as the initial crippling anxiety began to recede, and her physiological responses began to normalise, her mind remained on high alert. All synapses firing. Clarity of thought surfaced in her brain. She picked up her iPad and tapped a search into Google, the eerie glow from the tablet illuminating her tired looking face in the dark bedroom. Suddenly, her expression changed.

"Fuck me," she said.

After staring into space for a while, her mind racing with possibilities, she switched her device to sleep mode and, wishing she had a similar button herself, turned on to her side in what was unlikely to be a successful attempt at slumber.

28

17th May

Another day into the investigation. Another notch up in pressure, as evidenced by the uninvited presence of DCI Amanda Farrell and her boss, Superintendent John "Shifty" McNiven, at the briefing. Bankhurst looked at her team, and wondered what they would think of her suggestion, including her senior officers.

The door opened and Dr Louise McEwan joined the meeting, but positioned herself, this time, near the back of the room. Bankhurst had asked if she could reattend, and she had been quick to affirm.

"OK, ladies and gentlemen. Can we begin?"

The rhetorical question hushed the room.

"Following on from yesterday's briefing, I was doing a bit of research last night. One of the things I googled was a list of all of Aberdeen's parks and gardens." She tapped her keyboard and produced the list on a smart screen on the wall. "An asterisk indicates sites of murders this year."

*Seaton Park**
*Victoria Park**
Westburn Park
Duthie Park
Stewart Park
*Hazlehead Park**
*Johnston Gardens**
Bon Accord Terrace Park
*Union Terrace Gardens**
Persley Walled Garden
Allan Park
Queens Links
Westfield Park

All eyes in the room scanned the list, looking for something significant, something they didn't already know. No faces suggested any enlightenment.

"These are all public areas, be they parks, gardens or links. For ease, I'm just going to refer to them as parks. What do you see?"

"Just a list of parks, some more familiar than others."

"OK. How many?"

"Thirteen."

"Anything else you notice?"

"Is Allan Park not in Cults, rather than Aberdeen?" ventured Iqbal. "I think I've played cricket there."

"Might have known there'd be a cricket connection, Zafar, but, yes, Allan Park is in Cults."

"So, not strictly in Aberdeen?" continued Iqbal.

"Exactly!"

"I may be thick, but where are you going with this?" said Gillespie, his voice rumbling.

Bankhurst ignored the lack of respectful address.

"Well. If you exclude Allan Park, that leaves you with twelve Aberdeen parks. So far, we've had one murder per month in five different Aberdeen parks. There are twelve months in the year and twelve parks in Aberdeen."

She let her sentence hang in the air. The silence stretched as she hoped for the collective penny to drop. She wasn't disappointed.

A wave of nondescript noise and expletives rolled past Bankhurst and bounced off the wall behind her. Farrell and McNiven looked at each other.

She went to the nearest whiteboard and wrote in large capital letters:

SERIAL KILLER
12 MONTHS
12 PARKS
12 MURDERS

She invited quiet through outstretched, downturned hands.

The room hushed. Alert, interested faces focussed on their SIO. Only one person appeared different. Superintendent McNiven glowered at her, with a lowered brow and widened nostrils. She could almost imagine steam coming out of his ears. She quickly averted her gaze, but not before a small ball of anxiety formed in her stomach. She changed tack.

"Dr McEwan. Thanks for agreeing to come back at short notice. Do you have any comment to make?"

"Thank you, DI Bankhurst. This is certainly interesting, and could be significant. It certainly sounds more than just coincidence. A definite pattern. It could point towards something like arithromania – a mental illness, possibly an expression of OCD, where the person feels the need to count, or organise, their actions numerically. They are drawn to numerical patterns, around which they might plan activities."

"Do they tend to favour one number, or is it more generic?" Bankhurst asked.

"They don't usually stick with one number, though they may have several that are important to them. Possibly of some historical significance. I've never seen just a single number used, but, in theory, it could be possible."

"A dodekaphile, perhaps," prompted Babinski.

"Indeed," agreed McEwan, giving a nod to the DC to acknowledge his insight, before interpreting for the wider audience. "Someone with a strong affinity for the number twelve."

Several of his fellow officers turned and looked, with some amazement, at Babinski, but Bankhurst felt no element of surprise. She knew she had a nugget in her team. Somewhat socially awkward, but a font of knowledge, and an invaluable ability to think outside the box.

McEwan paused. "If the offender does have an OCD variant, this is potentially a worrying development."

Her audience looked confused.

"It's not a good combination with a serial killer personality. Meticulous. Attention to fine detail. Repeated checking of plans. Less likely to make a mistake. We need to understand the perpetrator better. This may be a significant step. The more we know about any previous patterns of behaviour, the more we may be able to predict future patterns. To get ahead of him. It's obviously an extremely worrying theory, if it is correct. We've all done the maths in our heads. Seven more calendar months, seven more parks, seven more…" Her voice drifted off.

DS MacDonald raised a hand. A nod from McEwan invited his contribution.

"What about the fact that all the MOs have been different, so far? Could that be another twelve factor? Is our guy looking to have unique MOs for every month?"

"That's an interesting question, er…"

"DS MacDonald, ma'am."

"Thank you. I really don't know, I'm afraid. I've never come across, or heard, of anything like that. I'll certainly do some research on it. Is that even possible? Are there twelve different ways to kill someone?"

A few seconds lapsed. Furrowed foreheads and raised eyes accompanied mental arithmetic.

"Yes, there are," said various people in unison, creating a hubbub of conversation that swirled around the room, only quelled when Superintendent McNiven stood up abruptly.

"DI Bankhurst. A word. My room."

He turned around and strode from the room, his face contorted in anger. DCI Farrell followed, and Bankhurst trailed behind, the small knot of stomach anxiety now snowballing into something much larger.

No words were spoken as the trio climbed the stairs to the senior officers' floor to McNiven's office.

"Shut the door behind you," he barked, as he hung his coat on a hook on the wall behind his bigger-than-it-needed-to-be alpha male desk. He settled into his leather chair, his face an impressive shade of red.

"Why the hell was I not informed of this, Bankhurst? If we hadn't decided to attend the briefing this morning, I still would be none the wiser."

"I apologise, Sir. I only just made the possible connection last night, and I wanted to run it past the MIT before taking it upstairs."

"Well, it's just not good enough. This whole thing could be an absolute bloody nightmare. Can you imagine what the press will make of it? We'll need a lot more evidence before we even entertain such a suggestion. Not just your musing, Bankhurst."

All about image, as usual.

She sucked the back of her teeth.

"Of course, Sir."

"It just won't do," he continued in a blustering tone.

"What do you think, DCI Farrell?"

"I agree, Sir… with DI Bankhurst."

Bankhurst couldn't help but glance sideways at her DCI. She had determined, non-bloodshot eyes and no hint of a smell of alcohol from her breath. The last thing she had expected was support from Farrell, and the look of surprise it created on McNiven's face was priceless. Her anxiety retreated a notch with an unexpected ally in the room.

"What?" said McNiven, surprised. He looked aghast that his DCI had the temerity to form her own opinion.

"I think DI Bankhurst is onto something. She's been banging the serial killer drum for a while but, to be honest,

I've not been an enthusiast. But the longer this goes on, the more evidence we gather, and with DI Bankhurst's astute work last night, I think we have to assume this is indeed the work of some kind of deranged serial killer. We should tackle it appropriately."

"But what of the consequences?" he blurted. "The Press. The panic. The effect on the city. The reputation of Police Scotland."

"We'll just have to manage them," she replied, calmly.

"We could maybe keep it from the press a little longer," suggested Bankhurst.

McNiven stared at her as if to say *Who asked you to speak?* but she avoided direct eye contact. "The public are not daft, and have already modified their behaviour around parks, even though they only know of three of the murders, and have no idea that these may be serial killings."

"You mean the same three murders that we know have *definitely* happened," McNiven interjected sarcastically.

Bankhurst ignored him. "There's been a reduction in footfall at the parks in the evenings and nights, which is when the killings have happened. They are effectively self-managing an out-of-hours parks embargo."

"But not everyone is," he said.

"No," Bankhurst agreed.

"And if you are right, these people are potentially at risk."

"Yes, but I think the greater risk would be tipping off the perpetrator that we're on to him. We need him to be smug. Overconfident. Make him think he's invincible. Then he might make a mistake. And then we will get him."

Farrell took over. "We could issue a general safety bulletin about keeping safe, especially after dark. Travelling in pairs, etcetera. Don't limit it to the parks. City wide. And no mention of a serial killer."

Bankhurst took over the baton and ran with it. "We could increase police presence around the seven parks that have not yet been used."

"And you think I have the manpower to do that, Bankhurst?" responded McNiven.

"Given the seriousness of the case, Sir..."

"Humph."

"If we don't have enough personnel we could, at least, site sentry cameras in each park."

McNiven drummed his fingers on the desk. Repeated the gesture several times. Deep frown lines persisted on his forehead.

"Very well," he snapped, "do what you have to do. I'll speak to the Chief Inspector. But keep the press out of it meantime, and I want to be kept up to date. Every step of the way."

"Yes, Sir." agreed Bankhurst and Farrell in unison.

As the two officers walked along the corridor, Farrell put her hand on Bankhurst's shoulder.

"I've gone out on a limb to support you, DI Bankhurst. Don't let me down."

"No, ma'am. I won't."

"And I want the full Met standard on this investigation."

"Of course, ma'am," she replied, trying to suppress a small grin so Farrell couldn't see it.

"OK, listen up everybody." Bankhurst was back in the MIT room.

"This is now a race against time. If we're right, our guy will be planning his next murder sometime in the first half of June. We have until then to catch him. We know from our victimology research and deep analysis of the friends, family and associates, that the victims seem unconnected. Totally random. The only thing they seem to have had in common was to be in an Aberdeen park at the wrong time. So, predicting the next victim is probably a non-starter. But can we narrow down the likely site? We believe it's likely to be one of seven parks. But which one?"

She looked at the list again.

Seaton Park*
Victoria Park*
Westburn Park
Duthie Park
Stewart Park
Hazlehead Park*
Johnston Gardens*
Bon Accord Terrace Park
Union Terrace Gardens*
Persley Walled Garden
(Allan Park – in Cults)
Queens Links
Westfield Park

"Rearrange them alphabetically and see if there's any pattern, either normal or in reverse order. Leave Allan Park out of it." Two minutes later, after DC MacLennan had typed in the laptop, a new list appeared.

Bon Accord Terrace Park
Duthie Park

*Hazlehead Park**

*Johnston Gardens**

Persley Walled Garden

Queens Links

*Seaton Park**

Stewart Park

*Union Terrace Gardens**

*Victoria Park**

*Westburn Park**

Westfield Park

"No. Nothing obvious there. What about postcodes? We think the perpetrator may be into numbers. Any sequence there? Also, what about the size or age of parks? Let's look into these. I also want, at least, two sentry cameras sited at each of the seven parks, and see how many mobile ANPR units we have available. I want them close to the parks. Can we also inform the drone, canine and armed units that we may need to deploy them at short notice sometime in the early June timeframe."

Bankhurst was in high gear, and the instructions flowed easily.

"We need to speak to Comms about organising a generic media campaign about safe practice around the city, particularly in the evenings and at night. Not a word about a serial killer, mind, and I want to see the draft before it's published."

"Ma'am?"

"Yes."

"We've got the data on the parks. The size varies from Johnston Gardens which is the smallest at one hectare to

Hazlehead at 180 hectares, but with no obvious patterns. Same for postcodes and ages of parks, I'm afraid."

"Damn. OK, thanks."

Bankhurst swallowed. Her mouth felt dry. A few beads of sweat surfaced on her forehead, and she had a faint sensation of dizziness. She realised she had neglected her fluid and food intake during the day and her physiology was telling her that her blood sugar was getting too low. She couldn't risk a hypo. Tempted as she was to scan her glucose metre on her upper arm, under her blouse, she demurred. Many of her colleagues didn't know she was diabetic, and she preferred to keep it that way.

A tactical retreat was necessary.

"OK, I'll leave you to it." She left the room abruptly, raising a few eyebrows in the process.

Back in her office, her glucose meter confirmed her tissue sugar was low at 4.1.

"Good excuse for a coffee and fine piece," she muttered to herself as she started out for the canteen.

Five minutes after devouring a jam doughnut, and half a cup of coffee, she began to feel better. Her dizziness resolved and she was thinking more clearly again. Something was on her mind. A mental itch she would like to scratch, and she knew the person who might be able to help.

"Lily!"

As ever, Dr Dexter Brewster seemed pleased to see his favourite detective inspector.

"What brings you to The Fridge?"

"Oh, just something that's been niggling away at the back of my mind."

"OK. Spill the beans."

"*Spill the beans?*"

"OK, I'm a dinosaur. What can I tell you?"

Bankhurst brought him up to date with the MIT thinking, including the perpetrator's possible interest in numerology, specifically the number twelve.

He sat back in his chair and stretched his arms, cracking his upper thoracic vertebrae.

"So, what can an ageing pathologist do to help?" he enquired, with a kindly look in his eyes.

"I wondered if you could pull up the details of the post-mortem you did on the Johnston Gardens victim?"

"The one who had multiple lower back wounds?"

"Yes. I obviously have your summary and a copy of the certification on cause of death."

"Exsanguination secondary to multiple sharp force traumas, I seem to recall," said Brewster.

"Yes. Exactly. Can you pull up the detailed post-mortem?"

"Of course."

Brewster swivelled in his chair, refreshed his computer screen and, with a few more taps, produced the report on his screen.

"Can you look at the bit describing the stabs?"

"Sharp force traumas, we prefer to call them in my world, Lily."

"Very well. Sharp force traumas... pedant!"

He grinned, and scrolled down to the relevant part.

"What would you like to know?"

"How many *sharp force traumas* were there?"

"Let me see."

He adjusted the glasses on his nose to bring the text more into focus.

"Well, I'll be damned."

"What?"

"Six on the left renal angle and six on the right renal angle. Twelve in total."

29

17th May

Hector McNeil was a study in concentration as he focussed on tying his latest fishing fly. Since being widowed he had converted a small room at the back of his house into a fishing sanctuary. Photos, trophies, river maps, rods and a taxidermy-mounted salmon adorned the walls. A large desk abutted against the wall, above which were two rows of small wall-mounted trays containing everything required for tying flies. A powerful ceiling lamp cascaded a pyramid of bright light down to the desk, where further illumination was supplied by an anglepoise lamp. In the middle of the desk sat his pride and joy, a top-of-the-range Stonfo Elite rotary vice, a present to himself a few months after his wife had passed away. He selected a size ten hook from a drawer, pushed his glasses to the top of his head and looked through a magnifying loop, before positioning the hook carefully in the vice.

Black Uni 6/0 thread was carefully wound around the shank of the hook, and back again. He then wrapped silver wire around the hook in a spiral pattern before securing it with further thread. Satisfied with his work he selected a pheasant tail for the next part of the procedure. Just as the tail was brought into focus through the loop, the doorbell rang. He looked at his phone to see who it was, and was surprised to see a familiar face holding a bottle up towards the doorbell camera.

Moments later he opened his front door.

"Peace offering," his visitor said, holding the bottle up again.

"Well, I wasn't expecting to see you," McNeil said. "Not after how our phone call went."

"No. I'm sorry about that, Hector. That's why I'm here, really. I felt very bad after our call. I was just a bit shocked to hear from you after so many years. Coming on top of Bob's death, I just overreacted, I think. Anyway, I was due to visit my mum in Ballater Nursing Home today, and I thought I would stop off at Aboyne on my way back to Aberdeen."

"Your mum's still alive?"

"Yes. She's ninety-two now. Pretty frail, but still on the right side of the grass, so to speak. Do you still like Campbeltown whisky, by the way?"

"I do."

"Well, I've brought you a Glen Scotia single cask malt."

"That's surely not the…?"

"Yes. It is. The thirteen-year-old. Voted world best single casket malt in 2024."

"Wow. How on earth…?"

"Oh. I've still got a few contacts here and there."

"Come in. Come in," invited McNeil, with gushing enthusiasm, and a sparkle of anticipation in his eyes.

"Have a seat. I'll get a couple of glasses."

He went to the cupboard and the glasses clinked as they came together.

"Here you go."

"Thanks."

McNeil watched in silence as the visitor poured the amber liquid in gentle glugs, into two unequal measures.

"Is that all you're having?" questioned McNeil.

"Well. I've got to drive home, and I'll be expected soon, so I can't stay long."

"You could always phone."

"Actually, my phone died on me just before I came out. I left it on charge at home."

"You could always use mine?" suggested McNeil, as he held his phone towards his visitor.

"No, no. You're OK. Thanks all the same. My supper will be ready, so I'll need to press on."

"OK. No problem."

"Hector. Could I trouble you for a little water? I've become a bit of a softie in my old age."

"Of course. I'll just get some from the kitchen."

McNeil returned with a small glass jug and pipette. He drew water into the pipette.

"Enough?"

"Perfect."

He emptied the pipette into the whisky. Both men raised the whisky, inhaled the aroma, and clinked the glasses together.

"Slainte mhath!"

"Slainte mhath!"

McNeil held the whisky in his mouth for a few seconds, before a slow and deliberate swallow. He looked up at the ceiling, as if searching for the right words.

"Heavenly," he offered, in a reverential tone.

"'Baked fruits and a salty, almost maritime finish,' according to the master tasters, though I'm not sure I get all that myself," replied his visitor. "All I know is it's a bloody fine dram!"

McNeil took another sip, relaxed back into his chair, and looked at his visitor.

"So, are you still getting some fishing?"

"Not as much as I'd like, to be honest. I've got a friend whose co-owner of a Speyside beat. I've been up there a couple of times in the last year, but there's not been that many salmon in the river. That's my excuse, anyway," he added.

"Aye," agreed McNeil, with a knowing look on his face.

"What about yourself, Hector?"

"Wherever and whenever I can, to be honest. Mostly The Dee, The Don, The Spey and The Deveron."

An empty glass was placed on the table.

"OK, Hector. I need to dash. I'll let you get back to your tying. Once again, apologies for my curtness on the phone. Hope you enjoy the rest of the bottle."

"I will. I will!" he replied, enthusiastically.

McNeil closed the door behind his unexpected visitor, and poured himself another generous measure of whisky. He switched the light off in his "fishing room".

"You'll keep until tomorrow," he muttered towards the fly.

He nursed his second drink for half an hour, before being enticed by the thought of an early bed. A pleasant, whisky-induced drowsiness quickly eased him into a deep sleep.

Three hours later he awoke with severe nausea. He rose and went into his en suite where he promptly vomited. He managed to get back to bed just before he started to sweat profusely. His heart started pounding and rapidly accelerated to what he knew must be a dangerous rate. Almost immediately he began to feel extremely breathless and light-headed.

I must phone for help.

His phone was on charge in the kitchen and he tried to summon strength to get out of bed again. He pulled back the duvet, and attempted to mobilise, but his legs were heavy and unresponsive. His breathing worsened. Fear gripped him.

I'm going to die.

In the "fishing room", the fly remained wedged in the Stonfo vice, obligated to remain forever half-finished.

30

18th May

Bankhurst was slightly early, and had entered the MIT room largely unnoticed. Some of the team were looking at their PC screens, but many were engrossed in their phones waiting for the meeting to start.

"Morning everyone. If you can pull yourselves away from your devices for a minute, we can get started."

Mobiles were promptly pocketed, and guilty faces focussed their attention on their SIO.

"OK. I'd like an update. Where are we at?"

"Nothing back of interest, so far, ma'am, on the Nike trainers, or the offshore workers with records."

"What about the association charts? Have we dug deeply enough? Anything turned up connecting the victims?"

"No, ma'am."

"Neil. Digital Forensics?"

"We've sent a phishing message to the unregistered phone used at Victoria Park. If he ever turns it on again, he'll get the message. If he clicks on the link, we'll be in."

"OK. Good."

"Sentry cameras in the parks?"

"Under way, ma'am, though what the team have found is quite interesting. There are already small cameras placed at strategic positions in many of the parks. No one seems to know anything about them. They're certainly not ours or council. We're wondering if the perpetrator has sited them for his own purposes. We've removed them, and they've been sent to Digital for analysis."

"OK. Good. Sounds promising. Let me know if anything turns up."

"Anybody got anything else?"

"Comms have emailed a draft of the press release about safe practice. Looking to get your OK to publish."

"OK. I'll have a look."

A hand was raised in the audience. "DC MacLennan, ma'am."

"Go on."

"I've been looking at anyone in the Portlethen postcodes area, with a criminal record. Something stood out this morning, Not so much a name, as an address. I thought I recognised it. When I checked, he shares an address with Mirena Loci."

"The nurse whose car was seen the night of Lennox's death in January?"

"Yes, ma'am."

"And his name?"

"Jim Liddell."

"What's on his record?"

"Aggravated assault."

"Right. Let's bring him in! In the meantime, let's get across as much of his digital life as we can. I want to be well prepared before he gets here. Good work, Hugh."

MacLennan nodded.

"OK. Keep it up, everyone. Remember, we're on a countdown until June. I really want our man in custody before then."

The room dispersed, and Bankhurst made her way towards the coffee machine for her first cup of the day. Iqbal would often follow her out for some coffee-machine banter, but, instead, she noticed, he returned to his desk and stared, somewhat vacantly, at his computer screen. He appeared lost in thought.

The other DS in the room, Hamish MacDonald, got up from his desk and approached DI Tony Ledingham.

"Hi Hamish."

"Boss, can I have a word?"

"No problem. What's on your mind?"

"Might be better in your office," suggested MacDonald.

Intrigued, Ledingham led the way out of the MIT room, along the corridor and into his own office.

"Can I show you something on your screen, Sir?"

Ledingham waved his hand to accede.

As he tapped in a series of instructions, MacDonald said, "I was a little economical with the truth, earlier, when I said we hadn't turned up anything of note in the offshore workforce."

Ledingham looked confused.

"There was one name that stood out a bit."

He finished typing with a slight flourish on the last tap and turned the screen to his DI. Ledingham ran his eyes down a list of names, before stopping at one entry.

"Well, well. Is that a black sheep, or is it not? Not exactly a common name."

"Appears he is, Sir. I checked him out. He has a sibling DNA match in the Contamination Elimination Database, with a serving officer in Police Scotland."

"Well, I'll be damned," the DI muttered.

"Philip Bankhurst."

MacDonald continued. "I've looked into him a wee bit. Was done for possession a couple of times. Intelligence suggested he was well mixed up with a Glasgow drugs gang. The weegie drug squad raided their lab and rounded up a number of them. Decent sentences handed down from the court. Bankhurst wasn't there that day, apparently. Taken in later on a minor charge. Got away with a ticking off."

"Lucky, or tipped off?"

"Who knows?"

"DI Bankhurst was working in Glasgow at the time, wasn't she?" said Ledingham.

"Think so, Sir. There wasn't any Bankhurst in the Drugs Squad… but there was a DC Lily Able."

He let the name, and inference, hang in the air.

"Maybe I should ask DI Bankhurst what her married name was back in the day?" suggested Ledingham.

"Or not, if you don't want to poke the bear," replied MacDonald.

"Fair point, detective sergeant, fair point. Though I might just keep it for a rainy day," he added, with a mischievous look. "Joking apart, we'll need to get him in for interview. He's on an offshore rota which places him shoreside for the first half of each month. And he's got a record. Lily Bankhurst can't be anywhere near him of course when he comes in."

"Shall I tell her, Sir?"

"No. No. You'd better leave that to me," he said with a sigh.

"Come in!" shouted Bankhurst, to the knock on her door. She had retreated, for a while, to her own room for peace and quiet. A chance to think. And a chance to check her social media. Although she gave her team a hard time about being glued to their phones, she realised, like almost every living adult, she had her own degree of digital addiction.

A serious looking Tony Ledingham entered and sat opposite her.

"We need to have a wee talk, Lily."

"Sounds serious."

"Listen. A name's come up in the list of offshore workers with a record."

"And?" She wondered what merited the sombre tone from her fellow DI.

"We think it might be your brother."

"What? I don't have a brother who works offshore."

"The DNA is pretty convincing," said Ledingham, sympathetically.

"Philip? I haven't spoken to him for years."

"Well, seems like he's an alive and kicking offshore worker, now."

"Bloody hell." A stunned face was all she could muster.

"Family falling out?" enquired Ledingham.

"Just him, really," confirmed Bankhurst. "Proverbial dodgy apple, is my brother. We haven't spoken since his conviction. That was the last straw to be honest. He had been a constant drain on the family, especially my parents, for several years. Common pathway in Scotland, sadly. Fell in with the wrong crowd. Substance use and abuse. Lies, petty thievery, even from home. You know the story."

Ledingham nodded.

"Anyway, I told him then, especially with the job I'm in, that I didn't want anything more to do with him. And, to be fair, he's very much kept off my radar since then. I think he sends a card to my mum and dad now and again, but that's about it."

Bankhurst paused and gazed straight ahead, as if she was recalling something about her brother. A faint ladder of lines climbed up her forehead.

"Mind you, although he's a scallywag, he's no serial killer."

"Fair enough, but we'll have to bring him in for interview when he comes onshore again."

"Of course," agreed Bankhurst.

"I'll let you know when he's coming and you can make yourself scarce."

"Thanks. Appreciate that, and appreciate the heads up about his name popping up."

"Only Hamish MacDonald and myself are privy at the moment. I'll see to it that we do the interview and, hopefully, no one else need know… as long as we can eliminate him."

"Of course," agreed Bankhurst. "I owe you one."

31

24th May

Lily was lost in thought.

"You look stressed," observed Tom.

"I am a bit, if I'm honest. It's this case I'm working on. We set up a special team last week, and all our lines of inquiry have dried up. I'm the SIO, so the buck kind of stops with me."

"And you'll be getting heat from above, no doubt?" suggested Tom.

She nodded.

"Listen, we don't have to stay if you don't want."

"Are you kidding? There's a *crema catalana* with my name on it. Not to mention the *tuile* biscuit, drizzled honey and toasted hazelnuts that come with it."

Tom smiled, and cupped his right hand over Lily's left. Normally she might have flinched at such an overt display of tenderness in a public place, but his warm, strong hand felt secure and comforting. She did nothing to end the moment.

"Listen, I know you can't speak about your work, but I imagine you're investigating one of these dreadful murders that have taken place in Aberdeen recently."

All of them actually.

"I couldn't possibly comment," she replied, in her best *House of Cards* accent.

"I understand. Same for me with patient confidentiality, but I'm here if you want to sound off."

"Thanks. Appreciate that," she said, "though if it's a choice between you and a *crema catalana* for comfort, you understand there's only going to be one winner, don't you?"

"Place in pecking order duly noted," he replied, with a generous smile creasing his face.

Lily responded in kind, but unbeknown to Tom, she was also ruminating about the imminent interview, at Nelson Street station, of her estranged brother. A family member as part of a serial killer investigation was not an easy thing to purge from your mind.

She had earlier received a WhatsApp from Tony Ledingham informing her that the interview was arranged for 8am the following morning, the inference being that she should make herself scarce.

Despite her best attempts to suppress it, and concentrate on enjoying her date, the swirling thought of her brother's interview rose periodically to her consciousness. She was impatient for it to be over, and realised she wasn't likely to be the best company until it was.

Despite her agreement with Ledingham, Bankhurst couldn't help herself. At 8:10am she slipped into the empty room next to where her brother, Philip, was already engaged with Ledingham and MacDonald. She stood in darkness looking through the one-way mirror at the sibling she hadn't seen for many years. His appearance took her back. He had hardly aged at all. In fact, he looked healthier, and possibly even younger, than the last time she had seen him outside a Glasgow courthouse, ravaged by drug abuse and malnutrition. He had put on some weight, but this appeared to be more muscle than fat. His face was tanned and relatively unblemished. A few grey hairs were evident in a thick mop of black hair which more than adequately covered his scalp.

No sign yet of the familial baldness.

She switched on the intercom to listen to the dialogue, finding herself wanting to hear her brother's voice, as much as what he had to say.

Memories came flooding back. Some good but mostly bad, tarnished by his behaviour leading up to the estrangement.

She focussed on the interview and noted the standard approach adopted by her colleagues. Although she had no real concern that her brother might be a serial killer, she was relieved when it became obvious during the interview that he could easily be excluded, not least of which because he had provable, cast-iron alibis for two of the killings.

After half an hour the interview was concluded. As Ledingham leant over to switch the recording machine off, Philip Bankhurst directed a penetrating gaze towards the mirror, and gave a tentative smile. It looked like he hoped his big sister was looking on.

Lily Bankhurst felt a slight shiver go down her spine.

Bankhurst had made her way, unseen she hoped, back to her own office when a ping announced the arrival of a WhatsApp message.

It was from Ledingham.

All good with your brother. Excluded from investigation. Was a bit weird looking at a male version of you across the table! See you at briefing.

Bankhurst thumbed a quick reply.

Thanks. Appreciate that. LB

The mood in the MIT room was flat all morning. Lines of inquiry had reached their natural end point, with little positivity to encourage morale. The sentry cameras found at strategic points in various parks were a common make. They seemed to feed to a central exchange, and then onwards to an untraceable destination. Similarly, the search for the purchaser of the size nine Nike trainers was fruitless. Even the interview with Jim Liddell, partner of Mirena Loci and with a record of aggravated assault, at one time highly promising, had turned out to be a dead end.

June was getting closer. They needed a decent lead. Bankhurst stood with folded arms looking at her tired colleagues, mostly engaged with their screens. *How to motivate?*

Carrot or stick?

Only one thing for it. Baked goods.

She slipped out the back door of the station and within

twenty minutes had returned, via her own room to take extra insulin, with two bags containing a variety of pastries from the local baker. Early grease stains on the paper bags hinted at the unhealthy, but tasty contents.

"OK. You lot. Let's have a break," she announced as she placed the bags on a central table.

The atmosphere in the room lightened immediately as the "carrot" did its job. Conversations started, punctuated by the odd burst of laughter. Bankhurst joined in. A pleasing hubbub of noise filled the room. After fifteen minutes of light-hearted banter, DC Babinski raised an arm. Never one to comfortably socialise, he had returned to concentrate on his PC. Little attention was paid to him by his colleagues who remained distracted by their baked goods and a break from work.

He spoke to grab their attention. "I think I may have something, ma'am."

Bankhurst looked over.

"Go on, Reflex."

"I've been having another look at the murder dates, ma'am. We know they've all been in the first half of the month, and we've assumed that time frame, for whatever reason, is the link. I wonder if we've been looking at it the wrong way."

He walked towards a vacant whiteboard, grabbing a pen on the way, and wrote a list of the murder dates.

7 January
8 February
5 March
5 April
3 May

Bankhurst nodded inviting him to continue.

"The day of the month that the murders were committed corresponds with the number of letters in that month. Seven letters in January, eight letters in February…"

Babinski paused to let his theory sink in, and allow others to quickly check the remaining months.

"Bloody hell, Reflex. You're bang on!" confirmed Bankhurst, excitement coursing through her at this new discovery. "It's so obvious now you've pointed it out. Well done. Great work. It would also fit with the offender having an OCD type thing about numerical patterns."

DS Gillespie chipped in with a typically dour observation. "I hate to piss on your wee happy parade, but if you're right, that means the next murder will be on the fourth of June. You don't need to be a mathematician to know that's not far away."

Bankhurst had already made the same deduction, but had been reluctant to leave the feel-good moment prematurely.

"True," she conceded, "but at least now we can target our resources around the fourth of June. We can flood the seven remaining parks with plain clothes, and monitor in and around with CCTV and ANPR cameras. We'll also have drones, dogs and armed colleagues on standby. If he so much as breaks wind in a park that day, we'll nab him."

Bankhurst patted Babinski on the upper back. "Good work, Reflex."

The DC nodded shyly, and made his way back to the comfort of his own workstation.

The following morning Bankhurst was in her office, having briefed Farrell and McNiven of the investigation's development. A lively debate had ensued about the pros and cons of informing the public, and therefore the perpetrator, or maintaining secrecy and the element of surprise. The latter had won out.

She looked up from her desk. Something had just blocked out most of the light coming through her open door. The not insignificant frame of DS George Gillespie had manoeuvred into the frame.

This is unusual. Something's up.

"Come in, DS Gillespie."

He waddled and wheezed into the room, carrying a newspaper in his right hand.

Why has this man not retired? He must be qualified on age and health grounds.

"Yes?" she said, in a clipped manner, a product of lack of sleep and medication. She had resisted visiting her top bedside drawer during the night but wasn't sure if mild withdrawal symptoms were any better than the morning sedation she would otherwise have had.

Gillespie didn't seem to mind. His type of verbal exchange.

"Hector McNeil," he said.

Statement or question. She wasn't sure. "Yes."

"Was that not the name of the guy Sharon Baxter interviewed in Aboyne last week?"

"Yes."

He dropped his paper onto the desk and rotated it for Bankhurst to read.

"I don't like coincidences," he said, in his usual laconic style.

She looked at the paper and focussed on a small

obituary titled Hector McNeil, underneath which was a photograph of him as a younger man.

"Well known, retired head teacher…"

She hastily read the article, and refocussed on the relevant dates. He died two days after his interview. More worrying was the funeral date. She glanced at her watch.

"But, that's today!"

"Aye, and he's going to be cremated," Gillespie added.

"Shit," said Bankhurst. "Why haven't we known about this before now?"

"His death notice wasn't in the *P and J* or nationals," responded Gillespie. "This is the *Deeside Piper*, which is only published weekly. I only know about it as the rag was shoved through my door last night. One of the downsides of living on Deeside."

Ever the little ray of sunshine.

"I've done a little digging. He was found in bed when the cleaner turned up in the morning."

"Cause of death?"

"Written up as myocardial infarction by the local GP. No post-mortem done."

"Shit."

Bankhurst rose from her chair.

"Thanks, George… er, DS Gillespie. I don't believe in coincidences either. I'm not sure how this fits in, but we're going to find out. And we have a funeral to stop."

32

24th May

The Baldarroch Chapel and Crematorium, at Crathes, sits sixteen miles to the west of Aberdeen and sixteen miles to the east of Aboyne, on the North Deeside Road. Since opening in 2016 it has proven a popular venue for funeral services for the Deeside population, and indeed Aberdonians looking for something a bit different.

The funeral was timed for 10:30am.

Bankhurst looked at her satnav. ETA 10:23am. She leant over and activated the blue lights. DS Sharon Baxter took the hint and depressed her foot on the accelerator pedal. Not quite trusting Gillespie's diplomacy skills, Bankhurst had decided to make the delicate trip herself. She had taken her friend, Baxter, along for support and distraction, but as they turned into the, quite full, car park she developed a crawling sensation in her skin. It felt almost surreal. Like something from a TV drama. Running in at the last minute to stop someone's final journey. And yet, here they were.

Putting their jackets on as they strode purposefully towards the chapel, the first few unmistakable chords of "Whiter Shade of Pale" spilled out of the chapel doors.

Inside they scanned the chapel for someone who might be in charge. A tall, serious man, in formal black clothes, was standing next to a smartly dressed middle-aged lady.

Funeral director and celebrant, assumed Bankhurst, though she was well aware of the dangers in doing so.

Bankhurst and Baxter approached the pair, showed their IDs and explained the need to postpone the ceremony. Family members, sitting in the front row, picked up on their stunned faces and invited explanation. As the funeral director spoke to them, Bankhurst went to the lectern. After tapping the microphone twice, confirming it was on, she faced the congregation, adopting her best serious face.

"Ladies and gentlemen, my name is DI Lily Bankhurst. I'm afraid I have to inform you that we are obliged to postpone this service. We need to investigate the circumstances around the deceased's death. I apologise, sincerely, for this inconvenience, but I would respectfully request that you all now leave the building."

Silence was followed by a low buzz of conversation as the congregation began to get up from their seats, carrying their order of service with them. As the last traipsed slowly out of the chapel, the playlist of McNeil's favourite music came to an end, but the loop of his photos on the wall-mounted screen continued in eerie silence.

Bankhurst consoled the family, while Baxter made a succession of quick phone calls.

She whispered in Bankhurst's ear. "That's the body-wagon organised, and Dexter Brewster has agreed to do

253

the post-mortem at 2pm; but only because it was you asking, he said."

After making sure nobody could see her, she stuck two fingers inside her mouth and made a gagging type movement.

Bankhurst didn't rise to the bait. A thought entered her brain. She pulled the undertaker aside.

"Are bodies usually embalmed for a cremation?"

"Not routinely," he replied, "only if the family wish the body to be viewed."

"And Mr McNeil?"

"No."

"OK. Good," she said, before rounding up Baxter and returning to their car.

2pm Police Mortuary

"You can't blame the GP, Lily."

"Why not?"

"Well, McNeil had a cardiac history, angina I believe, and was found dead in bed. Very likely to have been some type of cardiac event. Like an infarction."

"Heart attack, to me?"

"Indeed."

"So, he just had a guess at the cause of death?"

"In effect, yes. But GPs are often pressurised, by you lot in fact, into providing a best guess certificate, particularly in these sorts of circumstances. Much less paperwork for the police and fiscal."

Bankhurst nodded, acknowledging the truth in the statement.

"So, some people could literally be getting away with murder?"

"A few, no doubt, yes. Look, it's not a perfect system. If GPs reported all such deaths to the COPFS they'd be swamped, and the system would be overwhelmed. As it was, the GP did, in fact, on this occasion have a dialogue with the COPFS, and was told it was OK to go ahead and issue the certificate."

"Who was the fiscal?" enquired Bankhurst

"Let me see," replied Brewster as he pulled up a document on a nearby screen. "Andrew McCabe."

Bankhurst clicked her tongue. "Tosser McCabe. Might have known."

Brewster laughed. "Ha ha. Why tosser... Oh, I see. Tosser as in Tossing the Mc Caber?"

"No, tosser as in actual tosser. The man's a complete knob."

Brewster tilted his head back and roared with laughter. The mortuary attendant, and Lily, joined in with his infectious outburst. After the laughter had died down, and composure regained, he picked up a scalpel.

"Shall we begin?"

Brewster left his pathology technician to sew up the large Y-shaped incision. He removed his protective clothing and dropped them into a bin with practised ease. Looked at Bankhurst in the viewing gallery.

"So, in summary, there is no specific cause of death found in this 72-year-old man at this stage. I can confirm he had mild coronary artery disease, in keeping with his known history of angina, but there was no evidence to suggest myocardial infarction. Neither is there any evidence of foul play. Samples have been sent to toxicology for urgent analysis."

He clicked his voice recognition system off.

"Sorry, if that's not what you want to hear Lily."

"No problem, Dexter. It is what it is," she replied, though her face couldn't help betray her inner disappointment.

Had she stopped a funeral for nothing?

"At least we know it wasn't a heart attack," she offered meekly.

"Indeed," Brewster agreed.

It was mid-afternoon when Bankhurst got back to the MIT room, feeling slightly deflated. The rollercoaster ride of a serious crime investigation continued. Highs and lows. Apparently promising leads crashing on the rocks of reality.

She stood back, with arms folded and furrows creasing her forehead, scanning the boards for inspiration. None came. She sauntered round the room checking in with those present, but again was left disappointed.

She knew patience and graft were bedrocks of an investigation, but the looming fourth of June added an extra notch of pressure each day. She needed some kind of development. Sooner rather than later. Her sleep pattern couldn't take much more disturbance.

At 5pm, her thoughts were turning to what she had in the fridge for tea. Could she spin the chilli out for another night if she was generous with rice and nachos? Her phone rang. She picked it up on autopilot and didn't notice it was the mortuary calling.

"DI Bankhurst."

"Hi, Lily. It's Dexter."

"Didn't expect to hear from you so soon."

"I've just had toxicology on the phone. They've got some preliminary results."

"Tell me you've something interesting," she pleaded.

"Well, there was a moderate amount of alcohol, and also digoxin in his system."

"That's a cardiac drug, right? Not unexpected with him?"

"Perhaps not," agreed Brewster, "but it wasn't actually a drug he was on, and the serum level was ten times normal."

Bankhurst punched the air.

Brewster continued, "So, this is now an unnatural death. I'll be changing the cause of death to arrhythmia secondary to digoxin toxicity."

"Would there not be some evidence for that in the post-mortem?"

"No. Levels that high would almost certainly have caused an arrhythmia… a problem with the heart's electrics if you like… and ultimately a cardiac arrest, which leaves no post-mortem calling card."

"So, suicide or homicide?"

"That, Lily, is your department, but with the lack of any proximal medicine bottle or suicide note, I know which one my money would be on."

Bankhurst pointed at one of the side walls of the MIT room.

"I want a whiteboard for Hector McNeil started over there. Although, on the face of it, a completely different

257

type of murder, my gut says it's related to our case. He knew one of the other victims, and was murdered two days after being interviewed by us. Too much of a coincidence in my book."

DC Babinski picked up a marker pen and started to write.

Hector McNeil
Age: 72
Residence: Aboyne
Widower. Retired head teacher
No children
Date of death: 24 May
Time of death: 04:00 (estimate)
Place of death: Aboyne (home)
Toxicology: alcohol and digoxin
Cause of death: arrythmia secondary to digoxin overdose
(no evidence to suggest suicide)
Worked with Robert Lennox. No known connection to other victims

"OK. We need to throw the works at this. Let's get an SOC team out there ASAP. Cover all the usual bases, and ask them to round up any bottles of booze. We know he had alcohol in his system, and there were no needle marks, so we'll work on the theory that he had his drink spiked somehow. We'll need to get prints from his cleaner, GP and undertakers for exclusion."

"Ma'am."

"What about digoxin?" she asked herself, as much as the MIT. "Dr Brewster told me it's only available on prescription. He doubted there would be any on the black market. Could we cross-check people on digoxin with criminal records?"

"Doubt that would run, Lily," commented DI Ledingham. "NHS Grampian would never release personal confidential information. We might be able to get an anonymised total number, to at least give us an idea how many we're dealing with, but doubt we'd get individual names."

"OK, let's do that. Hugh, can you get in touch with the lead pharmacist at National Health Service Grampian (NHSG) and see what they can provide?"

DC Hugh MacLennan nodded his head, "Yes, ma'am."

Bankhurst paused, collecting her thoughts. She repositioned stray hair behind her right ear, and swallowed.

"So, how did our perpetrator get to Aboyne? Assuming he's Aberdeen based, that's too far to walk, and cycling would be a stretch. There may not be that many ANPR cameras on that road, but let's see what we've got. Also, we need every bit of CCTV along the North Deeside Road to Aboyne. We need to look at buses and taxi firms too. Any drop-offs or pickups in the area that evening?"

"Ma'am."

She paused again, having lost her train of thought slightly.

"Mobile data, ma'am?" prompted Iqbal.

"Yes. Thanks, Zafar. We obviously need to get McNeil's phone and any other devices. Let's look at Aboyne mast data for that evening. Whose phones were in the area, particularly near the victim's house? Any names that raise an eyebrow? Any non-registered phones?"

"Also, let's look at McNeil's own phone data for the couple of hours after his interview. Sharon Baxter had a gut feeling he was maybe holding something back. Was he spooked by the interview? Did he pick up the phone and call someone afterwards? If he did, has that call led to his death?"

"We also need to dive deeper into McNeil's past. I want a detailed association chart going back over the last thirty years or so."

"OK, let's get to it everyone. Feedback at four pm."

Bankhurst felt the need for caffeine, but before she pursued her first cup of the day, she thumbed a quick WhatsApp message to Louise McEwan, requesting the criminologist attend the afternoon briefing.

4pm briefing

"OK, everyone. Where are we at?"

"No ANPR hits, ma'am, and nothing, so far, on CCTV, but may take two or three days to round up all the footage. McNeil had a doorcam, but only a basic contract, so no data stored."

"OK. Keep at it." She looked round the room inviting further contributions.

"The SOC team is still working on the house. No sign of forced entry. Raises the possibility he knew his murderer. They also found two whisky glasses in the dishwasher and a quarter drunk bottle of Glen Scotia on the sideboard. Unfortunately, the machine had been on, and there didn't appear to be any usable prints on either glass."

"Damn," said Bankhurst.

"One of the SOCOs is a whisky buff. Reckons it's a high end, and quite rare, malt. Might be worth looking at sites where that can be bought? Might not be that many outlets."

"OK. Let's do it," agreed Bankhurst.

"They also found his calendar. Seems he was quite meticulous about keeping that up to date about appointments, commitments, etcetera. However, there was no entry for the evening he was poisoned, so presumably his visitor was unexpected."

Hugh MacLennan raised an arm.

Bankhurst nodded.

"NHSG's lead pharmacist was very helpful, ma'am. Ran a search, and was able to tell me within minutes that there are 1204 patients currently being prescribed digoxin in North East Scotland. Out of a total population of about 500,000."

"And no chance of getting a list of names?" enquired Bankhurst, with a hopeful expression.

"No, ma'am."

"Digital team?"

"We've got his phone and computer. Working on them, but early days. We *can* confirm he made a call, routed through an Aberdeen city centre mast, fifteen minutes after DS Baxter's interview. To an unregistered pay-as-you-go phone. Lasted for forty-nine seconds."

"Presumably different to the unregistered phone that was used to message Lennox inside Ashgrove Hospital?"

"Yes."

With contributions dried up, Bankhurst looked at her invited criminologist.

"Dr McEwan. Thanks for coming, once again. May we ask what your take is on this?"

"Thanks, DI Bankhurst. This is very interesting. If it is our man, and it seems quite possible that it could be, it's obviously a significant departure from his patterns of behaviour to date."

"This was a covert rather than overt murder. Reaction rather than action. Previously he has wanted to show us his handywork, the product of meticulous planning. He generally will feel invincible and want to demonstrate what he feels to be his superiority. But this murder feels different. And he wanted it hidden, not advertised. We have to ask ourselves, why?"

McEwan walked back and forwards with an easy elegance while formulating her thoughts, the cut on her expensive clothes highlighting her attractive figure.

"He has also had to deviate from his numerical script. His next murder should, in theory at least, have happened on the fourth of June. As he likely has a variant of OCD, he would have found this uncomfortable, vexatious even."

"There must have been a reason. This feels like a specific target, rather than random people in Aberdeen parks, who probably were just in the wrong place at the wrong time. The only exception to that was Robert Lennox who, as we know, was an associate of McNeil. Both men are now dead."

"In short, McNeil knew something and had to be silenced. This was a reactionary strike. The perpetrator wouldn't have had the luxury of meticulous planning. Perhaps that's why he tried to hide it. Because of this, he is more likely to have made a mistake. We need to try and find it."

"OK. Thanks, Dr McEwan. As always, very helpful."

Bankhurst turned to face the MIT.

"Right. Back to work everyone. Keep myself, or DI Ledingham, up to date with any developments."

Bankhurst went back to her office, logged into her computer and checked her social media on her phone. Her WhatsApp icon indicated a message had been received. She read the message, smiled, and tapped a quick reply, a frisson of excitement running through her body.

You're a naughty boy, Tom Donaldson.

She glanced at her watch, and decided to nip out to the local Tesco Metro for some essentials. When she came back after twenty minutes, one of the SOC team was waiting outside her door.

"Ma'am."

Bankhurst nodded an acknowledgement.

"We're finished at McNeil's house in Aboyne. Just to let you know, we've sent the whisky bottle to toxicology. And we wondered if you might be interested in this."

He held up a framed photograph.

"We noticed this on the wall."

Bankhurst looked at the eight male faces staring back at her. Clearly a fishing outing, they were suited and booted, ready for a day on the riverbank. She recognised McNeil and Lennox, standing next to one another, both grinning broadly, clearly comfortable in each other's company.

"So, they did know each other socially," she said in a low voice, "not just professionally, as McNeil had said."

She scanned the other faces but didn't recognise anyone else.

Who are *you?* she thought.

She flipped the photo over and read the inscription on the back.

Edinburgh Institute for Boys
Book, Line and Sinker Society outing 2004

Bankhurst groaned at the pun.

"Thanks. I'll keep this. We may have to track down some of the other people in this photograph. Twenty-five percent of them have recently died violent deaths. Seems unlikely to be a coincidence. Are the others at risk for some reason?"

"No problem, ma'am."

Bankhurst watched as the SOCO's car pulled away from the pavement before her eyes were drawn back to the photograph.

"What's for tea, Mum?"

"Fish pie."

Silence. "Can we have some chips with it?"

"What do you say?"

"Please."

"But, it's got mashed potato on top," said Bankhurst.

"I know, but can we still have some chips with it… please?"

Silence. "Oh, I suppose so," she relented.

The oven chips looked, and smelled, borderline freezer-burnt but, nevertheless were sprinkled over an oven tray and slid onto the shelf above the pie.

He'll never notice once he's added brown sauce, she thought, as she scribbled frozen chips onto the growing shopping list attached to the fridge door.

Bankhurst sipped at a glass of chilled white wine, and mindlessly surfed on her iPad while waiting for their tea to cook.

Once they'd finished eating, and not before Andrew had commented on the "funny tasting chips", Bankhurst tidied up. Andrew finished his homework.

Mother and son liked watching *Hunted* together on TV. There were not many programmes of joint interest, and Bankhurst looked forward to nestling up with Andrew on the sofa, an experience to be enjoyed before he got too old for it.

As she switched the TV on, the doorbell rang. She glanced at her Apple Watch, but it was dead. She couldn't see who was at the door.

"I'll get it," shouted Andrew.

Bankhurst took her Apple Watch off and placed it on charge. Andrew appeared at the lounge door, a perplexed look on his face.

"There's a man at the door, Mum. He says he's my uncle!"

"For f... Wait here, Andrew. Let me deal with this," said Bankhurst.

Lily walked along the hall feeling cool air and smelling newly cut grass. The front door was partially open and she quickly tidied her hair and adjusted her blouse before opening it fully.

"Philip. What are you doing here?" she said, in a slightly sharp tone.

"Nice to see you too, sis."

She hadn't heard that expression for a long time. Had she missed it? Perhaps.

"How did you know where I live?" Another, slightly accusatory, question.

"Guess you're not the only detective in the family, sis."

The siblings looked at one another for a few seconds. The tumbleweed moment was broken by Philip.

"Look, Lily. As you wanted, I've kept away from you and Andrew for years. As you'll no doubt know, I've been interviewed recently at Nelson Street... innocent I might add... and I could almost feel your presence when I was there. Don't know if it's a sibling thing, or what, but it got me thinking. I really wanted to see you, and Andrew, again. I'll never forget what you did for me..."

Lily glared at him with widened eyes saying *this conversation is not happening*. She looked over her shoulder, but Andrew was not in earshot.

"OK. OK," she relented. "You're here now. You'd better come in. But just for a short while. It's a school night."

Philip, holding up his hands to acknowledge the ground rule, followed his sister inside.

"Andrew. This is my brother, your uncle Philip."

Andrew paused, not quite knowing what reaction was expected of him. He knew of, but had no memory, of his uncle.

"Look at the size of you, Andrew!" Philip enthused, while patting his nephew's head.

Andrew grinned, pleased at the recognition of his physical development.

"The last time I saw you, you were just a nipper."

Unusually for Andrew, he seemed temporarily lost for words.

"Have a seat," invited Lily. "Would you like a glass of wine, or something?"

"No thanks. I've been off alcohol, and everything else, for four years now. Cup of coffee would be great, though. Thanks."

Lily cocked her head, and pursed her lips, in acknowledgement, though wondered if it was true. Her brother had a long way to go before regaining her trust.

She felt on edge. Suspicious. Why had he really come? She topped up her own wine glass with a generous glug.

"So, how have you been, sis? Mum tells me the odd thing, but you know what she's like. I, no doubt, got her edited version. She did say you were a DI now, and that you'd kicked Dave out a few years ago."

"Both true," she acknowledged. "Otherwise, you know, ups and downs of life. Like everybody else."

"Anyone special at the moment?" enquired Philip.

Lily blushed, and Andrew answered for her.

"Yes! And he's a doctor!" he exclaimed.

"Andrew," chided Lily, gently.

"Is he indeed," said Philip. "Sounds like a good catch, Lily."

"So far, so good," she said, "but early days yet. What about yourself?"

"Aye. I live with my partner, Elaine. We've been together two years."

"Where do you live?"

"Newtonhill. I've been working offshore for three years, so when we decided to get together it seemed logical to move closer to Aberdeen."

"Why offshore?"

"Good money. Plenty of free time. And a strict drug testing policy."

Maybe he was telling the truth, thought Lily, aware of

the regular urine sampling offshore workers are obliged to complete. *He's certainly looking good on it.*

Lily relaxed a little. Andrew was obviously comfortable in his uncle's company, and conversation began to flow more freely amongst the threesome. Before she knew it, forty-five minutes had gone by and Andrew's bedtime was approaching. Philip noticed her glancing at the clock on the wall.

"Time I was on the road," he said, standing up.

Just then, Lily's phone rang. DS Tony Ledingham's name appeared on her screen.

She held a hand up towards Andrew and Philip. "I have to take this," she said, and went into the hall.

"Hi Tony, you're working late."

"Yeh, I was just catching up on a few things," he replied in a serious voice. "Listen, Lily. The lab has been on the phone. They've finally managed to extract DNA from the Union Terrace Gardens semen sample."

"Brilliant! Tell me there's a match."

"There is," he replied, but without any enthusiasm in his voice. "I'm sending you the result now."

A ping on her phone announced the file had arrived. Bankhurst opened the document and scanned it with her eyes. She looked puzzled, and reread the report, this time slowly, from top to bottom.

"Is this a joke? This can't be right," she said.

"That's what I said," replied Ledingham, "but the guy at the lab said it was a one in a billion chance of being wrong."

"Bloody hell," Bankhurst muttered. "I'm coming in, Tony. Send me a car, would you? I've had a couple of glasses of wine."

"Done."

33

27th May

Two police cars and a police van cruised through the sparse Aberdeen traffic. At 6am there were few cars and buses, and only an occasional jogger or dog walker. The city was yet to get into its stride for what promised to be a warm, late May, day. Seagulls, scavenging from overfilled waste bins and discarded fast-food carry-outs, outnumbered humans.

The small police cavalcade negotiated the usual traffic challenges, including the newly added low emission zone and bus gates, before arriving, without fanfare, at their destination.

Engines were killed. The Method of Entry and arrest teams, including DI Ledingham, DS MacDonald and a contingent of armed officers, assembled on the pavement. The smell of fresh baking wafted towards them from nearby Aitken's Bakery, the only shop open in the vicinity. The distant siren of an ambulance faded to nothing.

Ledingham, wearing a body armour vest over a short-sleeved shirt, was already sweating and looked on edge. His pulse quickened. He looked at MacDonald, but even the laid-back Western Islander wore a tense expression, his bright pink, freckled face contrasting with his curly ginger pate.

Everyone knew their role.

Ledingham said, "Let's do it."

The first officer knocked firmly three times on the door of a small terraced house.

"Police! Open up!"

There was no response.

Three more knocks. Harder this time.

"Police! Open up!"

A curtain twitched in a neighbouring house.

Ledingham nodded towards another officer holding a red battering ram.

He advanced, steely-eyed, towards the door, but before he could do anything, it opened. A slim man in his thirties, dressed in gym gear and trainers, stood in the doorway. His colour quickly drained, but he remained calm, and made no attempt to avoid what was obviously about to happen.

DI Ledingham stepped forward and cleared his throat. He looked the man in the eye.

"Zafar Iqbal. I'm arresting you in connection with the murder of Oliver Bainton, and with possible involvement in the murders of Robert Lennox, Kayleigh Peters, Dawn Syme and Patrick Heggarty."

The man said nothing.

"You do not have to say anything, but it may harm your defence, if you do not mention, when questioned, something you later rely on in court. We also have a warrant to search your house, and retain anything that may be pertinent to the investigation."

Iqbal had a resigned expression on his face. He shook his head slightly.

"This is a mistake, Sir," he said, meekly.

"Keep it for the station, DS Iqbal," counselled the DI.

Iqbal turned around, and offered his wrists, which were promptly handcuffed.

"Can you make sure my house is secure, please?" he asked.

Ledingham nodded, before escorting Iqbal to one of the waiting cars. The walk of shame, witnessed by a few neighbours. His head was protected from the rim of the car door by the hand of one of the arrest team, as he bent to get into the back seat. He looked wistfully out of the car's side window as it accelerated away from the pavement, to the obvious disgust of a nearby, squawking seagull obliged to flap out of the way. Curtains stopped twitching. The smell of freshly baked rowies wafted down The Hardgate, and an HGV lorry rumbled up nearby Holburn Street. Everything returned to normal.

But it wasn't normal.

Something had happened.

And it wouldn't be long before the first image was posted on social media.

"God, you look awful, sis."

"Yeh. Not my best night ever," she agreed. "Some shit happened at work, and I couldn't sleep when I got back home. By the way, thanks for stepping up last night. Really appreciate it. I would have felt bad about dragging Olive over at that time in the evening, when she had only left a few hours before."

"No problem. Not the first couch I've slept on, and it was great getting to know Andrew a bit. Tell you what, he's a beast on the Xbox."

"Tell me about it," replied Lily.

"Do you want a coffee, or something?"

"No. Thanks. I need to get back to work. Andrew! Are you ready?"

"Coming." A distant reply from Andrew.

Philip got ready to leave, but paused. He had something on his mind. Lily had always been able to read him like a book, and the intervening years had changed little.

"What?"

"This seems a bit weird, sis, as we haven't spoken for years, but you know you can speak to me, right?"

Lily looked confused. "What are you on about?"

"Well. You know. I know you're under a lot of stress. That can be very difficult to live with… completely understandable if you needed some extra support."

"I'm none the wiser, Philip."

"How can I say it?" He paused, discomfort etched on his face as he sought the right words. "How long have you been using?"

"What!" she hissed indignantly.

"Look, Lily. There's not much I don't know about drugs. I can spot someone using a mile away. Variable mood, pinpoint pupils, and enough laxatives in your bathroom to sink a battleship."

"You went through my cabinet!"

"I was looking for some dental floss, as I didn't have my toothbrush with me. Wasn't expecting to stay. That's all."

Indignation softened in Lily's face as she accepted the reasonable explanation.

Rapid footsteps on the stairs preceded Andrew's appearance in the doorway. "Ready."

"Let's go," his mother said, tersely.

Andrew flashed her a *who's rattled your cage?* look. Lily avoided eye contact, shepherded him out the door, and whispered to her brother, "It's not what you think!"

He held up his hands in surrender, and kept quiet.

Iqbal sat, his head supported in cusped hands, looking at the featureless wall opposite him. His tired eyes drifted right and left. For the first time he was actually taking in the utilitarian features of the room he had spent many hours interviewing suspects in. Monotone colours, functional furniture, good lighting and a one-way mirror, inviting conjecture as to who might be watching from the other side. His right heel drummed on the floor as his knee bounced up and down to a nervous beat. A faint citrus smell, from the cleaner's visit, still hung in the air. On the table, an A4 pad (without any writing implement), a paper cup of water, and a digital AIRLight recording machine. In one corner, high up near the ceiling, a solitary CCTV blinked a red dot, as it scanned images to yet more interested parties.

Bankhurst was watching from the adjacent room. She often felt she was at the theatre when in the viewing room. Sitting quietly in the dark, looking through the mirror, like a proscenium arch, at the unfolding drama beyond. She was glad of the dark ambiance as, when she saw Iqbal sitting alone on the suspect's side of the table, her eyes moistened and the hairs on her forearm stood on end. She had no wish to share her emotions with her co-observer, Superintendent McNiven, who was sitting uncomfortably close to maximise his view. She could smell his aftershave, the nutmeg and star anise notes, immediately reminding her of her father.

My god, do they still make Old Spice? she mused, before quickly shutting down the thought and concentrating on the grave matter in hand. A matter that, twenty-four hours previously, she would not, even in her wildest dreams, have anticipated.

In retrospect, Iqbal had not been himself recently. Distracted. Less gregarious. Slightly distant. "Family problems" he had said, but clearly he had been carrying a much more onerous burden. She looked, side on, at her favourite DS. Her right-hand man. Emotions simmered, and sometimes bubbled, inside her. Pity. Anxiety. Fear. Anger. Sadness. Most of all sadness. And yet, as she looked at Iqbal, he seemed relatively calm. Not what she expected. Only the drumming of the leg suggested some inner disquiet, but his facial expression remained phlegmatic. Was this the cool detachment of a killer? Or perhaps a person relieved from the burden of carrying a monstrous secret? Was he somehow assuaged to be in custody?

The door opened suddenly. DI Ledingham and Superintendent Farrell entered the room and strode towards Iqbal. Without speaking they sat down and pulled their chairs in, making a grating sound on the floor. Iqbal assumed Farrell was there to lend gravitas to proceedings, but he doubted that her, little used, interviewing skills would allow her to play anything other than second fiddle to Ledingham.

Iqbal focussed on the DI. He looked tired and stressed. Dried sweat stains, from the early morning arrest, formed smile-shaped tidal marks under his armpits. He had loosened his tie slightly, presumably deliberately, but one side of his shirt had escaped his trousers and flapped loosely; presumably not deliberately.

The atmosphere was heavy and charged. A proverbial knife could have been used on either side of the mirror. Inside the room, they all knew their way around interview choreography, but few had experienced this particular dance before; one of their own on the most serious of charges.

Ledingham leant forward to start the recording. Iqbal could smell coffee on his breath and yearned for some caffeine himself.

"Interview commencing, room three, Force Headquarters, Nelson Street, Aberdeen. The thirty-first of May. 08:00. Present are the accused, Detective Sergeant Zafar Iqbal, Detective Inspector Tony Ledingham and Detective Chief Inspector Amanda Farrell. For the purpose of the recording, DS Iqbal has declined legal representation."

"Can you please confirm that you are Zafar Iqbal?"

"I am."

"DS Iqbal. Your DNA was found in a semen sample recovered from the rectum of murder victim, Ollie

Bainton. As you know, we strongly suspect this murder links with another four, possibly five, murders. We know the perpetrator is a male, fitting your age and body build, who has a keen forensic awareness. In addition, we have recently received new information, from our cyber team, about the phone call made by Hector McNeil, after the interview with DS Baxter at his house in Aboyne. We knew it was routed through a city centre mast but we have now looked at that data in more detail, and right in the middle of the mast's apron is Nelson Street Police Station. Duty rotas and CCTV place you in the station at the date and time the call was made."

Iqbal's facial muscles tightened and stretched his lips slightly. He swallowed saliva. He said nothing.

Ledingham continued, "Within two days of that call, McNeil was murdered."

Ledingham paused. Farrell shifted her weight on her seat, causing a slight creak, then silence.

"As you can see, DS Iqbal, this makes you a prime suspect for all these murders."

"Did you murder Ollie Bainton?"

"No."

"Did you murder Hector McNeil?"

"No!"

"Did you murder any of Robert Lennox, Kayleigh Peters, Dawn Syme or Patrick Heggarty?"

"I did not."

Ledingham allowed silence to develop, until it seemed to own the room. Iqbal was aware of the tactic, using silence as a third interrogator, but resisted responding. Ledingham changed tack.

"What is your shoe size, DS Iqbal?"

"Nine, as I'm sure you already know... Sir"

"So, as you know, we have a team turning your house over just now. Will they find size nine Nike trainers there?"

"Definitely not."

"You seem very sure."

"I am. I'm wearing them."

Ledingham and Farrell shared an awkward glance. In the adjoining room, McNiven scowled while Bankhurst, once again grateful for the darkness, couldn't suppress a small smile.

"I'll ask you again, DS Iqbal. How do you explain the presence of your DNA at the Union Terrace Gardens murder?"

Iqbal paused before he answered. Looked over towards the mirror and back again.

"I'm gay. It's as simple as that. Look, I'll naw deny it's my DNA. I had sex with Ollie Bainton in the toilet of The Knockscalbert pub on the same evening that he was murdered. I'm naw proud of it, but that's the truth, so it is. I had absolutely nothing to do with his death, or any of they others for that matter."

Farrell clicked her tongue. Brought a hand up and loosened her collar slightly. Ledingham said nothing, but squirmed slightly in his chair. He had started to sweat again. New beads of moisture began forming on his forehead.

"I havenae come out yet, though this has rather forced my hand. It's been difficult, but for various reasons... cultural, professional and sporting, I have kept it a secret. I don't have a partner, but I do have sexual desires like

277

most people. I'm a member of NEMESIS, under an alias, and use that service from time to time. And before you ask, I'm no' daft. I don't usually have unprotected sex with a stranger. I had a condom failure that night."

Farrell couldn't quite hide her apparent distaste for Iqbal's account.

He continued, "I've been over this a thousand times. My heid's been mince. Did I witness anything that evening that would have helped the investigation? No matter how many times I looked at it, the answer was no. That's why I kept quiet. I know it doesnae look good, but that's the truth. I'm telling you now, you'll no' find a shred of evidence, physical or digital, to link me to any of these crimes... because I am naw involved."

"That's all very well," interjected Ledingham, "but what about the phone call, via the city centre mast which covers this station, shortly after McNeil's interview?"

"I don't know anything about that. What I will say is that you'll no' trace it to me, and there are probably several thousand other people within that mast apron, both within and outside the station, who could have taken that call."

Farrell, going off script by the look Ledingham shot her, suddenly interjected. "Right. I've had enough of this. DS Iqbal, you are suspended with immediate effect. You will remain in custody while we look into this further. Even if what you say is true, you have, at best, wasted police time and, at worst, obstructed justice. Interview terminated at 08:30."

She reached over and pressed the off switch, with more force than was necessary, bringing her into the full glare of the powerful ceiling mounted light. It offered her no favours, her furrowed brow and flushed face highlighted, even to those on the other side of the mirror.

1ˢᵗ June

Clank.

Rattle.

Iqbal, who had been snoozing on his bunk, was roused by someone entering his cell. He swivelled to a sitting position in time to see Bankhurst enter, carrying his food tray.

"Lunch?"

"Don't suppose it's a Hilsa curry, is it?"

"Don't be daft," she responded, "this is Aberdeen. It's mince, peas and tatties."

Iqbal clicked his tongue, and accepted the tray with good grace. He was glad to see his DI; her looking relatively upbeat was a bonus.

She sat down on a single chair opposite Iqbal, looked around the cell and then eyed him up and down.

"I've seen you looking better," she said.

"You dinnae say," he replied with half-hearted sarcasm.

Bankhurst continued to seek out his eyes but Iqbal reverted his gaze downwards. His head dropped slightly.

"For god's sake, Zafar. It's the twenty-first century! Nobody gives a shit if you're gay," said Bankhurst.

Iqbal looked up again at his DI. "I know. I know," he said apologetically. "But look at me. Look at the colour of my skin. Look at my religion. Look at my job. I'm *polis*. Don't forget, I'm a Partick Thistle fan too. All ripe for possible bias or discrimination. I just thought I'd keep my sexual orientation to myself a bit longer. Can you imagine the comments I'd get from George Gillespie, or down at the cricket club for that matter?"

"Like *batting for the other side*," suggested Bankhurst, a mischievous twinkle in her eye.

"I rest my case," responded Iqbal, throwing his arms up in the air in mock protest, almost knocking the tray over in the process.

"Anyway," Bankhurst continued, "I have good news. There has been absolutely no evidence found linking you with the murders. We reviewed the CCTV footage from The Knockscalbert and, although you obviously did your best to avoid the cameras, we have picked up one grainy image, confirming your story. Your phone data and car telematics also place you there earlier in the evening, as you suggested. By nine pm you, or at least your phone and your car, were back home for the rest of the night. Cyber have drilled down into your NEMESIS app and found your exchange with Bainton setting up the liaison. Being single, and living alone, didn't help your alibi defence for the other murders, but on one occasion you were on duty and on another you were visiting family in Glasgow."

"Pity that wasn't checked before the rather public arrest," he said, ruefully.

"Word has it that you'll be released soon. You might still be suspended, but I'm going to see DCI Farrell about that. The clock is ticking. Only three days until the fourth of June. If we're right, that might be his next target date. I want my full team on this, and that includes you... you daft pillock!"

Iqbal stood up and embraced Bankhurst. As he held her tight, he sobbed.

2nd June

Iqbal had been released the evening before and gone straight home. After showering, and eating a carry-out, he had forced himself to address the matter that could no longer be ignored. His family. His sexuality. Thinking that he couldn't bear to see their faces he had elected to phone, rather than video call, his parents. His mother was generally supportive, and his father tried to be, but his voice betrayed something else. Disappointment? Embarrassment? Afterwards, relieved of the burden of the task, Iqbal felt more relaxed and ready for sleep. Just before he went to bed a WhatsApp message from Bankhurst told him she had called in favours with senior staff, though he couldn't imagine what, and his suspension had been lifted. He had barely put his head on the pillow before he fell into a deep sleep.

The next morning Iqbal was first in the MIT room. He tried to bring himself up to speed, but it seemed like the team had largely been focussed on investigating, and ultimately clearing, himself.

What a waste of time, he thought.

Pangs of guilt swirled inside him.

Slowly the room filled up, but the atmosphere was muted. Quiet industry and fixed concentration on screens suggested an unease at the correct situational etiquette. Iqbal felt conflicted. Freed from incarceration and the burden of his hidden sexuality, feelings of elation bubbled inside him, but fought against the potential damage he had done to the team and his dynamic within it.

Eventually Gillespie got up and slowly made his way towards Iqbal, his heavy footfall audible throughout the unnaturally quiet room. He shuffled to a halt, caught his breath and looked Iqbal in the eye.

"We had a whip round and got you something."

He explored a trouser pocket and extended a chubby hand towards Iqbal. A packet of extra strong condoms, complete with ribbon and bow, was presented to the DS.

"Very fucking funny," he snorted in reply.

Relieved faces turned away. Heads ducked down below half-height partition walls, a sense of broken ice in the room.

Bankhurst swept into the MIT room and was glad to see Iqbal having a chat with Sharon Baxter within the bosom of the team, accompanied by the normal MIT background hubbub. She had intended to arrive promptly, to facilitate Iqbal's return, but Andrew's missing football kit had delayed their departure from home, prompting a frosty atmosphere on the school run.

It had been a challenging forty-eight hours, since Iqbal's arrest had prompted a frenzy of activity and an emotional rollercoaster for his MIT colleagues. One of their own placed front and centre of a serial killer investigation. Although subsequently cleared, how had the group dynamic changed? Would he be accepted back without qualification? It seemed, on the face of it at least, that she needn't have worried. All appeared relatively normal, although she wondered what undercurrents were still swirling below the surface.

"OK, everyone. Can I have your attention please? First of all, welcome back DS Iqbal. It's been a tough forty-eight hours, but we need to put that behind us. I won't need to remind you all our killer is still at large and, if we're right, he may be planning another strike in two days. We need to double down on our efforts before then. Where are we up to?"

"Most of the new information concerns the McNeil murder in Aboyne, ma'am. Firstly, the lab confirmed there were no traces of digoxin in the whisky bottle."

"So, we have to assume the offender took digoxin with him, or her, and spiked McNeil's drink somehow," said Bankhurst.

"Yes."

"What else?"

"We've been looking at outlets who sell Glen Scotia malt. A sizeable chunk of sales are straight from the distillery in Campbeltown, the rest from numerous smaller outlets. We've been concentrating on sales within Scotland, particularly the North East. Still tracing and eliminating, but nobody of interest yet."

"OK. What about the people in the photo of the fishing outing?"

"Proving difficult, ma'am. Social media was in its relative infancy and the demographic in the photo were unlikely to be early adopters. The Society seems to have petered out a few years after that. In short, we don't have the normal digital data to mine. We've been in touch with the school where we think the society was founded, The Edinburgh Institute for Boys. There's nobody currently working there from that era, but they've given us a list of former teachers who they think worked there at the time. We've tracked two down so far. One lives in New

South Wales, Australia, and the other is six feet under in a cemetery in Inverness. Still working on the rest, ma'am."

"OK. What else?"

"We've been analysing data from our sentry cameras we've positioned in the seven parks. We've been particularly interested in anyone behaving oddly or looking like they might be casing the area."

"And?"

"A few drugs being sold, underage drinking and the like. Even an old-school flasher. All been eliminated."

"OK, but keep a close eye, meantime. He might be tempted to have a wee look before the fourth of June."

"Done."

"And, are we all set ourselves for the fourth?"

"Yes, ma'am."

"Extra personnel have been drafted in from the Tayside division. Each park will have five plain clothes officers on a shift pattern covering the entire twenty-four-hour period from midnight to midnight. We've also got sentry cameras, mobile ANPR units, uniform, canine and drone cover."

"OK. Good. If our man shows up, we will get him."

"Ma'am."

Bankhurst left the room and went down to the comms office to discuss a press release with the duty officer. The local press and social media had been frenetic since the arrest, two days previously, of someone who had turned out to be a serving police officer. The usual thing; "Police had declined to comment, but he had been named locally as Zafar Iqbal, a DS in A Division of Police Scotland."

Bankhurst wanted to make it clear that the male

arrested, whose identity had never been confirmed, had been released without charge, and had been eliminated from enquiries. She hoped it would get the media off their back slightly, though realised that any retreat would be temporary. The fourth estate was gathering momentum as it rode the multiple-murder wave.

Back in the MIT room, Bankhurst realised that most of the lines of inquiry, if not actually exhausted, were running out of steam. The team needed some oxygen, fuel for the investigative fire, but the thirty-six hours that followed, up until midnight on 3 June failed to deliver, and time passed slowly.

In the early hours of 4 June, a haar moved in from the North Sea, covering most of Aberdeen in a light damp blanket. To Aberdonians, a very familiar, if unwelcome, summer visitor. Only the western suburbs were spared the leading edge of the sea mist, being rewarded with sunshine and temperatures several degrees higher than the rest of the city. Bankhurst had spent a restless day at work. A fruitless wait for something to happen, and an inability to concentrate on anything else, had made it a long day. The haar, which remained fastened to the city all day, proved a mixed blessing. Fewer people, and therefore fewer potential targets in the parks, but less cover for her undercover officers, and challenging surveillance conditions, especially for the sentry cameras and drone unit. After a day of drinking too much coffee and eating unwisely, she drove home in a mood matching her gloomy surroundings. Moisture in the air triggered the car's automatic wipers and many cars had sidelights and rear fog lamps activated. Radio 2 played in the background, but she was in no mood for a singalong. Only as she neared Countesswells did she suddenly escape the haar's clutches, the bright western sun requiring an immediate adjustment to her sun visor.

After putting a lasagne in the oven, Bankhurst and Andrew went into the back garden, which remained bathed in bright sunshine. She sipped a white wine while looking at the edge of the haar, not five hundred yards away, a tidal wave frozen in time. Andrew played keepy-up with a football, occasionally requiring a reprimand for getting too close to the house windows.

He suddenly arrived at his mum's seat with an exaggerated gasp.

"Mum, can I have a drink and some crisps to keep me going until tea? I'm thirsty *and* starving."

She ran a motherly hand through his sweaty, unruly hair.

"Go on then," she said, in a manner that sounded as if she had made a significant concession.

She took another sip of the soothing wine, closed her eyes and tilted her head upwards towards the sun, feeling its warmth on her face. Her mood began to lift.

Less than three miles away, Mirena Loci had also tilted her head up and closed her eyes. But she had tilted her head to try and protect her airway, in response to the cold circle lapping her neck, and closed her eyes against the terror in front of her, uncertain if she would ever open them again.

34

5th June

"OK, everyone. Can we gather round please?"
Bankhurst called the MIT to order.

She stood with arms crossed, and a straight back, looking at her audience.

"Obviously, we have mixed feelings about yesterday. Clearly, we are pleased nobody was injured, or worse, but also frustrated that our man didn't show himself. I feel confident we would have got him if he had."

"We have to ask ourselves, why?"

"Could the weather have had something to do with it? Does he realise we're on to him, and has decided to back off for a while? Or, were we wrong in making our assumptions about the date and number of letters in the month? Could that have been a coincidence?"

She paused, but the team kept its counsel.

Even as she said the words, they sounded hollow. Deep inside, a strong forbidding feeling kept telling her that something had actually happened. They just didn't know what.

"Where do we go from here?" she continued. "Have we got the information on all the deaths that did occur on the fourth of June?"

"Yes, ma'am. Seven in the city and six in the shire. None thought to be unexplained, none in public spaces, and only one reported to the fiscal, a forty-six-year-old who died in hospital from complications of an RTA three days previously."

"OK. Thanks. What about the members of the Book, Line and Sinker Society? Any joy in tracing them down?"

"Not so far, ma'am."

"Anybody got anything else?"

Neil Jardine spoke up. "We've had a hit from McNeil's computer on the Epilog data recovery tool. He deleted some photos three years ago, but we were able to retrieve them. Child porn, I'm afraid. Young boys."

"OK," replied Bankhurst, "that potentially links with our suspicion that Lennox sexually abused boys. Looks like they were both up to their neck in it."

The haar ebbed and flowed a little, but it was 7 June before the city was finally freed from its grasp. The granite stone of many Aberdeen buildings shimmered in the sunshine, and the city's citizens had a small collective spring in their step.

Inside the MIT room, however, the mood remained sombre. Precious little progress had been made since 4 June, a day which, she had been reminded by Superintendent McNiven, had "cost an arm and a leg in resources with nothing to show for it".

Bankhurst sat at a desk in the MIT room. Consecutive nights of poor sleep had left her pale and gaunt. Heavy eyelids required a concentrated effort to stop them shuttering down. Even two double strength coffees had failed to provide any energy.

"Ma'am," called DC Alison Murray, "could be something or nothing, but you might want to have a look at the mispers data since the beginning of June."

Bankhurst summoned the energy to stand and walk to Murray's desk. She rubbed her eyes and forced herself to focus on her screen.

Murray continued, "Of the five people who had been reported missing, all have since returned or been found well elsewhere, except one. Mirena Loci."

Bankhurst's pulse quickened, and the weariness in her bones beat a slight retreat.

"She had been reported missing by her husband on the afternoon of the third of June, having failed to return home from a night shift at Aberdeen Royal Infirmary at 08:00 that morning. There has been no trace of her since, and no digital activity of any sort."

Bankhurst was now fully alert, the last traces of fatigue having quickly surrendered to the adrenaline circulating round her body.

She didn't like or trust coincidences.

Standing tall, she announced to the room, "Gather round everybody. This could well be important."

She allowed DC Murray the kudos of explaining the find, before taking over.

"For those of you that weren't attached to the MIT at the time, or have just forgotten, Mirena Loci, and her partner, have both been interviewed as part of this inquiry before. Mirena, because her car was in the vicinity of Ashgrove Hospital the night Robert Lennox died, and also in Portlethen when the perpetrator filled his jerry can with petrol. Her partner, Jim Liddell, was interviewed because of his criminal record, although he was eliminated from inquiries at the time."

"This has got to be connected. Someone known to the inquiry goes missing on the eve of the fourth of June and hasn't been seen since. This is more than a coincidence. What did we miss the first time round? Has he got her captive somewhere? Could she already be dead? If so, where is she?"

Iqbal chipped in. "Apart from the date, if she was indeed killed on the fourth of June, this would be a departure from his normal MO, in so far as there is no obvious body in a public place."

"True," Bankhurst agreed, "but, if he also murdered Hector McNeil, then that was also a departure from his norm."

Iqbal nodded an acceptance of his DI's logic.

"Right, we need to look at Mirena Loci and Jim Liddell again. Every tiny detail of their lives. I also want a detailed timeline for Loci in the forty-eight hours leading up to her disappearance. Physical and digital."

"Ma'am."

Bankhurst paused. Her eyebrows approximated slightly as she concentrated. Thoughts criss-crossed her brain. The silence was almost audible, finally broken by a rasping Gillespie cough, the deep rattling nature of which conjured unpleasant images of what was going on in his bronchi.

Iqbal leant towards Babinski, and whispered, "Check out Alison Murray, she's went all Procul Harem."

Babinski squeezed out a thin smile, though didn't look to have understood the reference.

Bankhurst came to life again.

"Maybe we need to look at things through a different lens? So far, we've had an incineration, a garotting, a stabbing, an overdose and a hyperthermia as MOs."

She added, "Possibly two overdoses, if you include McNeil, but he remains an outlier in the meantime. What other methods might the offender utilise, and where could a body be hidden?"

Responses came, thick and fast, from the floor.

"Gunshot."

"Asphyxiation."

"Manual strangulation."

"Poisoning."

"Electrocution."

"Drowning."

She raised a hand, and looked into the distance. Her focussed eyes narrowed. Animation flooded her face.

"Drowning," she repeated, nodding her head. "Yes. Yes. That could work!"

"Apart from The Dee and The Don, Aberdeen is full of little burns, criss-crossing the city. How many of them go through parks?"

"I can think of a couple off the top of my head," said Babinski.

"Are any of them subterranean or have subterranean sections?" enquired Bankhurst.

"...where you could hide a body." Iqbal continued the

line of thought, as it dawned on the MIT that they had not considered this possibility.

Bankhurst's fatigue was temporarily forgotten as she rode the momentum of the new idea.

"Right, I want a map of *all* waterways in Aberdeen, including subterranean ones, and then superimpose it on a map of the city, with particular reference to the parks. I want to focus, initially, on the seven parks that have not yet been the site of a murder. If they have burns, where are the entrances and exits? Are there any tunnels?"

"Will do, ma'am."

In less time than it took Bankhurst to visit the toilet and collect a coffee from the machine, the requested maps were displayed on a white screen.

"Let's see," she said, as she used a laser pointer to dance over the map, tracing the meshwork of waterways. Images of the thread veins on her granny's legs came to her mind.

"Bon Accord Gardens. No."

"Persley Gardens. Yes. The Scatter Burn runs along the northern border."

"Westfield Park. No."

"Duthie Park. Yes. No burn as such, but upper and lower lakes, connected by a waterway under a bridge."

"Stuart Park. No."

"Westburn Park. Yes. The Gilcomston Burn. Enters the park from a tunnel under Westburn Drive."

"Queen's Links. No."

"OK. Zafar, I want you to take a team round each of Persley Gardens, Duthie Park and Westburn Park ASAP. You might need divers for Duthie Park. Talk to the water authority, or council, or whoever's in charge. You might need help with access to drains and culverts."

"Yes, Boss."

"I want them all checked before close of play today."

Four hours later, the waterways of both Duthie Park and Persley Gardens had been checked and cleared. Iqbal messaged the news to Bankhurst, and that they were now on their way to Westburn Park. Her initial optimism was fading fast, another dead end staring her in the face.

Gilcomston Burn starts just north of Aberdeen Royal Infirmary, flowing in parts through the grounds of the hospital and the aptly named, adjacent, Burnside Gardens. It disappears underground again into a culvert, going underneath Westburn Drive, before surfacing for its journey through Westburn Park. It was initially called the West Burn of Gilcomston and, indeed, gave its name to Westburn Park. Before it exits the park, it disappears underground again and, apart from a short appearance in Fraser Place, remains subterranean until it joins the larger Denburn near Lower Denburn. The combined burns continue their underground journey eastwards until spilling into the Upper Dock of Aberdeen Harbour.

The team, led by Iqbal, nosed their vehicles gently along Cornhill Road, within Westburn Park, before parking a short distance from the burn, drawing curious glances from dog walkers and frisbee throwers. It quickly became obvious that the relatively shallow waters of the narrow burn, running through the park, would offer insufficient cover to conceal a body. Iqbal traced the burn to the western edge of the park where, behind an imposing iron grill, it succumbed to the darkness of the large culvert beyond. On closer inspection, he could see the grill was hinge-mounted on one side and fastened with a large padlock on the other. He crouched on his haunches and nudged the padlock instinctively, which creaked and scraped, before settling back in its previous dependent position. As he watched the motion of the large padlock, he became aware of a foul-smelling odour. He took a deeper inhalation through his nostrils. A putrid smell stung his nasal lining and turned his stomach. Forced to stand up and withdraw from the grill, he greedily inhaled the untainted air nearby. The nausea slowly began to settle.

He had smelt decaying flesh several times before in his career and was in little doubt about what his nose was telling his brain.

He activated his Airwave radio, which crackled into life.

"DS Iqbal to MIT control."

"Go ahead, DS Iqbal."

"I think we may have something."

35

7th June

Iqbal and Babinski donned Tyvek protective suits, boots, gloves and headlamps. Before completing his protection with a face mask, Iqbal dug out Vicks VapoRub from his pocket and smeared the cream just above his upper lip. An offer to share with Babinski was gratefully accepted.

"Bloody typical, it's a taps aff day, and we're havin' to pit all this gear on," he grumbled. "Any sign o' that cooncil man wi' the keys?"

"No, Sir."

"Right. I'm naw hanging about. Bring the cutting gear and get that lock aff."

With a crunch the padlock submitted to the strength of the bolt cutter. The gate slowly ground open. After checking his comms system and headlamp, Iqbal nodded to Babinski and led the officers into the tunnel.

The sudden change from bright and warm to dark and cool challenged their senses, the latter a welcome foil to the stifling heat inside the suit.

As they slowly waded into the culvert, natural daylight was quickly left behind, and the beams from their torches danced over the slimy, green brick walls.

Iqbal heard his own breathing, within the confines of his mask, magnified in the quiet of the tunnel, the only other noise a distant rumble of traffic passing overhead on Westburn Drive.

A rat scuttled past and disappeared up a gap between two bricks, the tail following like a sucked strand of spaghetti. Another rat, apparently dead, lay motionless on a small ledge.

Could the smell just be dead rats? Iqbal wondered.

He angled his headlamp downwards and then sideways. The water level was about a third of the way up his boots, approximately six inches deep, but the watermark on the side of the tunnel suggested the level regularly reached about eighteen inches.

After another ten yards, Iqbal came across another grill. Like the entrance gate it was a stout, cast-iron structure, but this time fixed at both sides with no hinge mechanism. Clearly not meant to allow passage. Some amorphous debris was snagged on the lower part of the grill. Leaves? A dead animal? Even through his mask, the smell of decay stung the lining of his nose. Another two steps. His pulse accelerated and he began to sweat. His keen eyes swept the scene before him trying to make sense of what he was seeing. Suddenly, he realised that the shape was not vegetation or a dead animal. It was a mop of dishevelled human hair. What he was looking at was the back of a head.

"Find! Find!" he shouted.

"Report in, DS Iqbal," came an urgent female voice from the MIT room.

"Female body in the culvert. On the far side of a fixed grill. Will need cutting gear."

"Fuck!" Iqbal heard Bankhurst swear clearly across the static-laden airway.

He crouched and shone his headlamp through the bars. The body was lying perpendicular to the grill, away from him, almost horizontal to the floor of the tunnel, partially submerged in water. The upper body and head were tethered to the grill with cable ties, the wrists similarly trussed laterally, in a crucifixion type position. It looked like she had been deliberately positioned, possibly alive, so that her face was just above the low water level, but would have been quickly submerged when the level rose only a few inches. The swish of waded water, and a new source of light bouncing around the tunnel, announced the arrival of a burly officer carrying a powerful looking cutting tool. He quickly assessed the situation, snapped protective goggles in position and set to work in a welter of tiny sparks. Twenty minutes later he removed a square section of the grill and Iqbal squeezed through.

Now on the other side, he directed the headlamp beam towards the head of the body, and gasped. The pale, gagged face of Mirena Loci was barely recognisable due to multiple small bites, and her left eye was completely missing, cored down to the bone at the back of the socket.

"Fucking rats," he murmured.

A downwards movement of the beam highlighted what appeared to be a blue nurse's uniform, short-sleeved top and generic trousers, stained and torn in places. Her badge declared her to be Staff Nurse Mirena Loci, Department of Surgery, ARI. Further down the light played on exposed feet which had suffered badly from rodent scavenging. The tissues looked decayed, the source of the putrid smell, he assumed.

He steeled himself to approach her head and neck to perform the formality of confirming death. Having missed a pulse once before, when palpating through a latex glove, he pressed firmly over the carotid artery.

Suddenly, Mirena Loci opened her right eye, and stared directly at Iqbal.

36

7th June

He reflexly pulled away and straightened up, cracking his head on the roof of the culvert.

"Bastard!" he shouted, and grabbed the top of his head.

"What's going on?" enquired Bankhurst.

"She's alive! She's alive! We need a medic here, now!"

He heard Bankhurst telling Hugh MacLennan to get hold of ambulance control.

"Speak to me, Zafar," instructed Bankhurst.

"It's Mirena Loci. I recognise her from photos and she's still got her nurse badge on. She's in a bad way, but she is alive! We're cutting her loose as we speak."

"Medics on way," confirmed MacLennan over the radio.

"Have you got a bodycam on Zafar?" asked Bankhurst.

"No, it won't work down here. Tried it earlier."

"OK. Describe the scene."

"She's cable-tied to the lower part of a solid iron grill,

almost like a horizontal crucifix position. Looks like she was positioned at a height just above the low water level, but below the high mark."

"She might just have been saved by the recent dry weather," suggested Bankhurst.

Iqbal continued, "She's in a bad way. Rats have been at her. Left eye's missing. Feet in a mess. Barely conscious. Have removed the gag, but she hasn't said a word yet."

"OK. Don't move from her side, in case she says something."

"Understood."

After increasing the size of the breach with the angle grinder, the three officers gently carried Mirena Loci from her site of restraint to the outside. Sunlight dazzled their eyes as they placed her on the grass. A small crowd of onlookers gaped in morbid fascination.

Iqbal spoke into the Airwave. "We need a team here ASAP, to secure the scene and control the public."

"Already on their way. Should be there any moment."

With that, a siren sounded demanding urgent clearance to get access to the park gate. A vanguard ambulance was followed by three police patrol cars. The well-trained public responded promptly, and the small convoy traversed the park on the narrow Cornhill Road.

Karl Poon, the paramedic who had been called to Dawn Syme's body in Johnston Gardens, and a paramedic known to Iqbal, was first to arrive by his side. Eager eyes quickly assessed the situation.

"Fuck me," he murmured to himself.

"Karl. How's it gawn?" said Iqbal.

"Nae bad," he replied. "Who have we got here?"

"This is Mirena Loci, a 43-year-old nurse. Misper since the third of June. We found her in the culvert. Attempted murder. Looks to be in a bad way."

"I can see that," confirmed Poon, as he quickly performed an initial assessment of airway, breathing, circulation, followed by oxygen saturation and a Glasgow Coma Scale, to determine the level of consciousness. Fast hands quickly attached a face mask, and the comforting hiss of oxygen signalled her resuscitation had begun. The back of an IV cannula, inserted into her right arm, flushed red as venous access was achieved. Poon pulled the needle from the cannula, and attached a bag of saline. As he secured the drip with tape he passed the saline bag to Iqbal.

"Squeeze that bag in for me, would you, Zafar? Let me know when it's nearly done."

"Nae problem, pal."

Poon phoned the emergency line at Accident and Emergency at Aberdeen Royal Infirmary, to brief them and say he was on his way. Geographically he was less than half a mile away from the resuscitation unit, with a correspondingly short transfer time, but his stressed face leaked concern that Mirena Loci might not even make it that far.

Ten minutes later the swing doors swished closed behind Mirena Loci as she was sucked into the resuscitation unit. A bank of serious faces immediately busied themselves around her trolley. Iqbal reluctantly ceded to the request to sit outside, a cheap plastic chair with a warped back offering little prospect of comfort. Suddenly tired, as if the adrenaline that had fuelled him for the last hour had been switched off, he slumped in the chair. From behind the doors, a murmur of unintelligible voices fed his imagination as to the flurry of medical activity being undertaken to try and save her life. Not blessed with the strongest constitution, a shiver ran down his spine as he contemplated the various devices and orifices that might be involved. He focussed on posters on the wall opposite preaching good hygiene practice and, somewhat out of date, Covid social distancing advice. His phone pinged. He dug it out of his pocket, welcoming the distraction. It was Bankhurst.

Any update?

In resus. Looks touch and go. Hasn't regained consciousness.

OK. Hang around in case she does. I'll arrange relief for you. We'll need her guarded 24/7.

Will do.

He slid his phone back in his pocket and began reading the posters again for the umpteenth time.

37

7th June

Mirena Loci
Age: 43
Italian
Lived in UK for 10 years
Partner: Jim Liddell
No children
Staff Nurse at ARI
Reported missing: 3 June
Found in culvert in Westburn Park, 7 June
Attempted murder (possible failed drowning)
Currently in ARI. In coma
Previously interviewed as part of Between the
Rivers Investigation

Bankhurst looked at the nascent whiteboard for Mirena Loci. She adjusted her hair, a stress mannerism she was aware of but accepted, as her eyes danced back and forth to the others:

Robert Lennox. 7 January. Incineration. Victoria Park
Kayleigh Peters. 8 February. Garotted. Seaton Park
Dawn Syme. 5 March. Stabbed. Johnston Gardens
Patrick Heggarty. 5 April. Overdose. Hazlehead Park
Ollie Bainton. 3 May. Hyperthermia. Union Terrace
Gardens.

Loci had been abducted on 3 June, and by Iqbal's description of her body, it was likely she had been lashed to the culvert grill the same day. She assumed the expectation of the perpetrator was that natural fluctuations in water level over the following twenty-four hours would have led to her drowning on his chosen date, 4 June. This, in turn, would have satisfied his sequence compulsion. One death each month, in an Aberdeen park, a different MO each time, the day of the month determined by the number of letters in the month.

It all fitted. Satisfaction that the perpetrator had confirmed the MIT's working theory was heavily tempered by crushing disappointment, and guilt, that another victim had been attacked in the process. Self-doubt and self-incrimination littered her thoughts, a gnawing anxiety crawled in the pit of her stomach.

She felt an arm on her shoulder.

"This wasn't your fault." DI Tony Ledingham spoke in a low, sympathetic voice.

"Huh. Am I that transparent?" she said, dropping her shoulders slightly.

"SIO can be a lonely role," he continued. "If it's any consolation, I would have made exactly the same decisions."

"Thanks, Tony. Appreciate that," she replied, before adding, with a weak smile, and a raised, inquisitive eyebrow, "don't suppose your spirit of collegiate support would extend to taking the press conference tomorrow, would it? Comms are saying the shit has really hit the fan. They'll no doubt be looking for blood."

Ledingham held his hands up in the air, as he began walking away, as if to say *that's a step too far.*

Against the rhythmic, faint gasping noise of the ventilator, and bleeping from the cardiac monitor and automatic infusion pumps, Staff Nurse Jake Menzies looked at his friend and colleague, Mirena Loci. It was 2:30am and he was half way through the first of three consecutive night shifts in the intensive therapy unit (ITU). As his body clock faced the rigours of changing from daytime to night-time existence, a creeping tiredness had already pervaded his body. Although his professionalism tried to temper it, his face, and moist eyes, displayed the burden of his task as he worked diligently on the forlorn figure of Mirena.

Her initial assessment in A and E had shown that she was in multiple organ failure and septic, thought to be secondary to infected gangrene of her left foot and lower leg. After initial resuscitative measures in A and E, she had been transferred to ITU, where she was placed in a medically induced coma, intubated and ventilated. After a multi-team discussion it was decided, despite the fact she was a poor anaesthetic risk, she required all dead and dying tissue excised, to remove the primary source of infection. The on-call orthopaedic surgeon performed a left below knee amputation along with debridement of wounds on her right foot and what little remained of her left orbital contents. Having survived the surgical trauma, she had been back on the ITU ward for an hour.

Menzies was well used to the paraphernalia that engulf a typical ITU patient, and adopted a professional detachment from his charges, but the sight of his diminutive colleague before him was hard to bear. Even if she survived, her life would be forever changed. He began to busy himself again with the many routines of intensive care and noticed, with dismay, that there was only about 30mls of dark coloured urine in the catheter drainage bag. Her failing kidneys were not producing their most vital product.

That's not good. He shook his head slightly.

The door swished open and Dr Tom Donaldson followed, with less enthusiasm than the door, appearing about as tired as Menzies felt. He looked like he had spilled tea down his scrubs top, and either didn't know about it or couldn't be bothered to change.

"Busy night?" the staff nurse enquired.

"Just a bit," Dr Donaldson replied, wearily. "How's our patient doing?"

"About as well as could be expected, I suppose… given everything. I'm worried about her urine output, though."

Donaldson followed Menzies' eyes to the catheter bag, before studying the urine output chart, fluid balance sheet and latest kidney function results. Concern was etched on his face.

"Yes, she's definitely on a sticky wicket," he agreed. "I think all we can do for now is keep her sedated, her vital organs supported as best we can, and continue the high dose, antibiotic cocktail. The next twenty-four to forty-eight hours will be critical. At least she's had the source of infection removed. Let's hope that improves her chances a bit."

"Do you know her?" enquired Menzies.

"Not really. I've probably come across her in theatre a few times… but then we're mostly behind masks in that environment."

"Oh, you wouldn't miss her. Small stature, but big Italian personality. Didn't… doesn't… suffer fools gladly."

"Not sure I have then," replied Tom. "She does sound as if she'd stand out from the crowd! I'll come in past in a couple of hours, but let me know if there's any significant change in the meantime. Oh, and we'll need up to date bloods and gases before the changeover round."

"No problem," confirmed Menzies.

Bankhurst woke abruptly at 7am after another fitful sleep, punctuated by sweats, palpitations, nightmares and one panic attack. No measure of refreshment had been drawn from her time in bed. She wished Tom had been there. His physical presence, his flesh on hers, intimate or otherwise. She had started to develop real feelings for him, beyond the transient excitement, intrigue and lust a new relationship brings. Confused by her own emotions she wasn't sure if she was laying down a strong emotional platform, from which to build a lasting relationship, or a temporary scaffolding to get her through a challenging time in her life.

She looked at her phone. With a sigh, she realised there was only another fifteen minutes until her alarm went off.

There was no point trying to get back to sleep. A small red circle, nesting a number one, on the WhatsApp icon caught her eye. She opened the app and her facial muscles tightened to a faint smile when she saw it was from Tom.

Hey. Hope when you read this, you'll have managed to get some sleep ahead of the press conference. Been a busy night here. It seems our worlds have collided. I know we don't normally speak about our respective jobs, but the patient I've been looking after tonight is likely to be on your books too. No names obviously, but I'm sure you know who I mean. Hanging in there but on a bit of a shoogly peg. Hope to speak to you after I've had a kip. Good luck!
XX

Cheered slightly by his message, she stepped into the shower hoping that hot water would vitalise her. Having lingered there for five minutes longer than usual, Bankhurst got out, dried herself and her hair, and gave Andrew his first morning shout. After dressing she stood in front of the mirror. Despite adding finishing touches to make-up and running a brush through her hair, the face looking back at her reflected her feelings. Tired. Forlorn. A little desperate.

"Come on, girl. You've got this," she cajoled herself, but even as the words came out of her mouth, she realised they were only words, and she had failed to drag any conviction from within herself. She stifled a yawn as she padded through to the kitchen, knocking loudly on Andrew's door as she passed. The kettle hissed as the first smoke from the burnt edges of toast began to whisper upwards from the toaster. Although she had no appetite, she forced herself to eat tea and toast to guard against the nightmare of a hypo during the press conference. As Andrew got ready, she cupped the mug in her hands and sipped at the last of her tea, staring blankly into space and fretting about the day ahead.

"Christ, Lily. You look awful."

Bankhurst was slightly taken aback. Not because of Farrell's forthrightness, nothing unusual there, but the familiar, almost friendly address.

"Yes, ma'am," was all she could think to say in response.

Farrell's face was set in a determined mode. "Right, I will take the press conference. You'll do the morning MIT briefing, and then go home for the rest of the day."

Farrell could see the beginnings of an objection in Bankhurst's eyes, but before she could say anything Farrell cut her off.

"And that's an order!"

"Ma'am."

Relieved of the intimidation of the press conference, Bankhurst was pleased to feel an elevation of mood and energy as she walked sprightly, coffee in hand, into the MIT room. Her arrival was noted. Heads and bodies began to turn in anticipation of the briefing.

"Right, everyone. Let's see where we're at. The update from ARI is that Mirena Loci remains critical but stable. She's likely to be in a medically induced coma for another two or three days, at least. So, no prospect of any interview in the meantime. We've got a twenty-four-hour guard outside her door, and ARI will let us know if there's any significant change in status."

"As you know, I don't like coincidences. I find it hard to believe she, unlike other victims perhaps, was selected randomly. Was she chosen for her diminutive size, to make it easier for the offender to transport her along the culvert, or was she taken for the offender to tie off a possible loose end?"

Bankhurst walked over and pointed to the wall-mounted map of Aberdeen and surrounding area.

"As we know, her car was in the vicinity of Victoria Park the night of Robert Lennox's incineration, and in Portlethen, the night the offender bought fuel at the petrol station there. We had wondered if she might have been linked to, or seen, the offender, but we subsequently ruled that out. What if it was the other way around? What if the offender had seen, and recognised, her? Perhaps he had been worrying that she might have seen him and could ID him, sooner or later. To keep his sequence going he would have planned a murder for the fourth of June anyway. If he targeted Loci, perhaps he was thinking *two birds with one stone.*"

Heads nodded at the plausible theory.

Bankhurst continued, "Where are we on Loci's timeline leading up to her disappearance?"

Iqbal responded. "She finished the dayshift at 8pm on the third of June and left surgical theatre three, as witnessed by several colleagues, shortly after. We've got her on CCTV, apparently acting normally, within and at the exit of the hospital, but we lose her for part of her route in the ARI grounds. She was in the habit of parking her car on Westburn Road," he pointed to the location on the map, "and would normally walk straight there after a shift. We know she never made it there, as the car was still parked where she had left it in the morning. We traced her phone which seemed to go dark on Burnside Gardens, which is just adjacent to the hospital site. We've had a team look at Burnside Gardens in detail. It's a no through road, with little traffic, save for residents. There's a secluded area at one end with bushes and trees giving cover, where you could easily park a vehicle with little chance of being seen. Also, there's no CCTV coverage of that area. What we did find, however, is a sizeable manhole cover giving access to the culvert which runs under Westburn Drive and into Westburn Park. By the look of the rim of grime around the manhole cover, it had been disturbed recently. A SOC team is working the scene as we speak."

"So," Bankhurst interjected, "it seems that Loci was abducted, in broad daylight and with presumably plenty people around I should add, somewhere between leaving the surgical theatres and her car on Westburn Road. She was then, presumably, subdued and taken to the culvert where she was gagged and bound awaiting her death. And nobody saw a single thing?"

"No, ma'am."

"And we put an appeal out for witnesses on NHSG Global email?"

"Yes, ma'am."

"Seems bloody hard to believe," she muttered.

A thought occurred to her. "Was there anything on the toxicology screen?"

"No, ma'am, though it wasn't collected until the seventh of June so any sedative used might have been out of her system by then."

"Mm." Bankhurst nodded, pensively.

"Ma'am," interrupted DC Alison Murray. "That's the press conference about to start." Heads turned and eyes were raised to the wall-mounted TV, as Murray, with remote control in hand, increased the volume.

Farrell, her name and rank scripted along the bottom of the screen, had a steely look in her eye. She cleared her throat, eyed the main camera directly and began.

The MIT remained in rapt attention for twenty minutes as Farrell expertly controlled proceedings. Having sized up her audience for the first few minutes, she then worked them to her advantage, giving time to the reasonable, and minimal opportunities to the unreasonable, or downright aggressive. She remained calm and forthright. Ambiguous and unambiguous as appropriate and, never once, losing control. She finished with the hackneyed, but somehow still appropriate, appeal for people *who will know this man* to come forward, and then she left in the blink of an eye, inviting no protraction of the conference.

"And that, ladies and gentlemen, is how you do a press conference." DI Ledingham could not hide his admiration.

"Bloody hell," agreed Bankhurst, blowing her cheeks out, although she also wondered if Farrell had perhaps enlisted some Dutch courage to assist her. "Worthy of the Met indeed," she said.

"Did you see how she handled that wee bawbag from *The Scotsman*?" added Iqbal. "Pure class, by the way."

Murray switched the TV off, and attention refocussed on Bankhurst.

"OK. I want us to look at Mirena Loci again. I know we've already done so to some extent, but I want us to drill deeper. Who are her associates? Has she any connections with the other victims? Recheck all her social media. Also, reinterview her husband again. No stone unturned."

"Yes, Boss."

"I won't be on-site the rest of the day, but you can get me on my mobile if there are any significant developments."

"One last thing before I go. The top floor has decided that, until further notice, there will be a curfew on all Aberdeen parks from 6pm to 8am, with regular and visible patrols during the daytime opening hours. They're also going to close the parks all day on the fourth of July, the next sequential date, though aren't going to advertise that in advance. The offender will know we're on to him now, but he might not know that we've cracked his method of choosing his attack dates. We'll keep that to ourselves in the meantime."

As Bankhurst left by the rear of the police station, the last of a brief summer shower petered out and the clouds released their grip on the Aberdeen sky. A surprisingly warm sun gratefully accepted the gaps created. The smell of warm summer rain on concrete filled the air as faint steam vapours rose from the nearby road. She navigated the city centre, and drove towards Countesswells, her mood increasing and anxiety decreasing in equal measure. After a brief stop at Aldi to buy fresh ingredients for tea, she wended her way the last few streets to her home in the quiet Aberdeen suburb. An old man, with a hunched back and a walking stick, made slow progress along the pavement while a middle-aged woman, waiting to cross the road, was giving more attention to her phone than her cockapoo companion.

She unloaded the car before crashing on top of her bed. Sleep took her quickly and, for a change, held her undisturbed until releasing her back to consciousness three hours later. After refreshing with her second shower of the day, she dressed in casual clothes, texted Olive to say she would pick Andrew up from school, and started preparing vegetables for their dinner, distracted by the simple pleasure of food preparation.

Having enjoyed a quiet evening with Andrew, Bankhurst read in bed for a while and, despite her afternoon nap, drifted off to sleep quickly. An electronic bleep roused her at 4:30am. With bleary eyes she looked at the message from night shift DS Hamish MacDonald.

Mirena Loci died at 03:45 this morning. HMacD

38

9th June

Dr Dexter Brewster put down his scalpel and invited his anatomical pathology assistant to sew up the Y incision he had made ninety minutes previously on the trunk of Mirena Loci. His eyes looked over his glasses, perched on his nose, towards the viewing gallery. DIs Bankhurst and Ledingham looked on expectantly.

"So, going on blood analysis and post-mortem findings, the cause of death is..." He paused to marshal his thoughts and take a breath. "Cardiac arrest, secondary to hyperkalaemia, secondary to multi-organ failure, secondary to sepsis, secondary to rodent trauma."

He paused again. "In layman's terms, infection introduced by the rats caused multi-organ failure, including the kidneys. This, in turn, caused raised levels of potassium, that's hyperkalaemia, in the blood, which was well documented in her pre-mortem and post-mortem bloods. High levels are known to be cardiotoxic, with cardiac arrest a recognised complication."

He paused again, longer this time, and reached for copies of the blood results. Moments passed. He ran a hand through his hair.

Bankhurst caught his hesitation.

"Anything twitching your sixth sense, Dexter?"

"Well... I stand by my assessment as cause of death, but looking at the results, with the supportive therapy she was getting, her renal, that is kidney, function was actually beginning to improve, and yet her potassium was, if anything, getting higher."

"Meaning?" prompted Bankhurst.

"Well, it's a long shot, and I realise the implications, but was she getting some potassium from an external source, to hasten her demise?"

"But, that's impossible," countered Bankhurst. "She's been under twenty-four-hour guard since she was admitted."

"OK. Fair enough," he replied, "must just have been the potassium level lagging behind the other results as they improved."

He clicked his microphone off, tore away his apron, mask and gloves, balled them together, and threw them in a pedal bin.

"Anyone for coffee? A wee birdie told me we've got rowies in the staff room," he said, in a muted voice, with less enthusiasm than normal, the gravity of the latest victim's post-mortem still showing on his face.

Bankhurst excused herself as she and Ledingham left the morgue. She strolled the nearby streets, somewhat aimlessly, with vacant eyes and contemplative face. After twenty minutes she found herself outside the imposing iron gates straddling the entrance to St Nicholas's Church. Without making a conscious decision, she entered the churchyard and, avoiding other people seeking respite from city centre bustle, found a bench bathed in a beam of sun which had somehow found a path through the rustling tree canopy. She enjoyed the warm, caress of the sun and the noise of the ancient trees gently exercised by the summer breeze. The occasional sound of laughter, or the sudden gasp of a drink's can being opened, flirted with the periphery of her consciousness, but she remained lost in contemplation. Ten minutes later, she started back to the police station. She knew what she had to do, but she wanted to pick Dexter Brewster's brain once more before visiting DCI Farrell.

Brewster lowered his newspaper slightly and looked over the top as Bankhurst entered the coffee room.

"Thought you might still be here," she quipped.

"This paper won't read itself," he said, with a grin.

"Who even reads a newspaper these days anyway, Dexter?"

"Fair point," he said, thoughtfully. "Just dinosaurs like me, I suppose."

"So, what brings you back so soon?"

"I've been mulling over the post-mortem, particularly the... what did you call it? Hypokalaemia?"

"Hyperkalaemia," he corrected. "Raised potassium is fine, if you prefer."

"We'll obviously look at the CCTV, but as far as I'm aware, there have only been health personnel and her husband in that room, and he was never there alone. If there was extra potassium given to her, someone on the ARI staff would need to have done it."

"Indeed," agreed Brewster, "and likely to have been a nurse or doctor, in order to have accessed the potassium and administered it intravenously. Wouldn't be the first medic to go to the dark side."

"Do you think it would have been a once-off dose, or added to the infusion?"

"The latter I think, as if they had pushed in a bolus dose it would have created an obtrusive, and suspicious, spike in the blood potassium level, whereas adding it to the infusion would have caused a slow increment, difficult to discern from the natural processes going on in multi-organ failure."

Bankhurst continued her thought processes. "And if there had been interference, this would have been much less likely to have happened when she was in theatre, than in an ITU room?"

"On the basis of more witnesses being present there you mean?"

"Yes."

"I suppose so, though not really my line of work," he continued, with a tilt of his head.

"OK, so at least that would narrow down who we may have to look at."

"You're going to look into it, then?"

"Yes. I sincerely hope it's a dead end, but I just can't ignore it."

"Well, in that case, there's one more thing that has just occurred to me," said Brewster.

Bankhurst nodded encouragement for him to continue.

"I'm thinking back to the other cases."

"And?"

"It's mostly anaesthetists who staff the ITU."

"And?" Bankhurst repeated.

"Anaesthetists sometimes use ketamine."

39

9th June

"Are you alright, Lily? You don't look so good."

Lily could see Brewster's lips moving, but couldn't understand what he was saying.

The panic attack trapdoor had already opened and she had rapidly been sucked through. There was no stopping the physiological process unleashed within. A familiar feeling of terror rose from her core and spread rapidly to the rest of her being. Her breathing and pulse accelerated rapidly. The first patches of damp quickly began to show on her blouse. She wanted to reassure Brewster that she would be OK, but no words came from her mouth, itself encircled by a ring of pins and needles.

Similar tingling began to prick her fingertips and spread up towards her wrists, as her chest tightened like a vice.

"I think you should lie down, Lily."

She raised an arm. "I'll be OK," she managed to splutter, "just give me a minute."

Brewster put a comforting arm on her shoulder. She knew he understood what was happening.

"It's OK," he said, in a soothing voice, "you're safe here."

A few minutes later, Bankhurst was past the worst.

"Sorry about that."

"Don't be silly," reassured Brewster, "our daughter used to have panic attacks. I'm well used to them. How long have you had them?"

"About eighteen months or so."

"More or less since…?" Dexter let the sentence dissipate.

"Yes, I suppose so," agreed Bankhurst.

"Are you seeing anybody?"

"I went to a couple of sessions, but didn't think it was for me."

"Lily…" Brewster couldn't prevent a slightly disappointed parental tone in his voice.

She held her hands up to say *I know, I know*.

"What brought that on just now?"

"Oh, nothing in particular," she said, lying. "They're a law unto themselves sometimes." But, she knew, within herself, that Brewster linking ketamine to anaesthetic practice, and the possibility that a key witness had been murdered before being able to testify, narrowed the accusatory focus to only a few individuals. Dr Tom Donaldson was very much one of them.

This cannot be happening.

Having refreshed herself in the morgue toilet, Bankhurst made the short journey back to the police station and, with trepidation, climbed the stairs to the second floor.

She checked her clothes and hair before knocking on DCI Farrell's door.

"Enter."

Bankhurst closed the door behind her, and stood in front of Farrell's desk, awaiting the invitation to speak.

The DCI finished typing and looked up at her SIO.

"I hope you bring good news."

"Er... probably not what you'd call good news exactly, ma'am."

"Tell me the worst," she said, with a sigh.

"Dr Brewster certified Loci's cause of death as cardiac arrest secondary to high blood potassium levels. In all probability this was secondary to her kidney failure, but he did raise the possibility that someone could have injected potassium, at some point, to increase the possibility of an arrest. I want to investigate all the staff involved in her care in ARI, especially the medical and nursing staff."

"Sounds reasonable," agreed Farrell, with a slightly perplexed face. "So, what's the problem?"

"Em... I'm seeing one of the doctors involved."

"For fuck's sake, Lily."

Bankhurst hung her head slightly.

Farrell paused for a moment.

"OK. It is what it is. You'll make yourself scarce for the next seventy-two hours, and Tony Ledingham can lead the team meantime. How many people are we speaking about?"

"Well, if we concentrate on ITU, and exclude females, that leaves us with three doctors and one nurse."

"OK. That's not so bad. We should be able to do background checks, interviews and check their digital history over the next couple of days. If it all turns out OK, you could be back as SIO in two to three days."

"Thank you, ma'am. That sounds good."

"Goes without saying that you should have no communication with the team, or your doctor shag, in the meantime," she stated, with a stern look above the rim of her glasses.

"Of course, ma'am."

"OK. On your way, then. Bring Tony Ledingham up to date, and then go home. You'd better tell him why you're taking a couple of days, but no need to tell the rest of the team, at this stage anyway."

"Thank you, ma'am. Appreciate that."

Bankhurst, dismissed with a swish of Farrell's hand, made her way downstairs feeling her encounter had gone a bit better than expected.

After briefing Ledingham, Bankhurst went home as ordered, but found herself unable to relax. Magazines and internet browsing failed to secure her interest. Thoughts of the case, and Tom, reverberated inside her head squeezing a variety of emotions to the surface; confusion, anxiety, shame, anger. A spur of the moment decision prompted a phone call to her parents in Glasgow and a short conversation with her mother, whose maternal instincts were aroused by the time of the call and the subtle change in the timbre of her daughter's voice.

Half an hour after Andrew arrived home from school, mother and son had joined the crawling, early evening exodus from the city as they headed south for a weekend break; Bankhurst hoped that putting distance between herself and the case, along with family distractions, would ameliorate the weekend.

She lasted until Sunday evening before curiosity muscled obedience aside and she WhatsApped Ledingham for an update.

Hey. I know I'm not meant to make contact but this is doing my head in. How's it going?

OK. Most people alibied out.

Most people?

Well, your guy had some difficulty there. Guess that's what happens when you live on your own. He was on duty one night at the hospital on the date of one of the murders, so that helped.

Anything from Cyber?

No

OK. Hopefully see you tomorrow or Tuesday.

OK. Will let you know when we're finished.

Thanks Tony.

No problem. Night.

Night.

Ledingham put his phone down on his desk and sighed. He took his glasses off and rubbed the bridge of his nose between thumb and index finger before repositioning his lenses. After refreshing his screen, he reread the email he had received from Hugh MacLennan.

"Hi, Boss. Just thought you should know that we've turned something up on Dr Tom Donaldson. He attended Aberdeen High School for Boys at the same time Robert Lennox was a teacher there."

"For fuck's sake," he muttered, "why is nothing ever simple?"

40

12th June

Bankhurst awoke with the sound of a WhatsApp message arriving. She stretched, rubbed her eyes and reached for her phone. It was from Tony Ledingham.

> *Things taking a bit longer than anticipated. Will need you to keep your distance for another day at least, I'm afraid. Just going through processes. You know how it is.*

> *Anything I need to know about?*

Despite typing a speedy reply there was no further response from Ledingham.

She frowned. She flicked through her other social media and email accounts, and then back to WhatsApp.

Surely Tom would have been cleared by now.

With Farrell's specific instructions still fresh in her memory, she resisted sending Tom a message, but she did pull up his chat thread on WhatsApp. Tom had not checked his messages since late Friday afternoon, and his phone was currently unavailable. *Digital Forensics must still have it*, she thought.

The hairs on her neck stood to attention.

"Speak to me, DI Ledingham," commanded Farrell.

Tony Ledingham cleared his throat.

"Drs Chettie and Neilson, along with Nurse Menzies, were excluded fairly easily, within twenty-four hours. We've been focussing on Dr Tom Donaldson since then."

Farrell raised her eyebrows.

"DI Bankhurst's..." she struggled to find the right word, "liaison?"

"Yes, ma'am."

"And the bottom line...?"

"Well, he's the right build, and has shoe size nine. He potentially had opportunity in ITU and, as an anaesthetist, would have access to ketamine and potassium. He also has no alibi for four of the murders. Finally, we know he had a connection with one of the victims; he was at Aberdeen High School for Boys at the same time Robert Lennox was a teacher there."

"OK. Interesting, I grant you... but all very circumstantial. Any evidence that actually connects him to any of the murders or Loci's death, bearing in mind that, in her case, we don't even know there was any crime committed in ITU."

"No, ma'am. Specifically, we have no eyewitnesses, physical or digital evidence. We've dug deeply into his phone, computers and car telematics. There's absolutely no evidence, including geolocation data, linking him with any of the murder sites."

"And this is a man with a completely clean record?"

"Yes, ma'am. And, for the record, everyone speaks very highly of him at ARI."

"So, a man of average build and shoe size, who went to a local school along with thousands of others, with an impeccable record and absolutely no evidence that he is involved. We need to leave it there. For now, at least."

"Yes, ma'am."

"Oh. By the way, you can put DI Bankhurst out of her misery."

"With pleasure, ma'am."

Feeling somewhat guilty, Bankhurst walked through the MIT room to her desk, expecting to draw inquisitive eyes. Despite what she thought might be an awkward moment, she was largely ignored, and the collective body language and behaviour of the MIT appeared normal; the usual mixture of noises and smells, good and bad. All seemed well.

With a sense of relief, she sat down, pulled her chair in and booted up her computer.

Iqbal noted her arrival and came over. Non-specific pleasantries were exchanged and he updated her on the case. Most of the MIT had been involved in investigating the four male members of hospital staff. Little progress had been made elsewhere, except that an exhaustive scrutiny of the lives of Mirena Loci and her partner, Jim Liddell, had failed to yield anything of note.

Bankhurst checked her phone and noted Tom was now online. She fired a quick message.

Hey. Really sorry about all that you've been
through. Maybe I could make it up to you by
cooking you some food tonight?

Yeh. Wasn't the best weekend ever, have
to admit. Your guys were very thorough!
Understand the reasons, though. Managed to
get a game of golf in, so not all bad. Food sounds
good. What time do you want me?

7pm?

See you then. X

With her mind more settled, Bankhurst refocussed on
the case, with an occasional foray onto Pinterest seeking
inspiration for the home-made meal she had committed to.

Tom burped, tasting garlic and red wine again in his
mouth.

"Excuse me," he said, with a double tap of satisfaction
on his abdomen. "Sign of a good meal."

"More wine?" Lily held the bottle of Merlot up in her
hand.

"Go on, then," he agreed.

She topped up their glasses, before going to knock on
Andrew's door.

"Game off, Andrew. Bedtime."

"OK," came a muffled, begrudging reply.

Lily nestled up to Tom on the sofa, sensing his body
warmth and aftershave. She kicked her shoes off and bent

her knees to bring her feet up beside her. They sipped from their wine.

"Tell me something," said Tom, "did you ever suspect me? Be honest, now."

"No. Not really."

"Not really? That doesn't sound too convincing." There was a note of exaggerated hurt in his voice.

"The trouble with being a detective is that, over the years, you learn to believe nothing and trust nobody. It goes with the territory. It's nothing personal. Plus, you didn't tell me you'd been to Aberdeen High School."

"To be fair, you never asked."

"You told me you were brought up in Huntly."

"I was, but my parents, for whatever reason, wanted me to have a private education. It was a wee bit far to commute to Aberdeen, especially in winter, so I boarded Monday to Thursday and went home every weekend."

Lily turned to Tom and gave him, what she hoped, was a reassuring kiss on the cheek.

"It's OK. I get it," he said. "I looked after Mirena Loci, and had a tenuous connection with Mr Lennox… though I haven't seen Bobby Ballbag for years, far less knew he was in Ashgrove Hospital."

"Bobby Ballbag?"

"Well, he was always a bit of a sleaze, and had a reputation of getting close enough to rub his *equipment* against you."

"Did he indeed?"

"Well, that was the buzz around the school. Never did it to me mind you, but I believe he did that, and worse, to other boys."

Bankhurst nodded thoughtfully.

"Are there many other Aberdeen High School former pupils working at ARI?"

"Oh, yeh. Quite a lot. Even a few in anaesthetics. We're one of the biggest departments in the hospital, actually. Over a hundred doctors, and I think we've got three or four, apart from myself. But they're all good guys."

Lily caught a look in Tom's eyes that she couldn't interpret. What was she not telling her?

"What is it?"

"Ach, it's nothing."

"No, go on, tell me."

Tom hesitated. "This is a bit difficult. I don't really want to say it."

"What?"

"It just occurred to me that one of the High School guys does an electroconvulsive therapy list occasionally at Ashgrove Hospital, and would likely have come across Bob Lennox."

"But we cleared the ECT doctor. What was his name... something double-barrelled... Dr Alexander-Robbie, I think."

"Oh, Cameron. Aye. He's a good guy. But when he goes on holiday, one of the ex-high school boys subs in for him."

"And who is that?"

"Kevin. Kevin McIvor. He was a couple of years above me at school."

"What's he like?"

"Oh," Tom continued, "he's fine enough. You don't get many laughs out of him though. Very organised and precise. A wee bit anal perhaps, but he's a good anaesthetist. Had a tough time towards the end of last year. Went through an acrimonious separation from his wife."

Lily raised an eyebrow. "Excuse me a minute," she said, sliding away from the muscular warmth of Tom's body. "Be back in a jiffy."

Having closed and locked the bathroom door, she dug her phone out from her trouser pocket and, with a slightly tremulous hand, punched in the direct dial number of the MIT room.

"OK, listen up everybody, for those of you who don't know we have a new person of interest," Bankhurst announced, her voice conveying some of the conviction and confidence she had carried since the previous evening.

She walked forward purposefully and stuck a photo onto the wall. A Caucasian male with narrow eyes and a stern face, enclosed by short dark hair, looked out at the MIT.

"This is Dr Kevin McIvor. Thirty-seven-year-old anaesthetist at ARI. Married, but acrimonious separation from wife last year. No kids. No priors. Former pupil at Aberdeen High School for Boys, where he would have come across Robert Lennox. We now believe that Lennox was likely to have been involved in sexual abuse of some of the boys at the school. This may explain why he moved, or was moved on by head teachers keen to avoid a scandal, around the country to different schools. Louise McEwan said that there may have been a trigger that caused the initial attack, before the lust for killing itself took over."

"So," Iqbal interrupted, "if he was stressed from his separation and then, accidentally, came across someone who had abused him as a child, that might have been the tipping point."

"Exactly," agreed Bankhurst.

"But he wasn't one of the staff involved in the care of Mirena Loci," pointed out Tony Ledingham.

"True, but we don't actually know if there was a crime or not in ITU. Perhaps that's been a red herring. But he would have potential access to ketamine, which was used in some of the victims, and would be skilled in its administration."

"And." Bankhurst hesitated before paraphrasing Tom's character assessment. "I believe, from speaking to one of his colleagues, that Dr McIvor is hyper-organised, bordering on OCD, which would fit our profile."

Ledingham shot her a glance aware, unlike the others, of her likely source of information.

Bankhurst caught the look, but pressed on. "We tried to pick him up last night but he wasn't in, and his phone was switched off. He was due at work this morning but hasn't turned up, which is apparently very unusual for him. We're waiting for an emergency warrant and will go back to the house ASAP. In the meantime, I want us all over his physical and digital life. I want everything there is on Dr Kevin McIvor. This could be our man. Make sure his car registration is on ANPR surveillance and alert all divisions of Police Scotland, the English forces, airports and ports."

"Yes, ma'am."

Bankhurst watched as the police van in front left the A96 between Blackburn and Kintore, and weaved and bobbed its way up a potholed drive, towards McIvor's converted steading.

Tall, wispy grass by the side of the road, swayed in the wind, only partially protected by the drystone dykes behind. Two magpies, disturbed by the police vehicles, flapped up indignantly into air thickened by dust from the entourage, both the stour and the birds settling to their previous positions as the vehicles climbed the hill away from them.

After taking a wide berth on the final corner to avoid a particularly large pothole, the steading came into view.

A slated roof, seemingly plunging in several different directions, capped stone walls containing small, square windows. A well-maintained front door was flanked by standard bay trees and smaller tubs of red geraniums, all perfectly symmetrical. Further along the front of the house was an electric car charging station and, beside that, a reinforced bicycle strongbox.

"No one answering the bell and no sign of life in the property, ma'am," reported the burly, mode of entry sergeant, who looked like he could have done with an armoured vest one size bigger.

"OK. Let's ram the door," said Bankhurst, who was happy to stand in the background with Iqbal and Babinski, while the uniformed team secured the premises.

After a series of faint "clears" from within the steading, a thumbs up from the sergeant at the door invited the detectives in.

A division of the tasks enabled the three detectives to assess the steading in under thirty minutes.

"Anything?" Bankhurst enquired.

"I've bagged up a laptop, but nothing apart from that," replied Iqbal. "Very neat and tidy for a man living on his own. Put my place to shame, so it would."

"Reflex?"

"Looking at the size of the clothes hanging in the wardrobe, it would certainly seem to fit our guy... and there are size forty-three shoes in his bedroom."

"In old money please, Reflex," requested Bankhurst.

"Size nine, ma'am."

She nodded. "Does it look like there are many clothes missing?"

"No. Not really."

"So, it looks like he left in a hurry. Wonder what it was that spooked him."

Nobody answered.

Bankhurst wandered through to the kitchen, her gaze drawn through a small, curtained window to the back garden. At the furthest point was a septic tank and nearer to the house, on the right, an isolated oil tank. On the left, half way down the garden, was a sturdy looking shed and an adjoining roofed area for log storage.

"Better have a look at that, I suppose," she said, and nodded in the direction of the shed.

Compared to inside the steading, the light outside was dazzling and, for a few seconds, the detectives shielded their eyes as they made their way across the paving slabs to the shed. A large padlock discouraged uninvited entrance.

"Seems a bit heavy-duty for a shed," said Iqbal.

Bankhurst took the padlock in her gloved hand.

"Four digits," she muttered.

"Let's see." Bankhurst rotated the number wheels to 1212. No response.

"What about a palindrome, using the mirror image of twelve?" suggested Iqbal.

1221. No response.

"This is wasting time," said Bankhurst. She tutted. "Get the guys to bring the bolt cutters."

"Just a minute, ma'am," said Babinski. "Try 1100."

"What is that?"

"Twelve expressed as a binary," he said, with a disdainful look suggesting that it should be common knowledge.

Bankhurst laughed. "You're something else, Reflex."

1100

Click. The padlock opened.

41

13th June

Iqbal ventured in first, dipping to avoid the low door frame. He fumbled left and right. The click of a switch followed, and the inside of the shed was bathed in weak light from a naked bulb suspended from the ceiling.

Bankhurst and Babinski followed him to be met by the smell of petrol and creosote. It was cramped, and each detective had to rotate on their own axis to take in the contents of the shed; makeshift shelving and an old-fashioned piece of bedroom furniture, its life extended as a multi-storage shed unit. Cobwebs, dangling from the high corners, oscillated in the draft from the open door, drawing the brief appearance of a spider looking for prey.

Paint pots, white spirit, fertilisers and weed killers crowded the shelves while a variety of garden tools hung neatly from wall hooks. A jerry can, and lawnmower, had been pushed hard up against the back wall.

With some persuasion the top drawer of the dresser creaked open revealing labelled plastic containers of nails, screws, bolts and washers.

Iqbal flexed his knees to access the lower drawer but found it locked. A hand holding a key appeared over his right shoulder.

"This was hanging on the back of the door," said Babinski. "Looks about the right size."

"Cheers, wee man."

Iqbal encouraged the rusty key into the lock until it would go no further. With a clockwise rotation and a clunk, the lock opened.

He pulled the drawer out and aimed his flashlight to illuminate the contents.

"This looks promising, ma'am," he announced, pulling out black gym trousers, a matching hoodie and Nike trainers.

"Yes!" shouted Bankhurst. "Get in there!"

Iqbal returned his flashlight beam to the drawer.

"Jesus Christ! You need to see this, ma'am."

Iqbal stood up and handed a monthly calendar to his SIO.

Bankhurst took the calendar to the door and allowed sunlight to fully expose the horror she could see unfolding before her. Her face tightened and she felt the hairs on the back of her neck rise. Nausea gripped her stomach and she had to fight the urge to retch.

She leafed through January to June without saying a word, every page a sickening sight. In each month the date of the murder was highlighted, and beside that a photograph of each victim.

"Fuck's sake," she muttered, repugnancy lacing her tone. She passed the calendar to Iqbal and Babinski. "What a bastard!"

Bankhurst felt her eyes moisten, but she managed to refocus before tears escaped her lower lids.

"Right. Get the SOCOs up here ASAP. When we find this guy, I want every shred of evidence to throw at him. Also, get Comms to put out a press release with full details; name, photo, car description. The lot. Advise caution and that he is dangerous. Not to be approached."

"Yes, ma'am."

Iqbal approached Bankhurst, holding the calendar ahead.

"Did you notice this, ma'am?"

Iqbal turned the calendar to July inviting his DI to have a look.

The fourth was already circled.

"OK. Where are we at?" Bankhurst demanded the following morning. The MIT, energised like hunters closing in on their prey, were quick to respond.

"We've found DNA from five different people on the clothing; three from the victims, McIvor himself, and an unknown. Also, the mud and silt on the soles of the Nike trainers match samples taken from the culvert in Westburn Park, where Mirena Loci was dumped. The tread on the trainer also matches partial treads found in Johnston Gardens."

"Excellent," replied Bankhurst. "Now we've just got to find the bastard!"

"He'll naw get far, ma'am," said Iqbal, "the whole

country's looking for him. He's across every media platform you could name, and all the ports and airports are on alert. We've cancelled all his cards and frozen his accounts. We're also monitoring his family and associates in case he reaches out for help."

"No ANPR hits on his car?"

"Not so far, ma'am."

"Perhaps he's changed…"

"Ma'am. Ma'am," shouted Hugh MacLennan. "Got someone on the tip line. Says he's looking at a red Kia Sportage, reg DR32 7GW, right now!"

"Where is he?"

"By the old bridge over The Dee at Milltimber."

"Wouldn't be the first time someone has parked there before throwing themselves in the river," observed Gillespie.

"Bastard," muttered Bankhurst. "Right, get the guy to send a photo to make sure he's not a time waster, and let's get over there. Give SOC the nod to meet us there. And we might need the river search team, too."

"Ma'am."

42

1st July

"The bastard must have topped himself," declared Bankhurst. "That's getting on for three weeks and not a dicky bird."

"I would still like to see a body," grumbled Gillespie. "He might have staged it."

"Possibly," agreed Jardine, "but it's actually very hard to stay completely off grid, these days, for that length of time. We know his passport hasn't been used, and there's not been a single physical or digital hit on him, or his associate network, in that time frame, to suggest he's alive. I think it's likely he's just been washed out to the North Sea."

"Fucking coward," continued Gillespie, to no one in particular.

"For that matter," continued Jardine, after Gillespie's interjection, "his whole digital life seems to be clean over the last year."

"We know he was forensically very aware," commented Iqbal. "Perhaps he was equally digitally aware, and deleted everything."

"Ah, but you can never erase everything," responded the IT expert. "You know my feelings on that, I think, DI Bankhurst?" He nodded in the direction of the SIO.

"Oh, digital *tattoo* as opposed to digital *footprint*?"

"That's the one."

Iqbal's face invited further clarity.

"People may think they have deleted their footprint, but there is always something to find, somewhere. A permanent stain. Hence, digital tattoo."

Iqbal nodded his understanding.

Bankhurst could feel the frustration within the depleted MIT, their numbers reduced by redeployment. The sense of anticlimax. The hard yards of the investigation had eventually paid dividends, but they had been denied the satisfaction of looking the offender in the eye, of seeing him in court. His body would have offered some compensation, but with each day that went by, it seemed less likely to happen.

"It's naw all bad," said Iqbal, with his usual optimism. "The top floor is happy and the press bawbags are off our backs as well."

"Who said we were happy, DS Iqbal?" enquired a stern sounding DCI Farrell, who had entered the room unnoticed.

"Sorry, ma'am. I didnae see you there."

Farrell held up conciliative hands.

"It's OK. Relax. As it happens, myself and Superintendent McNiven feel the team's work at times has

342

been…" She paused searching for the right words. "*Quite* good."

Several eyebrows rose in simultaneous surprise.

"However, we're now at the stage where we need to wind down the investigation. We'll keep a core team, for a period, tying up loose ends, but the rest of you will be reassigned tomorrow."

"That's all," she finished curtly, before turning around and heading to the door in a businesslike manner. With a hand on the door handle, she looked over her shoulder. "By the way, I've put £200 behind the bar at The Craigard. Have one on me tonight."

As the door swung to closure behind her, an excited ripple spread round the room. Even DS Gillespie was unable to prevent a smile creasing his florid face.

After two large glasses of wine, and about as many anecdotal stories as she could tolerate, Bankhurst began to look for an exit strategy. Fortuitously, it was Friday night and Andrew was at a sleepover. She WhatsApped Tom.

Hi. What are you up to? Fancy picking up a slightly pished DI? Could be worth your while.

Where are you?

The Craigard

I'll be there in ten.

Thanks!

Relaxed by the wine, Tom's company and a home-measured G and T, Lily made her way to Tom's bedroom and lay on the bed. Tom tidied up and went to secure the doors. By the time he arrived in the bedroom, Lily was fast asleep. He carefully removed her outer clothes, positioned her under the duvet and switched the bedside light off.

Lily woke in the early hours with the July sunshine already streaming through a crack in the bedroom curtains. She lay on her side, with Tom's protective arm over her.

The blue stone in his signet ring dazzled in the direct rays of sunshine, highlighting the purity of the colour. The simple symmetry of the design, like a small pound coin, appealed to her minimalist tastes. She found herself wondering what stone it was, and if it was a birth stone. As a girl, after taking a liking to dressing up in her granny's clothes, high heels and jewellery, she had, for a while, developed an interest in birth stones. Enchanted by the mysterious stones with exotic names, she had developed her own mnemonic to try and remember the sequence.

How did it go? she mused.

Gems Are Dear...

Gems Are Actually...

She went over it in her head but the answer eluded her. As she continued to ponder the conundrum, her eyelids became heavy and sleep slowly reclaimed her.

Lily's eyes opened quite suddenly.

That's it!

At a subconscious level her mind had continued to work through her recollections and had finally produced clarity.

Gems Are Always Dear Except Promotions Reduce Prices Some Of The Time.

Yes, yes. That's it.

She extrapolated the mnemonic to the stones representing January to December. She whispered, counting fingers as best she could. "Garnet – January, Amethyst – February, Aquamarine – March, Diamond – April, Emerald – May, Pearl – June, Ruby – July, Peridot – August, Sapphire – September, Opal – October, Topaz – November, Turquoise – December."

Feeling self-satisfied, she cast another glance at Tom's ring. Different shades of blue and green scattered from the single hued stone.

Has to be turquoise.

"So, possibly a December boy," she whispered, looking at Tom. She made a mental note to ask him in the morning.

43

2nd July

For the remainder of the night, Lily tossed and turned, rising to the brink of wakefulness before descending again into deeper pockets of sleep. Minutiae of information and images ricocheted around her brain. When she finally awoke, she felt anxious and ill at ease, but the sensation felt different to the familiar signature of a panic attack. She lay still, concentrating on her breathing, to see what the next few minutes might bring. Next to her, Tom's slow expirations, with slight puffing of cheeks against pursed lips, suggested he remained fast asleep.

She tried, as a soothing measure, to synchronise with the effortless, unhurried rise and fall of his chest, but still she felt uncomfortable.

Suddenly, she realised why.

Her eyes opened slightly wider and her pupils dilated. A crawling sensation started to form in her stomach.

She carefully removed Tom's arm from around her, glancing again at his ring. The ring shaped like a pound coin. A twelve-sided coin. The dodecagon gold frame housing a solitary turquoise stone. The birth stone for December, the twelfth month. With her pulse rising, Lily carefully reached for her phone and brought it to life, quickly switching it to silent mode.

She remembered that, not long after they had met, she and Tom had swapped their contact details via WhatsApp. She clicked on Tom's profile and scrolled down. Birthday: 12 December. The twelfth day of the twelfth month.

No. No. No! she screamed internally. *This* cannot *be happening!*

She carefully eased herself from the bed, collected her clothes from the back of a chair and tiptoed through to the lounge. She dressed swiftly and quietly, tears welling in her eyes, as multiple thoughts careered around inside her head. Certain jigsaw pieces began to fit together... if she considered the most unpalatable thought. That Tom could be the killer. She ran through the points in her mind, but found little comfort.

He fitted the physical profile, and owned a powerful e-bike which he could have used to traverse the city speedily, without registering on ANPR. He had the specialist skills, and potential access to drugs, of an anaesthetist. He only had an alibi for one of the murders, Robert Lennox in January; he was on night duty at Aberdeen Royal Infirmary, which was immediately adjacent to Ashgrove Psychiatric Hospital. Perhaps he had the opportunity to slip out of the hospital for an hour?

He looked after Mirena Loci in ITU. If she had

regained consciousness, and the blood work suggested she was slowly improving, then she would have identified him. He would have needed to take her out, and had the opportunity to add potassium to her infusion. Around the same time, McIvor became the prime suspect. But only after Tom had effectively delivered him to the MIT, by offering a potential link between McIvor and Lennox, via the electroconvulsive therapy list.

What if it was the other way round?

What if McIvor had mentioned to Tom, in the anaesthetists' common room for instance, that he had come across their old teacher, and abuser, while doing the list? Could that have been the trigger to ignite Tom's serial killing rampage?

If he had deliberately misdirected the investigation towards McIvor he must have done so safe in the knowledge that his colleague was already taken care of. If McIvor was indeed in The Dee, perhaps it wasn't of his own volition? What about the physical evidence at McIvor's house? That would have been easy enough to plant. The padlock with encrypted code? An unnecessary extra touch, fuelled by narcissistic confidence, perhaps. It would have been a risk to leave the physical evidence, as his own DNA must have been all over the clothes, the fifth "unknown" profile found on analysis. But he was being backed into a corner, and perhaps had been forced into precipitous action, reassured his own DNA was not in the system. He had been *invited in for questioning*, neither charged nor arrested, so DNA had not been collected.

She recalled Jardine's words. McIvor's digital record was completely clean. The absence of even a trace of a digital *tattoo* should have rung more of an alarm bell. She cursed herself under her breath.

No, no. There must be an alternative explanation.

The previous mantra returned. *This cannot be happening. This* cannot *be happening. Not again.*

Once before, through capricious and ill-thought-out action, she had placed herself in danger at the hands of a killer. Almost paid with her life, leaving Andrew an orphan. Her son deserved better, and she had vowed then never again to be as irresponsible.

But, her instincts were hard to ignore. Was she now not only potentially dancing with the devil again, but had invited him into the bosom of her family?

Although crushed by mixed emotions, and fighting a basic instinct to flee, her CID autopilot kicked in. Continuing on tiptoe, she crept through to the bathroom. A quick search failed to identify what she was looking for. She opened the mirrored cabinet above the sink and on the first shelf found a toothbrush, toothpaste and dental floss. Satisfaction briefly flickered on her face as she quickly pocketed the toothbrush and slowly brought the doors towards closure. As they clicked softly together, and the mirrors aligned, she caught a brief glimpse of Tom behind her – just before she felt damp gauze being placed, with force, over her mouth and nose, a sweet pungent smell stinging her nostrils.

She kicked and struggled to no avail. Tom was too strong for her. His left arm encircled her trunk trapping her arms while his right hand, strengthened by many years of holding masks onto patients' faces, easily kept the ether-soaked gauze in place. It wasn't long before Lily felt an all-encompassing sleepiness spread over her. Her limbs went completely flaccid as she slipped into unconsciousness.

"DS Iqbal?"

"Aye."

"This is the duty desk sergeant, Ian McLeod. I've got a woman here who says she's a friend of DI Bankhurst. Her son was on a sleepover at her house last night, and DI Bankhurst was due to pick him up at ten this morning. She never turned up, which is very unusual for her, apparently. She phoned around a few friends and went to Bankhurst's house, but couldn't raise her. She left it until after lunch but became worried, and decided to come in to report it."

Iqbal paused, his mind racing.

"Are you still there?" enquired McLeod.

"Aye. Sorry. Send her up, please."

"Will do."

Dawn Watson appeared to be in her late thirties. She was thin, bordering on skinny, and wore sports shoes, three-quarter length white trousers and a striped top. Her pale, freckled skin sat well with red eyebrows, but less so with, rather obviously, dyed blonde hair. A perfunctory smile did not hide her concern.

"Thanks for seeing me."

"Nae problem. I'm DS Iqbal. I work with DI Bankhurst… Lily."

"Oh, yes. I've heard her speak about you. Nothing bad," she added, with another weak smile.

"I got the details from the desk sergeant," said Iqbal. "Who all have you phoned?"

"Lily herself, obviously, and several mutual friends."

"And you've been to her house?"

"Yes. No sign of life there… and no car either."

Iqbal glanced out the window. Bankhurst's car remained where it had been parked all day the day before.

"OK. Thanks very much. We'll take it from here. Are you OK to look after Andrew for a bit?"

"Yes. No problem."

"OK. Thanks. Can you leave your contact details at the front desk? Let us know immediately if she turns up, or gets in touch, please."

"Yes. Of course."

As Dawn Watson headed back towards the front desk, Iqbal picked up his phone.

"I don't like this," he said to himself, "naw one wee bit."

Within an hour, DCI Farrell had joined Iqbal and the duty team in the MIT room. The door swung open and a pink faced DI Tony Ledingham walked swiftly towards the group huddled in the middle of the room.

"Any word?"

"No."

"Fuck."

"Where are we at?"

Iqbal acted as spokesperson. "We've triangulated her phone. It was with her when she was with the rest of us in the pub, and it then moved to an address in Viewfield. Tom Donaldson's address. Went dark there at 07:14 this morning."

Farrell cleared her throat. Looked around the group. "For those of you who don't know, and I think it's important you do now, DI Bankhurst and Dr Donaldson are in a relationship."

After a tumbleweed moment, with several quick glances exchanged, Iqbal continued.

"We've tried contacting Donaldson, but his phone is switched off."

Farrell noted Iqbal's omission of a first name, or title, when he mentioned the anaesthetist, sensing suspicion, distrust or both. Iqbal confirmed as much. "I've had a squad car go round to his house, but it's all quiet. There's something about him that's gnawin' at me, so there is. I cannae put my finger on it, but there's something bugging me."

An uneasy stillness cloaked the room.

"OK," said Farrell, suddenly and with purpose, "here's what we need to consider. Is DI Bankhurst missing? Has she been abducted? If so, by whom? Could McIvor still be alive? After all, his body was never found. If not him, do we need to consider someone else? Is Donaldson now a suspect given his address was the last known location of DI Bankhurst's phone? Is it even possible that DI Bankhurst and Donaldson are both victims, and they have been abducted together?"

"I don't like this, ma'am," added Iqbal, "especially as it's the second of July."

"I know," she nodded gravely, aware of the proximity of the next circled date on the calendar recovered from McIvor's steading, 4 July.

"This is potentially a race against time. Let's pull everyone back into the MIT. I want us all over this. Get a team over to his house and turn it over. No stone unturned."

3rd July

"How's Andrew doing?" enquired Farrell

"Naw bad," replied Iqbal. "He stayed at the Watsons last night. They told him his mum was working on a difficult case. No point in alarming the wee man at this stage."

Farrell nodded, and couldn't help consider the consequences for Andrew if her DI did not return safely.

"Any progress?"

"Naw really," replied Iqbal. "We're going over every scrap of information we know about Donaldson and McIvor. No leads as yet."

"And his house?"

"Nothing so far. His bed was unmade, and there were indented pillows on each side. Looks like two people slept there. No obvious sign of a struggle. His computer and e-bike have been taken to the lab for forensics and we've sent samples to Genetics for urgent DNA analysis."

"OK, keep me in the loop."

"Ma'am."

Something continued to niggle Iqbal. Looking for inspiration he walked through to the coffee machine, and distracted himself by rehearsing drives from an over pitched ball outside the off stump. He kept his eye on the imaginary ball until well after it had left his imaginary bat. The focus on the ball reminded him of his golf swing.

Something clicked. He turned and jogged back to the MIT room, leaving his coffee dribbling from the machine into the waiting plastic cup, a whisper of steam rising slowly upwards.

44

3ʳᵈ July

"I've got something, Boss!" shouted Iqbal.

Farrell walked smartly to the DS's desk.

"I remembered that Donaldson mentioned, when he was in for interview, that he'd played in the weekly medal at Craibstone that same weekend. That's my home golf course too as it happens, so it is. Us golfers are a nosy bunch, and a couple of days later I went on to HDID to see what Donaldson's handicap was, and what he'd scored."

"HDID?" enquired Farrell.

"Sorry, ma'am. Howdidido app. Pretty well all golfers use it to enter their scores and monitor their game. Donaldson had scored a respectable net seventy-three, I seem to remember. Anyway, that's naw the point. What is the point, and this is what has been niggling me subconsciously for a while, is you need to enter your score in real time through the app, when you're playing the round."

"On your mobile?" interjected Farrell.

"Aye!" said Iqbal, "and Digital Forensics had his mobile here that whole weekend."

Farrell joined the dots. "So, he's got a second phone."

"Yes! I asked the digital team if they could analyse a data dump from the local phone mast that covers Craibstone, for the morning that Donaldson played golf. There was only one phone in the area, at the time, that was a non-registered, pay-as-you-go phone. I've just got more information from Digital. That same handset, albeit with different sim cards, was present near the sites of three of the murders in the two weeks before they took place. Probably casing the scenes. The perpetrator obviously thought he was safe switching sim cards. A rare error from him. And, crucially," Iqbal continued, "there were two pings at Tom Donaldson's home address... *12* Viewfield Circle."

"Fuck!" declared Gillespie in his usual guttural voice, encapsulating, in one word, the feeling of the room as they realised the list of several possible scenarios had just been distilled into one highly likely one. Dr Tom Donaldson was the perpetrator. He had DI Bankhurst captive, and there was a strong possibility he would kill her the next day.

"OK. Excellent work, DS Iqbal. Worthy of the MET."

Iqbal blushed, and looked at his feet, slightly uncomfortable with the unexpected praise. Suddenly, the door opened and Superintendent McNiven strode in, his casual clothes and fierce demeanour suggesting he expected to be somewhere else.

"Well, this is a shit-fest!" he barked, his face darkening towards the colour of his red Barbour sweater. "What is this going to look like?"

"We've just had a very positive development, actually," countered Farrell, with the clipped tone she usually reserved for lesser ranks, "due to DS Iqbal's astute work." She shot a stony look towards her superintendent.

"Humph," replied McNiven, apparently unimpressed.

"I may have something else, ma'am," shouted Reflex towards DCI Farrell, ignoring the senior officer present.

"Go on."

"I've been looking through all of Donaldson's accounts. He's mostly RBS, but the guys at his house found a Santander card at the back of a drawer which links to a current account. There's a monthly direct debit to a property leasing company. Too small to be rental for his house. I've managed to track someone down from the leasing office. They say it is for a lock-up, under the arches, on South College Street."

"You jazzer!" shouted Iqbal, as he punched the air.

Farrell stepped in decisively, "Right. Let's get down there, now! We'll need some specialist firearms officers with us. No lights or sirens."

Wearing protective vests and grim expressions, Iqbal and Farrell eased themselves quietly out of their vehicle. Their noses twitched. The unmistakable faint smell of fish hung in the warm July air, having drifted across The Dee from the processing plants in Torry. The specialist firearms officers, already in place, looked impatient for instruction.

Minutes later, a solitary officer crept towards the closed doors and fed a small, flexible telescopic camera underneath. With one hand he manipulated the camera while holding, and looking at, a screen in the other.

He spoke into his headset.

"No obvious movement or occupants. Weak horizontal thermal hotspot towards rear of property. Possible body."

"No. No!" shouted Iqbal, as he started to run towards the lock-up.

"Wait there, son!" commanded the lead SFO. "We haven't cleared the premises yet."

Reluctantly, Iqbal held his ground, to be joined by Farrell at his side. The pair watched from a distance as the SFO team breached the door and swarmed inside.

"Clear. Clear. Clear."

Iqbal and Farrell needed no further invitation and sprinted forward.

"Over here," shouted an officer crouched over what appeared to be a body.

With dread coursing through his body, Iqbal fell to his knees. A motionless, feminine body lay before him on a dirty mattress, a black hood enveloping her head. Iqbal ripped the hood off and inhaled sharply. The pale, gagged face of Lily Bankhurst gave no hint of life. Iqbal placed his fingers on her neck and thought he could feel the hint of a pulse. He tilted her head forwards and undid her gag. She exhaled softly.

"Medic! Over here. Now!"

He pulled Lily towards him and hugged her.

"I've got you, Boss. I've got you. You're going to be OK."

She opened her eyes and whispered something, which Iqbal couldn't hear. He put his ear closer to her mouth.

"Tom. Tom. Tom."

A tear ran slowly down her cheek.

45

3rd July

"They call them *gaviotas* in Spain, Emma."

"What, Granddad?"

"Those."

The three-year-old followed the direction of her grandfather's slightly gnarled index finger, screwing her eyes up against the glare of the sun. High above, numerous grey and white birds circled and swooped effortlessly over The River Dee.

"Seagulls," he explained.

"Will they eat me, Granddad?"

"No, no, Emma. They prefer fish. That's why they like it here. Close to the sea and close to that fish factory over there." Duncan Irving changed the direction of his pointing finger to indicate the processing plant on the other side of the river.

"What's a factory, Granddad?"

"Where they make stuff."

"Do they make fish there, Granddad?"

"Er. No. Not exactly…" He paused, looking for an escape from the line of questioning. "How about we go for an ice cream?"

"Yes, please!"

As grandfather and granddaughter headed towards Duthie Park, high above the seagulls a low noise, quadcopter drone was nearing the end of its battery power. Its remote pilot was about to bring it back for a recharge, when he spotted something of interest, zooming the camera in to have a closer look.

His radio crackled into life as he spoke.

"Single person, probable male, heading towards the south end of South College Street."

The message was picked up in the control centre and relayed to all officers stationed in and around the lock-up, focussing minds and alerting bodies.

"Turning into South College Street now."

Minutes passed.

"Eyes on! Eyes on!" The urgent broadcast from the ground team pierced the silence.

"Suspect confirmed. Eyes on Tom Donaldson. Walking towards lock-up."

"Stand by everybody," announced Farrell. "Body cameras on."

Then she muttered to herself, "And don't fuck it up."

Tom Donaldson walked up towards the lock-up with the relaxed shoulders and comfortable gait of someone at ease with himself. Only when he reached for the padlock did his demeanour change. His body stiffened and he looked around furtively.

"Armed police! Stay where you are! Lie on the floor. Now!"

He hesitated before suddenly swinging the door open and disappearing inside.

Straight into the six officers waiting for him.

4th July

"Look at that bastard. Cool as a cucumber."

Iqbal and Farrell stared through the one-way mirror at Tom Donaldson, sitting alone in the interview room.

"Still not saying anything?" enquired Farrell.

"No. Says he'll only speak to DI Bankhurst."

"And refusing a lawyer?"

"Yes."

"How is Lily?"

"Got home this morning, I believe. No lasting physical damage. Psychologically, who knows?"

Donaldson suddenly turned towards the mirror and stared directly at them, with unblinking eyes.

He mouthed something.

"Turn on the microphone," said Farrell.

"Tick. Tock. Tick. Tock."

A thin smile spread over Donaldson's face.

"What the fuck?" said Iqbal, as he turned to Farrell. "What's he getting at?"

"It's the fourth of July," responded Farrell, grimly. "Could he still, somehow, have a plan to continue his sequence?"

"Even in custody?"

"Wouldn't be the first time someone has used a timed device. Bomb? Chemical release?"

"Or he could just be pulling our chain, ma'am. Manipulating us to get DI Bankhurst in," said Iqbal.

"But can we take that chance? Even with the obvious conflict of interest, never mind the emotional stress."

"Tick. Tock. Tick. Tock."

"Ba'bag!"

Farrell looked at Iqbal, unsure as to what exactly he had said in his Glaswegian accent, but she caught the derogatory tone.

"Thanks for doing this, Lily," said Farrell.

"No-brainer, ma'am," Bankhurst said, softly, "given the circumstances."

"You don't have to face him. You could stay on this side of the mirror."

"No, ma'am. I want to see the white of his eyes."

"Understood."

Bankhurst had her hair up in a simple bun, wore no make-up and her clothes looked like they were the first to come to hand. They were. Her haggard features and body language betrayed her recent stress, but a steely glint remained in her eyes, the pinpoint pupils of which a legacy of the dihydrocodeine she had taken to salvage some sleep.

She took a deep breath in, entered the room, and sat down without speaking. Leaning over towards the wall she pressed a button on the recorder and stated the time, date, and her own details as she would for any other interview.

She looked at Donaldson and held his gaze, trying not to blink. She searched, but failed to find, any hint of the evil inside. Some nuance that she had missed. But all she saw was the same doe-eyes she had fallen for.

"Thanks for coming, Lily."

"DI Bankhurst," she corrected stiffly, as she shifted position in her chair and straightened her back. "I believe you have something you wanted to say to me."

"Yes."

Donaldson leant forward so that only Bankhurst could hear.

"There's going to be another death today," he whispered.

He sat back, his face suggesting he had nothing more to say.

"Would you care to repeat that out loud?" responded Bankhurst.

"No comment."

"Did you just say to me that there is going to be another death today?"

"No comment."

"Have you anything else you wish to say?"

"No comment."

Bankhurst wasn't in the mood to play games.

"Interview terminated at 14:25 hours."

She left the interview and stepped into the adjoining room, with turned out palms and raised eyebrows asking, *What do you make of that?*

"It's all about control for that bastard," suggested Farrell, coolly. "Even now he wants to feel in charge."

"But what's he getting at?" said Bankhurst.

All three of the officers turned to look at Donaldson, contemplating their next move. He seemed to sense their attention and turned his gaze towards them. Slowly, his face tightened to a grin. When it had reached its extent, he held it for several seconds before suddenly turning in his chair and bending forward. His hands worked furiously in front of him.

"What's he doing?" said Iqbal.

"I don't know, but get in there and find out," ordered Farrell.

Bankhurst and Farrell watched as Iqbal sprinted to the door and entered the adjoining room… just long enough for Donaldson to put something in his mouth and swallow.

Iqbal looked towards the mirror, but his DI and DCI were already on the move.

With a supercilious air, Donaldson watched the officers cram into the room. On the table lay the turquoise stone from his signet ring, prised from its dodecagon gold setting.

"The bastard's taken something," shouted Iqbal.

"You're too late," replied Donaldson. "I'll be dead very soon. My birth stone has become my death stone. Well, the wafer underneath it has."

He smiled at what he perceived was clever wit, but it was curtailed by a spasm of coughing. He began to sweat profusely and his normal look of absolute self-confidence was replaced by a more anguished expression. The expression of someone who knew they were about to die. Seconds later he collapsed to the floor. His breathing quickened as he began to gurgle and wheeze. At the same time as his skin reddened and started to swell into weals.

As his conscious level visibly reduced, he beckoned Bankhurst to him.

She knelt down on one knee.

He tried to speak but his voice was now croaky and weak and he could only manage one word at a time between breaths. She couldn't understand what he had said and lent a little closer, being careful not to touch him.

"I… didn't… kill… McNeil."

The effort of his last sentence seemed to accelerate Donaldson's downward spiral. Moments later he was unconscious. His lips and fingers turned blue, the final act before his breathing stopped altogether.

Iqbal slipped on gloves and felt Donaldson's neck.

"No pulse."

"Don't even think of CPR," ordered Farrell. "He's a biohazard. We need to get out of here."

46

5th July

"But, why would he lie about it?" questioned Bankhurst.

"I don't know," replied Farrell, "but I'm getting a lot of heat from McNiven to wind things up. He's seeing it as a result. Case solved. Offender dead. No need for a costly trial and long-term imprisonment."

"Even if it makes us look a bit inept. Killing himself in front of us."

"Why did he even still have that ring on his finger?" lamented Farrell.

"I've looked at the police custody and security officer's notes. Specifically, his risk assessment," said Bankhurst. "The ring was too tight to come off and Donaldson refused to have it cut off, citing high sentimental value. Wasn't thought to be a danger."

"Anyway," continued Farrell, "McNiven says he can live with that, as the positives outweigh the negatives. I believe he's brushing down his uniform, as we speak, to take the press conference."

"I bet he is," said Bankhurst, her words laced with innuendo. *He's never slow at taking plaudits* was left unsaid.

Farrell nodded her understanding.

"I'm still uneasy with it, ma'am. McNeil's death was different in several ways. It wasn't on a sequential date, it seemed reactionary rather than planned, and was covert rather than overt. Add in Donaldson's last words…"

"I know. I know. But we now know McNeil and Lennox were connected both via their school and likely child abuse. So, there's a link that can't be denied. Anyway, it's pie in the sky as the order is clear. You can wind down the MIT and take a few days off. That's an order, by the way," she added, with a raised eyebrow.

"Thanks, ma'am."

6th July

Bankhurst showered before dressing in jeans, an unironed T-shirt and Skecher shoes. Unable to face breakfast, she reduced her morning dose of insulin and brewed strong coffee.

Sitting at the breakfast bar, she cradled the coffee between two shaky hands. She stared into the middle distance, frowning.

Questions flooded her brain.

How did this happen? How could I have been so stupid? Will I ever trust a man again?

With forensic zeal she sifted through memories of Tom, looking for clues she had missed. Data to beat herself up with. Even their first date was worthy of scrutiny. He had refused empty tables while waiting for *his table*. Was that subtle evidence of OCD, always preferring the same table? Worse still, could it have been table twelve he was waiting for?

Snippets of conversation tugged at her brain.

His house. 12 Viewfield Circle. "It wasn't a perfect fit, but for some reason it kept calling me," he had said.

His bike. "It's a Boardman Adventure e-bike. Twelve gears."

Something else nagged at her. It rose to the surface and crystallised into a single thought. She picked up her phone and typed into the search engine *Rush. Canadian band. Biggest hit.*

Numerous hits appeared, all telling the same message.
2112

She shook her head in disbelief. "For fuck's sake. Even his ringtone. A reverse mirror image of twelve."

Bankhurst swirled the last of her coffee around the base of the cup before swallowing it. Grimaced at its cold temperature. Slowly, the self-recrimination loop had been interrupted by other thoughts. Doubts and questions about Hector McNeil's murder.

She opened her laptop and pulled up photos from the Aboyne crime scene. After twenty minutes with no inspiration, she buried her weary head in her hands and rubbed her eyes. Suddenly, she looked up. Refocussed eyes quickly scanned the pictures again until she found the one she was looking for. She picked up her mobile and dialled.

"Ah. I was hoping you might still be there, Reflex."

"Ma'am."

"Do you know if McNeil's house in Aboyne has been cleared yet?"

"Don't think so, ma'am."

"How do you fancy a wee drive out there... off the record?"

"Don't see why not, ma'am. The mood's a bit flat here, anyway. What am I looking for?"

"I've been looking at the crime scene photos. In one of them, in his fishing den, there's a trophy. Presumably some kind of fishing trophy. It's difficult to see when I magnify the image, but it looks like on the wooden plinth under the trophy, there's a plaque where you might inscribe previous winners. I'd like to have a look at that."

"OK, ma'am. No problem."

"Could you maybe drop it off at my house in Countesswells on your way back?"

"Sure."

Bankhurst jumped as the doorbell rang. She checked her phone and was relieved to see her DC on the doorbell camera. She put her palm on her chest to help calm her racing heartbeat. Her pulse slowed.

She removed the security chain and unlocked the door.

"There you go, ma'am." Babinski held out a trophy.

"Thanks, Reflex. Come in. Let's have a look."

She placed the trophy on the breakfast bar.

Book, Line and Sinker Society
Annual Outing
Winner of Biggest Catch

1998 P Davidson
1999 N O'Neill
2000 No fish caught
2001 A Henderson
2002 R Hamilton
2003 No fish caught
2004 J McNiven
2005 H McNeil
2006 C Torrance
2007 H McNeil

Bankhurst raised half an eyebrow and looked at Babinski. His face told her he had made the same observation.

"Surely not?" she said.

She brought up the photo taken in 2004 and scanned the faces again, pausing at the fourth from the left. A brimmed hat, with a variety of fishing flies piercing the khaki material, partially obscured the smiling Caucasian face. Bankhurst magnified the image but lost definition.

She looked at Babinski.

"Could that be a younger Superintendent John McNiven?"

He shrugged.

"Not impossible, ma'am, but why would he be in an Edinburgh school photo?"

Bankhurst's mind raced. If it was McNiven, he clearly had a connection with two of the murder victims, who in turn were very likely involved in child sexual abuse. There had also been the phone call from McNeil, after his interview with Sharon Baxter, to the unregistered phone at, or near, the police station. Previously it was considered it could have been Iqbal who took the call. Could it, instead, have been McNiven? And did he take action after the phone call? To silence McNeil.

He had also been quick to order the investigation be closed after Donaldson's suicide. Coincidence or opportunism? The chance to bury a murder in a serial killer's portfolio.

"OK. This is a potential shit-fest, Reflex. We need to keep this between ourselves in the meantime. Not a word to anyone."

"Understood."

"We need more information, but I can't come in, meantime. Might look suspicious, and I'd probably just be sent packing by DCI Farrell, in any case. Can I count on you to do a bit more digging, under the radar?"

A nuance of discomfort showed across his face.

"I'll take the rap if it all goes to shit."

"Ma'am."

"We need to take a look at McNiven's mobile, and car data from the night of the Aboyne murder. If you can look into that I'll do a bit of research, from home, on his career. See if he was in Lothian and Borders Police at the time of the photo. I'll also see if I can track down any of the other names on the trophy."

By late afternoon, lack of sleep had caught up with Bankhurst. After spending a couple of fruitless hours on the phone trying to track down other historical members of the Book, Line and Sinker Society, she rested her head on the table and succumbed to sleep.

She woke suddenly as the ping on her phone announced a new WhatsApp message. She glanced at her watch to see who it was from.

Reflex Babinski.

She stirred herself, rubbed her eyes and sat up straight. She picked up her phone and opened WhatsApp. Babinski had sent a voice note.

"Hello, ma'am. This is Reflex, eh, DC Babinski. Just an update. Superintendent McNiven's phone and car seem to have been at home all that evening. However, I did a bit more digging, and there is another car registered at that address. Under his wife's name. That car *was* picked up on ANPR that night heading in the direction of Aboyne and returning two hours later. Mrs McNiven, or her phone at least, spent three hours at an address near her house. It appears it's the local village hall where they hold a weekly bridge evening. I checked with the organiser and Mrs McNiven was there all evening. So, someone else drove her car out and back from Aboyne."

Bankhurst replayed the message then switched her phone to standby. Just as she did, it rang. Unknown number. She answered.

"DI Bankhurst."

"Hello. This is Andy Henderson. You left a message on my phone earlier."

"Ah. Yes, I did. Thanks for getting back to me." Bankhurst prepared herself for another dead end. "This is DI Bankhurst, from Aberdeen. I don't know if you can help or not, but we're actually looking for a Mr A Henderson who, we think, used to work at Edinburgh Institute for Boys, about twenty years ago."

"Yes, that's me," he replied, "though I've been retired for a few years now."

Bankhurst sat up straight. She tried not to sound too enthusiastic.

"We're particularly interested in the Book, Line and Sinker fishing outings."

"Ha," he said, laughing. "Many a good day out I had with that lot. Though often it was more about the chat, and a few beers, rather than the fishing."

"Was it exclusively teachers who went on the outings?"

"No. Mostly, but not all. To make up the numbers, people sometimes brought a friend with them."

"Do you remember if there was ever a policeman on an outing?"

"Let me see. Yes, yes. I do remember. There was a chap who came a couple of times. What was his name? McNish, I think. No, McNiven. Yes, John McNiven. Bit of a rising star I seem to remember. I believe he went on to quite high office."

"And do you remember who brought him along?"

"Yes. I think it was Hector McNeil, if my memory serves me."

"Thank you, Mr Henderson. That's been most helpful."

47

7th July

Chief Constable Grant McCulloch sat grim-faced behind a large wooden desk, his neatly-pressed dark uniform reflecting his sombre mood. He shook his head in disbelief.

"John McNiven. I can't believe it. You'd better be one hundred percent sure. Speak to me."

Farrell nodded at Bankhurst indicating the floor was hers.

"Firstly, we've been able to establish that Superintendent McNiven, while he was at Lothian Police, knew both Robert Lennox and Hector McNeil when they worked at the Edinburgh Institute for Boys. We feel it is highly likely they were both involved in a child sex abuse ring. We know that McNeil phoned an unregistered number within the apron of the mast that covers Aberdeen Police Station shortly after he was interviewed by DS Baxter. At that interview he would have been made aware we were treating Lennox's death as suspicious and not a suicide. We think he got spooked and may have reached out to another member of the child sex abuse ring."

"*Think*, DI Bankhurst? I need more than your thoughts," interrupted McCulloch.

Bankhurst cleared her throat. "On the night of McNeil's murder, Mrs McNiven's car was driven to and from the Aboyne area, while she was at her bridge club. Superintendent McNiven's own car, and mobile, were left at home."

McCulloch raised an eyebrow, acknowledging the suspicious behaviour.

"Today, we've received some further information. DC Babinski traced an online purchase for Glen Scotia whisky that was made via PayPal. It turns out that PayPal account was linked to a Bank of Scotland current account held by Superintendent McNiven. Also, we got an urgent warrant this morning to look at his medical records, which confirm he is on a regular prescription for digoxin for a heart condition."

McCulloch's face invited clarification.

"The drug that was used to spike McNeil's whisky. Looks like he was taking out a potential loose cannon. Lennox was already dead and by killing McNeil he was removing the link between himself and the past he wanted to forget."

"Jesus H Christ," McCulloch whispered to himself.

"OK. OK." He held up his hands in submission. "Bring him in. But I want you two to do it," McCulloch stated, looking over the top of his glasses, "with professional courtesy. We need to hear his side of the story."

"Yes, Sir," Bankhurst and Farrell replied in unison.

Superintendent John McNiven was struggling with the last corner of *The Scotsman* crossword. His drought of inspiration had taken him to the edge of sleep and he was startled when his phone chimed. It was from the Ring device at the entrance to his gated property. From his phone he saw DI Bankhurst standing in front of the camera. Behind her, he could make out two cars, one unmarked with DI Farrell in the passenger seat, and then a marked police vehicle.

He swallowed but his mouth had suddenly become dry.

"Who is it, John?" said his wife, Grace.

"Just some colleagues, dear. I, erm, actually forgot they were coming. I need to look out some documents in the garden room. Can you maybe leave it a couple of minutes and then let them through the gate. When they get to the house, just point them in the direction of the garden room. I'll be ready by then."

Grace McNiven did as bidden and welcomed the police officers. She was intrigued, and suddenly worried, by the presence of so many of her husband's colleagues, looking matter-of-fact and serious. It was very unusual for her husband to have colleagues visit him at home, and it seemed an excessive number just to be collecting documents.

She directed the officers through the house and then out the back door.

"He's down in the garden room," she said, pointing to a modern, stand-alone structure at the foot of the garden.

"Thank you, Mrs McNiven," said Bankhurst. She led

the small group of uniformed and plain-clothed officers along a slabbed path bisecting a well-tended lawn.

Bankhurst knocked on the garden room door, but received no answer. She stepped sideways and looked through the window. McNiven was dressed in a polo shirt, casual jumper, chinos and slippers. It was the grey, checked slippers that caught her eye, swinging back and forth. Four inches above the ground.

Epilogue

Bankhurst looked in the mirror. Her eyes, already darkened by smudged mascara. Another tear fell softly down her cheek.

How had it come to this?

She picked up the bottle of dihydrocodeine and poured its contents into the palm of her right hand, forming a small, potentially lethal pyramid. Suppressing a sob, she looked at the tablets, then back in the mirror, and took a few slow, contemplative breaths. Conflicting thoughts swirled around her head. She needed to reach a decision.

She turned and dropped the tablets in the toilet, flushing them away.

Picking up her phone she punched in a number.

"Hello. Police Scotland. Occupational Health."

"Hello," Bankhurst replied, weakly. "This is DI Lily Bankhurst, from Aberdeen. I need to make an appointment with the clinical psychologist. I need help."

Glossary

Glaekit	stupid
Wan	one
Na	no
No'	not
O'	of
Hame	home
Hawd on	hold on
Nae	no
Didnae	didn't
Waen	child
La dracu	damn (Romanian)
Rowie	Aberdeen roll (aka buttery)
Ne'r	never
Clout	article of clothing
Ken	know/you know
Kent	knew/known
Saft	soft
A'body	everybody
Dinna	don't
Wasnae	wasn't

Fit	what
Mare	more
Doesnae	doesn't
Havenae	haven't
Heid	head
Taps aff day	tops off day (a hot day)
Pit	put
Cooncil	council
How's it gawn	how's it going
Shoogly peg	a loose peg (touch and go situation)

Acknowledgements

I would like to acknowledge Dr Sally Lawton and Professor Henry Watson for proofreading. I would like to say a big thank you to my wife, Julia, for her unstinting support, encouragement and keeping my plot ideas on the straight and narrow.

About the author

Ewan Wallace, originally from Campbeltown in Argyll, graduated from Aberdeen University Medical School in 1983. After a career in general practice in Aberdeen, he retired in 2021. His interests, apart from family, include golf, gardening, ballroom dancing and travelling.